Baby on the Doorstep

Lori Copeland

Cassie Edwards

Susan Kay Law

HarperPaperbacks
A Division of HarperCollinsPublishers

HarperPaperbacks
A Division of HarperCollins*Publishers*
10 East 53rd Street, New York, N.Y. 10022-5299

Copyright © 1997 by HarperPaperbacks
"The Woman Next Door" copyright © 1997 by Susan Kay Law
"Tomorrow's Promises" copyright © 1997 by Cassie Edwards
"Daniel's Song" copyright © 1997 by Lori Copeland
All rights reserved. No part of this book may be used or
reproduced in any manner whatsoever without written
permission of the publisher, except in the case of brief
quotations embodied in critical articles and reviews.
For information address HarperCollins*Publishers*,
10 East 53rd Street, New York, N.Y. 10022-5299.

ISBN 0-06-108498-0

HarperCollins®, ®, HarperPaperbacks™, and HarperMonogram®
are trademarks of HarperCollins*Publishers* Inc.

Cover illustration by Jeff Barson

First printing: July 1997

Printed in the United States of America

Visit HarperPaperbacks on the World Wide Web at
http://www.harpercollins.com/paperbacks

❖ 10 9 8 7 6 5 4 3 2 1

TABLE OF CONTENTS

Baby on the Doorstep

PROLOGUE

Mooretown, Minnesota 1864

Davinda trudged down the road with her hand pressed to the ache in her lower back. She had no sense of how long she'd been plodding on, mechanically putting one foot in front of the other, but the thickening darkness of the murky sky told her sunset must be near. Her need to find shelter warred with the insistent urge to keep going, to put as much distance between herself and her family as possible.

She couldn't afford to be caught. In all the months they'd kept her locked in her room—since the instant her parents had discovered she was carrying Johnny's child—this was the first opportunity she'd had to escape. And now her time was nearing; she'd probably never get another chance.

A cold spring wind tugged at her shawl, flapping the end of it in her face. She shivered and drew the ragged swatch of wool closer around her.

Though Mill Valley was only two miles south of

1

her father's farm, she'd chosen to go north instead, braving the much longer route to Mooretown in the hope that her family would search the other way first. Even so, she'd kept to the still-barren fields for a solid hour before she'd dared risk the road.

The harsh whisper of the wind muted other sound, and she didn't hear the approach of the wagon coming up behind her until it was nearly upon her. Frantically, she searched for a clump of brush to hide herself in, but only wide, empty strips of plowed earth sprawled on either side of the road.

But it was not her father, thank God, only a bulky farm wagon pulled by two sturdy draft horses, driven by an unfamiliar figure on the front seat. Davinda lowered her head and walked on, hoping the man would take no notice of her and simply drive on by.

No such luck; why would she ever have thought she'd be blessed with good luck now? The wagon slowed, keeping pace with her.

"Need a ride?"

Davinda kept her head down and her feet moving. "No, thank you." The pain in her lower back crawled forward, drawing around the lower swell of her belly. *Go away,* she silently urged him, *go away!*

The team's hooves thudded, slow and steady, in the damp dirt of the road, the wagon rumbling along at her side. She quickened her pace and her breath came hard.

"I'm thinking maybe you should take me up on it, ma'am. A woman in your condition shouldn't be strollin' along out here by yourself. 'Specially not at this time of day."

She stopped, now certain that the man wasn't

going to give up easily, and just as certain she wasn't going to be able to keep on like this much longer, anyway.

He looked ordinary enough. Simply dressed, healthy features rimmed by a floppy brown felt hat and a thick beard nearly the same shade, he must be near her father's age. But there was no other resemblance for, though his gaze was squarely focused on her rounded stomach, she couldn't find a hint of condemnation in his eyes.

"Perhaps I could use a ride, at that."

He helped her up to the front seat, and she couldn't hold back a deep sigh as she sank down. Despite the dangers of accepting a ride from a stranger—the more people she came in contact with, the more likely that someone would be able to tell her father where she'd gone—she couldn't regret it. Exhaustion bruised her, muddling her thoughts, pulling her in and out of almost-sleep.

Her benefactor turned out to be talkative. She didn't mind. Tom Schmidt was a farmer from outside of Mooretown, on his way back from delivering a load of grain to Mill Valley. He seemed to expect nothing from her but a nod now and then, and his chatter distracted her from all the problems she had no answer for. Where would she go? How would she survive? How could she care for a child, all alone, penniless, unmarried?

Enough! she scolded herself. She'd had no choice. She'd manage because she had to, by worrying only about the things she could handle, surviving the next few hours, and letting the future take care of itself.

The road turned east along the Mississippi, winding

its way high up along the bluffs. Down on the river, she glimpsed the lights of a riverboat and wished it was full daylight so she could see the ornate decks shining white in the sun.

She turned on the seat, watching the boat until it disappeared around a bend. If she could just find her way to the docks, sneak on board, she'd be safe. She'd escape downriver, to Dubuque or St. Louis. Anywhere where her family could never find her and steal her child. They intended to give her baby to distant cousins who needed more hands to work their farm, now that they'd stopped birthing their own. And her father planned to force her to marry the old lecher who he claimed was "the only one who'd have her now."

They rolled into the outskirts of Mooretown. Light-filled windows edged with lace gave glimpses of families settling down to supper, bowing their heads in prayer. An ache kicked up in her chest, nearly doubling her over. Her child deserved that, damn it, the simple act of closing a day with family and food. The war and her parents had ruthlessly taken that simple gift from her, and Davinda had no idea how she could ever make it happen.

The next house drew into view, and she caught her breath on a pained gasp.

It was *her* house. Exactly. The one that she and Johnny had planned a dozen times, in happy, dream-filled detail, before he'd left for the Civil War. Two stories, white, a narrow, roofed porch prettying up the plain front. Melted-butter light spilled from the first-floor windows, warming a small front yard edged by a whitewashed fence, all presided over by a massive, bare-limbed oak. The wind dragged at the branches and set a rope swing wildly in motion.

"A perfect house," she said to no one in particular.

"Nice, ain't it? That's the Collins place."

"Collins?" she repeated. Lost in the memories of the daydreams she and Johnny had shared, she'd forgotten the man by her side.

"Yup." He chuckled. "Never seen a man so happy as that one, when he found out his wife was carryin'. Put up that swing the first day. Sure was a shame about—" He fell silent.

"What?" She swung around to find Mr. Schmidt staring at her stomach, his face glum. "What?" she repeated. She couldn't have said why it mattered so much to her, why she simply had to know what he'd intended to say. "*Too bad about what?*"

Averting his eyes, he shrugged. "He went off to the war. Got himself shot."

"Was he . . ." The words lodged in her throat.

"Naw, he got back all right."

She waited, but for the first time since she'd met him he seemed to run out of words. When she looked back, she could no longer see the house.

"You might as well let me off now." She'd gotten this far safely. There was no point in continuing to ride along with Mr. Schmidt. Surely, somehow, she could make her way to the river from here.

He sucked on a tooth and eyed her carefully. "How long you been havin' them pains?"

"Pains?" One was coming on right then, and the word came out a bit breathlessly.

"Before I picked you up, even?"

There was no point in denying what she'd been trying to ignore for too long. "Yes."

"Best I get you to Doc Mickelson, then."

"No!" She had no money to pay a doctor. And surely the story of a stranger, all alone, suddenly showing up on the doctor's doorstep and giving birth would make its way through the town all too quickly. "No, please."

He stared at her, clearly debating. Perhaps he saw her desperation, for finally he nodded reluctantly. "You come home with me, then. My Lizzie's had six of our own, not to mention pulling more calves 'n I can count. She'll take good care of you."

She did. Davinda didn't know what Mr. Schmidt told his wife, but Lizzie asked no questions, merely lent her a billowy nightdress, set her up in the daybed in the front parlor, and scarcely left her side.

Birthing her child proved to be much harder than Davinda had ever imagined. Night bled into day and back to night, a timeless blur of struggle and pain.

Something was wrong. Davinda knew it, from the anxious looks that Lizzie tried to hide, from the urgent tone of her voice when she stepped to the door and whispered to her husband. Finally, Davinda allowed them to send for the doctor. It didn't matter; he couldn't come, for he was already with another patient. In the end, they'd managed on their own, the baby slipping free in the blackest part of the night, halfway between midnight and dawn.

Davinda drifted in and out of sleep, bone-deep exhaustion losing out to the absolute wonder of the little girl a few feet away, sleeping away her own fatigue from the hard birth in a deep, speckled enameled dishpan padded with soft rags.

Her daughter! Hers and Johnny's, tiny and red and wondrously beautiful. She'd named her Jonnie, of course, on a fragile wave of hope that began with her baby's first cry.

Perhaps it would all be all right. Maybe it had all been fated—the chance to escape her family, her coming across Mr. Schmidt just when she needed him. Now they could—

Harsh, angry voices pulled her from her dreams. She dragged herself from the bed and scuffled to the front window, brushed aside the heavy drape, and peered out.

No! *Nononono.* Her mind, her heart, could form no other words. Her father stood only feet from the door, gesturing wildly, shouting. Mr. and Mrs. Schmidt faced him calmly, shoulder to shoulder.

She couldn't let him find her. She simply could not. Davinda grabbed a heavy blanket from the bed, throwing it around her shoulders, and struggled to lift the pan that held her daughter. She ignored the pain that shot through her battered body as she crept slowly, painfully, toward the back door. The only thing that mattered now was protecting her baby.

She would never know how she made her way back to Mooretown. Stumbling through the fields, following a spring-swollen creek, her bare feet frozen and bleeding from small cuts. Time had no meaning, only survival did, and the child that slept on, warm and lulled by the motion.

Darkness haunted her. It seeped down from the bruised sky that only grew blacker as the day went on. Worse yet was the bleak, cold darkness that seemed born deep inside her, that spread through her limbs and blurred her vision.

She stopped only once, in an old, abandoned shack, to put the babe to her breast. She wanted to stay there, in the sheltered space, Jonnie in her arms. But it wasn't far enough away. And what if she died there? The thought terrified her—her baby, crying piteously, starving beside her cold body. And so she struggled on.

When she reached the town, the streets confused her. She couldn't remember the way to the river. She kept to the shadows, well back from the empty roads, slipping behind buildings, wandering, praying, searching for something familiar.

The ominous sky made good on its threat, unleashing cold rain that hovered on the edge of sleet. She set Jonnie down and dragged the blanket off her shoulders, draping it over the pan. Her daughter had to stay warm. The thin, overwashed nightdress she wore was immediately soaked, flapping hard against her body in the strong wind, and she saw the dark red-brown stains on the bleached white.

Her arms trembled as she lifted the dishpan again. It was so heavy, and she was so tired. She staggered, leaned briefly against a fence post.

Her house. There it was, the neat little porch, the swing just made for little girls to play in. The life her daughter should have had.

Darkness blotted her vision, and she fought it off once more, now certain it was death itself she held at bay.

Her house. Johnny's house. Perhaps his spirit had

led her here, and shown her what he wanted her to do.

She made her way across the rutted road, through the gate, up the front stairs, her eyes holding the image of the snug little house with the warmth-filled windows.

Carefully, she placed Jonnie on the porch. She was beyond tears, beyond hope, torn by a pain that would surely kill her even if the darkness didn't. Dear God, how had it come to this?

If only there was something she could give her daughter besides life. A little bit of herself, so she would know that she had had a mother who loved her. She bent down to arrange the blankets, and her locket swung free, catching a glint from the light that spilled through the glass panes.

Of course. Johnny had given her the necklace before he'd gone off to war, along with his pledge that he'd come back and marry her. In return, she'd given him her body as her own promise. She slipped the chain over her head and gripped the cold metal in her palm. It had begun with this. Fitting that the locket stay with the child created that night, a gift from both her father and mother.

But Davinda could not bear to take nothing with her. She opened the locket, bent back the lid, the delicate hinge snapping easily, closing one half of the broken locket in her palm. She tucked the chain amongst the blankets, careful not to touch the baby. For she knew if she touched her, felt that fine, whisper-soft skin, warm with life, she would never leave her. And she could not take her daughter into the darkness with her.

With a last burst of strength, she knocked sharply on the door, then dashed across the yard, hiding herself in a clump of stripped, ragged bushes.

The door opened. The man who stepped out was tall, dark, hard-featured, his broad frame outlined in flickering gold from the firelight inside the house. A soldier, a strong man, like her Johnny. A man who could protect a child.

She saw him bump the dishpan with his foot. He looked down, surprise and shock written clear on his face. He ran out into the rain, and Davinda shrank back into the tangled brush. He was shouting something, she couldn't tell what; the wind ripped at his words and carried them away from her. Finally he rushed back to the porch and lifted the dishpan with gentle, extreme care. He shouldered open the door, taking her baby into the light-filled warmth of the house, out of her life and into his own.

And Davinda Norris faded into the darkness.

PART 1

The Woman Next Door

1

A baby.

Dear God, a baby. What damn-fool idiot would leave a baby on *his* doorstep?

As soon as Michael Collins had taken the child into the shelter of the house, he'd raced back outside, hunting the yard and the street for any sign of who'd knocked on his door. The road was empty except for the spray of icy rain and bare, broken branches.

Unwilling to leave the baby alone any longer, terrified something would happen to it, he'd finally given up and rushed back home.

It hadn't disappeared while he was gone. He'd been nearly convinced that it would, and wasn't quite sure whether he should hope for that or not.

He sagged into the nearest chair, his hands hanging loose between his knees, and stared at the dishpan and the neatly tucked bundle of cloth it held. He'd peeled back the blanket that draped loosely over the top only once, only long enough to see what it held.

He didn't even dare touch the pan again. What if he did something wrong? What if he hurt it? Dear

God, what in the hell was he supposed to do with the thing?

Ever since Michael had returned from the war, he'd done everything he could to avoid babies. When he walked through the streets of town, he kept his head down; on the rare occasions that a mother brought her child into his smithy, he averted his eyes, keeping them carefully on whatever bit of metal he was working.

He had to. It was asking too much of him, to be confronted so vividly with all he'd lost. It was too much pain to live with, and so he didn't. He survived only by keeping it ruthlessly boxed away. And by carefully, sometimes rudely, staying away from any reminders of what could have been, if only he'd been less stubborn. Less plumb self-righteously stupid.

But he couldn't keep his eyes off the blue-speckled dishpan and its living cargo. Was it breathing all right in there? What if the blanket sagged down and blocked its tiny nose? Maybe there was something wrong with it. Maybe whoever had left it on his doorstep had confused his house with Dr. Williams' next door, not realizing the doctor had left nearly two years ago to run a Union hospital.

He leaned over and gingerly lifted the faded wool blanket.

Jesus, it was so small. He couldn't decide if it was the ugliest thing he had ever seen, or the most beautiful. Skin pink as a sunburned pig, blotchy in the wavering firelight. A head no bigger than a misshapen orange, crowned with delicate fuzz the pale white of dandelion tufts. Little bitty features, eyes screwed shut with lids so thin they looked almost translucent.

Jesus Christ.

It could be sleeping. Or it could be dead. How the hell was he supposed to know?

Carefully, he brought the tip of his forefinger under a nose that was barely the size of his fingernail. He caught a whisper of delicate warmth, a current of air so insubstantial, at first he wondered if he imagined it. It was breathing, then. Good.

Now what?

It squirmed a little, opened and closed its mouth a few times.

Then it started hollering.

He jumped back. "Damn it!" He *knew* he shouldn't have gone near the thing. And now look. He'd barely touched it, and already it was wailing away.

"Aw, come on, don't do that."

He picked it up, dishpan and all. Even with the sturdy metal pan and what had to be a few dozen yards of cotton and wool gauze, it still seemed lighter than even a small horseshoe.

"Please, please, don't do that."

It didn't listen. Who would have thought a creature that small could scream so loud? At least he knew the lungs were in working order.

"*Please* be quiet," he pleaded, not at all sure why he thought it would respond to politeness. It just seemed like the thing to do.

He cautiously jiggled the pan a little. The baby's face was rapidly turning from pink to all-out beet red, looking like it might head right on to purple.

"Shit!"

Michael Collins was no fool. He knew when he was in over his head.

He flipped the blanket back over the screaming child, sheltering it from the cold rain outside, and went straight for the door.

Perhaps Katherine Williams had imagined opening her door to see Michael standing there a few times. Okay, maybe even more than a few times, when her defenses were down. Even so, she'd never really expected to find him there. And certainly not warily cradling a cloth-wrapped bundle from which resounded the unmistakable sounds of a very angry infant.

"Michael!"

"I know it's late, I'm really sorry," he said in a desperate rush, "but can I come in?"

"Of course." She stepped aside to let him enter, her shock rapidly giving way to a vibrant curiosity. What in the world was Michael doing with a baby?

"Here." He shoved the pan in her hands so quickly that she was grateful for efficient reflexes. "I don't know what I did to it, I swear. I just checked to make sure it was breathing, and it woke up and started screeching and I don't see how I could have hurt it, I barely touched it, and—"

"I'm sure you didn't." She swallowed a smile, knowing he wouldn't appreciate it. That was more words than she'd heard from Michael in the previous six months put together, and it pleased her. "Doesn't sound hurt to me, anyway. That's a mad cry if ever I heard one."

She set the baby down on the sofa and began unwrapping the layers of cloth. "Let's see what we have here now, hmm?" she said soothingly. "You sure are a loud one, aren't you?"

Hovering over her shoulder, Michael shifted awkwardly from foot to foot. "Is it? It sounded awful loud to me, but I didn't *think* I could have hurt it so bad. Maybe I scared it."

"Oh no, you're fine, aren't you little one?" She lifted the baby into her arms, charmed as always by the thistledown weight and new-sweet smell of an infant. She swayed, an even, soothing motion, and the crying eased a notch. "Of course, if Michael doesn't stop all that twitching, it's no wonder you're a tad upset, is it?"

He froze. "Sorry."

Katherine broke into laughter. "Relax, Michael. It's only a baby."

He shot her a look of pure disbelief. "How do you know it's all right?"

"Well, now, my sisters have eleven between them so far, not counting the one Anne's expecting any day. I *do* know what I'm doing."

"Then what's the matter with it?"

"Hmm." She bent her head, so she could brush her nose over the softness of the fuzz on the baby's crown and fill herself with the scent. It had been too long since she'd held such a little one. "Needs a britches change, would be my guess. Or perhaps the babe's hungry."

"Well do it!"

"All right." Fortunately, she kept a stack of diapers in the linen closet. It was easier than her sisters having to pack a supply every time they brought one of their children to visit. She fetched one, and changed the baby right on the embroidered brocade of the sofa—her mother would have had a fit, but who would tell her?—while Michael perched uneasily on a chair nearby, as if he couldn't quite decide whether he should bolt.

"Now." She lifted the child to her shoulder, and she burrowed in, nuzzling the side of Katherine's neck. "I've got some questions, but first we need to feed her. She's hungry."

"She?"

"Yes, she. Didn't you notice?"

"I didn't look!" he said, clearly aghast.

"Of course not." She turned to head for the kitchen, but the look in his eyes made her pause.

His eyes had always drawn her. Not only with their color, a deep, unusual green, like pines hidden in the shadows of a forest glade, but with the life they held, the secrets, the fierce intensity.

But ever since Sarah had died giving birth to their stillborn child, and he'd limped home from the war over a year later with a bullet in his hip and that bleak emptiness in his eyes, she'd looked into them a hundred times, searching for something, anything, a vague spark of the power that had once been there. There'd been nothing . . . until now.

His gaze never left the child. Half of him was terrified, certainly; but there was also a tentative, unmistakable yearning, so fragile it nearly broke her heart just to look at it. And if it could hurt so much just seeing him that way, how much worse must it be for him, to be feeling it?

"Here." Her decision made, she placed the baby in his arms before he had time to think about it and backed away. His big hands, rough, scarred from his work, shiny with red patches where he'd burned himself on the red-hot metal, nearly swallowed up the tiny body.

"But I can't—"

"Of course you can," she said calmly. "Or I wouldn't let you touch her. Just keep her head supported."

"I know that much!" he snapped.

And, before he could protest again, she disappeared down the hall without so much as a backward glance.

"Lord." He wondered how many times he'd begged help from Above tonight. He'd thought he'd given up that useless habit long ago. Back when he'd lain in a Union hospital and prayed for death and even that release had been denied him.

The crying picked up volume again. It astounded him that she could keep it up that long. He tried the swaying he'd seen Katherine use, rocking back and forth, and was immensely relieved when it seemed to help.

The warmth of the child, perceptible even through the layers of blankets, surprised him. He wouldn't have guessed she would be so warm. And he would never have guessed that he would like the feel of her in his arms so much.

Which, of course, was exactly why he had to get her off his hands and out of his life as soon as possible, before he started to like it *too* much. Because there was no way in hell he was ever going to allow himself to go through losing someone he would miss ever again.

"Here we go."

When Katherine reappeared at his side, Michael gratefully moved to hand over the baby, but she shook her head. "Oh no, you go ahead and feed her. Might as well get used to it." She handed him a small tin bottle topped with a black rubber nipple.

He was about to protest the "get used to it" when the infant let out a renewed wail. Desperate, he jostled to free up one hand, tucking her more firmly in the crook of his elbow, and nudged her mouth with the tip of the nipple.

She latched on with such ferocity that he nearly jumped, her cries instantly replaced with the sounds of lusty suckling.

"What the heck did you put in there, anyway?"

"Just water, mostly. A teaspoon of sugar and cream." Katherine played her fingers lightly over the baby's head. Elegant fingers, long and slender; a musician's hands. "She's too young to handle anything richer yet, I think."

"Young?" He looked up to find Katherine close beside him, her head bent over the child in his arms. Closer than he'd been to a woman in months . . . years. Her hair was loose, falling softly over her shoulder, the firelight picking out strands of red in the rich, glossy brown, and his belly contracted painfully.

It had been his choice, the absence of women in his life. His punishment, for not having been there when Sarah needed him most. For being off hammering horseshoes on military nags while she struggled for her life, and the life of their child, and lost. It hadn't been nearly penance enough—not even when he talked his commanding officers into letting him leave the army smithy and fight at the front instead.

After Sarah's death, just the idea of touching another woman seemed sordid and sacrilegious.

He could live without the sex. It was the other things he missed more, the soft, daily things. The feel of warm, damp woman's skin right after her bath or the curve of a secret smile that was just for him. Once, a few months after learning of Sarah's death, he'd counted out enough money for a prostitute the night before battle. Not to sleep with; he'd known he wouldn't be able to bring himself to do that, as much as he would have welcomed the oblivion. He'd just wanted the chance to bury his nose in the silky coils of a woman's hair and breath in that sweet scent one more time. Instead, though, she'd stunk of smoke and whiskey and other men, and he'd left feeling worse than before.

But this was Katherine. Katherine, his wife's best friend, whom he'd always liked in a vague sort of way but never thought more about than that. She lifted her head, her blue eyes dark as twilight in the shadowed room, and she was close enough to kiss, and he was utterly shocked that the idea had even occurred to him.

Hell! He didn't want this. Didn't want it, didn't need it, couldn't handle the complication of it. He survived each day only by removing himself from even the possibility of feeling anything, not pleasure or pain, and certainly not this sudden, sharp flicker of unwelcome attraction.

"How old do you think she is?" he asked, looking for distraction.

"You don't know?"

"No, I—" His gaze whipped to hers. "You don't think she's *mine*!"

"She's not?" She wasn't, of course, and Katherine knew it. Michael would never suspect that half of her almost wished the child *was* his. She would rather have him be a man, even a flawed and careless but obviously *alive* man, than the cold, stiff monument to grief he'd made of himself.

"She's not."

"Well, she's certainly brand new. No more than a day or two, I'd say." Unable to resist, she let her fingers drift over the baby's scalp, taking pleasure in that impossibly tender skin. "She's small, though. And had a bit of a rough time of it. See how her head is misshapen from being pushed through the birth canal?"

Though it was hard to tell in the dusky light, she could have sworn he blushed, and was utterly charmed by it. Katherine supposed it wasn't the sort of thing a lady of any delicacy should say to a man. But childbirth was not a modest undertaking, and she'd gone through it with her sisters and friends often enough that she was no longer embarrassed by any aspect of it.

"Is that what it's from? I'd wondered," he said.

"Mmm hmm. It'll go away, though, soon enough." He looked so fine with a child in his arms, she decided. Even so obviously uncomfortable. There was something about a big, hard man with a new life held safe in his battered hands that would always get to any woman with a heart. And she had one, as hard as she'd tried to steel it against him. "Are you going to tell me where she came from?"

"Here. You take her."

"Does it bother you to hold her?"

"No." He was surprised she asked; he was so accustomed to people carefully choosing their words around him, never touching on any subject that might remind him. Even more surprised that his answer was the truth. He would have guessed it would hurt more, expected that he could hardly bear to be so near a newborn. But two years had passed, and it was hard to mourn something that was a possibility more than a memory. Hard, too, to remain distant and unfeeling with the soft weight of a child in his arms.

When Katherine settled on the sofa, he took a seat in a nearby chair. Better not risk being too close to her, he reasoned. Though he'd known her for years—seven? eight?—and never felt it before, that was no guarantee that the odd, and surprisingly potent, burst of attraction would go back where it came from. He dared not take the chance.

"Now then," she prompted.

"Someone left her on my doorstep."

"Just like that?"

"Just like that." It still seemed impossible to him. Who could abandon a child like that? And who would be idiot enough to give over care of an infant to *him*?

The baby squirmed and gave out a fussy cry. He yanked the bottle from her mouth and frantically looked to Katherine for help. God, wasn't she *ever* going to rescue him? Couldn't she see he was utterly helpless? "Hell, she's gonna start hollering again."

Katherine grinned, clearly unconcerned, and just as clearly having far too much fun at his expense. "You probably just need to bubble her."

"Huh?"

She motioned with her hands, demonstrating how to bring the baby to his shoulder and gently pat her back.

"What if I hit her too hard and hurt her?"

"You won't." He had no idea where she'd developed this unshakable faith in his abilities. Until now, he'd always considered her a fairly intelligent woman. And he refused to be flattered by her confidence in him.

"Worst thing that could happen," she continued, "is she'll lose her dinner all the way down your back."

He looked up abruptly and she burst into laughter. The woman was *giggling* at him, damn it, her eyes dancing with amusement and firelight.

"You might as well get used to that, too," she said.

"I'm not getting used to anything!" he said, with enough force that the baby startled. "Can I put her down now?"

"Of course. She's probably ready to go back to sleep, anyway."

Even after so brief a time holding her, surely less than an hour, he felt the reluctance to give her up, knew that he would miss the feel of her against his chest. And since he understood, far too well, the danger of growing accustomed to having something warm and sweet in his life, he moved to return her to her dishpan bed as fast as he could.

He carefully tucked the blanket in around her, and caught a glint of metal, hidden deep in the folds of cloth. Curious, he probed the blankets, drawing out a delicate chain spun of gold, fragile as the strand of a spider's web. An oval disk twirled from it, catching flashes of the flames from the hearth and throwing them out into the darkness.

"What is it?" Katherine asked.

"Here." Taking care not to accidentally brush her fingers with his—who knew what the result would be, in a night that seemed completely beyond his control—he dropped it into her waiting palms.

"A locket," she murmured, fingering the edges of the oval. "Half of one, at any rate. From her mother, I suppose." She glanced up at him. "Why are you standing there? Sit."

This time, there was no inconspicuous way to select a place comfortably far from her. Uneasy, he took a seat on the far end of the couch. Even from there, he imagined he could smell her, a drift of soap and toilet water.

"What are you going to do now?"

"Do?" He'd been too busy trying to survive each moment without doing that fragile infant permanent harm to give much thought to what came next. He'd been hoping Katherine would simply take over and save him the worry. "I'll find her mother, I suppose."

"It might not be that easy." Or even desirable, in Katherine's opinion. A woman who could abandon a child on the doorstep of a stranger should hardly have the right to such a precious charge. "She was probably quite desperate, to leave her child like that. Or perhaps . . . oh, I know. Maybe, in her shame, she threw herself into the river. She was unmarried and alone, cruelly cast off from her family, and the stranger who attended the birth couldn't keep a motherless child, for she already had six of her own she could barely keep fed. Before she took her tragic leap to join her murdered love, the mother begged the kindly stranger to find her daughter a good home. And the good woman selected you."

"Did you just think of that?" he asked, caught between admiration and sheer astonishment.

"Well . . . no," she admitted. "Mother's off to Anne's until after the baby's born—the twins are only eleven months, you know. So I've been reading at night to occupy myself." She leaned forward, drawing him into her conspiracy. "*Novels*. And if you tell her, I'll make you very, very sorry. I promise I will."

"Oh, I believe you would. Clearly, you're much more imaginative than I am. Who knows what you'd come up with." He gave a mock shudder.

Then he added one more extraordinary thing to an already extraordinary night—laughter. How long had it been? Long enough that he barely recognized the sound of his own laughter. He tried to feel guilty, tried to stop his inappropriate response, but he couldn't find the will. It felt too damn good.

Katherine sobered, and he had the oddest urge to do something silly, just to see if he could make her laugh again. And if *that* wasn't silly, he didn't know what was.

"What if you can't find her mother?" she asked.

"I will." There was nothing else to be done.

"And what will you do with her until then?"

"You could take her," he suggested hopefully.

Katherine drummed her fingers on her knees, considering. She'd take the child, in a moment, if it came to that. But if she did, she knew what would happen. She'd noted how quickly he'd rid himself of the baby after she finished her bottle. If the baby stayed with her, Michael would retreat back into his comfortable, sterile isolation. She had no doubt of it. That tender glimmer of interest and emotion she'd seen when he looked at the babe would be gone as if it had never existed.

She knew of no better way to mourn and heal than to hold a child.

"Oh, I don't think so," she said slowly. "I have work to do. Who would care for her when I teach? Or play at the Sunday services? Mother won't be home for two months, at least."

Obviously, it had never occurred to him that she would refuse. His eyes went wide, his mouth opened and closed, as if he felt the need to say something but couldn't quite figure out what.

"I guess you'll have to keep her yourself."

"What!" *Now* there was clear emotion in his eyes— pure and unmistakable panic. "That's"—he cast around for a word strong enough—"impossible!"

It was patently unfair of her to use a confidence he had no idea she knew. She was going to do it anyway.

Sarah had told her once that the reason Michael was so obviously and completed devoted to his new family was simply because he'd never had one of his own. He'd been raised in an orphanage and hated every second of it. She suspected he'd cut off his own arm before consigning another child to the same fate.

"I suppose," Katherine said, as if thinking aloud, "That we could consult Reverend Hartman. Perhaps he knows of a good orphanage that would be willing to take her in, poor thing." She was faintly surprised that she'd managed speak the words so calmly, for she hated the idea herself, and would never let a child go into one of those cold and lonely places if she could possibly prevent it.

For a moment she thought she'd badly miscalculated. His expression went dead cold and Katherine was afraid that, once again, Michael had managed to detach himself from everything—and everyone—around him.

"No," he said flatly. "She's not going to an orphanage. Ever."

Her relief was muted by the distinct possibility that he would never forgive her for making the suggestion. Still, she'd had little choice. Nothing else had ever lured him back from his icy grief; if this worked, she would gladly live with his anger in return.

"Do you have any other suggestions?"

"I still don't understand why you can't. You can't have lessons more than a few hours a day. I've got my own work to do."

"Yes, well . . ." He was right, darn it. She'd hoped to get this settled before he had time to think it through. "I . . ." She sniffled loudly. "I think I'm getting a cold, though. It wouldn't be good for her to be around me all the time. At least until I'm not sick anymore."

"A cold?"

"Oh yes." She rubbed her neck. "My throat's real scratchy."

"And I suppose she could catch it."

"Of course. Wouldn't do at all."

"I guess not."

"If you keep her, I'll help you all I can," she suggested quickly. "I'll teach you everything you need to know. You can drop her off on your way to the smithy in the mornings. I'll watch her any time I don't have lessons to give."

"What about your cold?"

"Oh, as long as she's not with me *all* the time, it'll be okay. I'll be careful."

Truth be told, he'd probably be heartily sick of her presence before this was over. Though she was absolutely sure of the baby's welfare—Michael was intelligent, capable, and sensible, and that was, in her opinion, far more important than his sex in the ability to care for a child—he was a tad short on practical experience. But what brand new parent wasn't? Still, she fully intended to live in his pocket, at least for a while.

"Whatever you need, Michael, just remember I'm right next door."

Afterward, he really had no idea how it had happened, how he'd ended up taking charge of a newborn baby.

Katherine spent more than an hour showing him what to do. Diapering took practice; his big, clumsy fingers simply weren't made to tuck and tie cloth around such a tiny creature, and, even when he'd thought he'd gotten it right, he'd lifted her up and the diaper sagged right off her little butt. The entire time, Katherine kept up a steady stream of advice until his head spun like he'd downed half a bottle of whiskey.

Just past midnight, she sent him home with the baby tucked under one arm and a flour sack of supplies over his shoulder. He clutched a sheaf of papers, the pages filled with what seemed like thousands of directions in Katherine's small, neat writing, the words swimming before his dazed eyes. How to skim the rich top cream and warm it with water and cane sugar. The way to store the nipples in soda water and boil used diapers with borax. The importance of keeping a cork marble fastened over the navel with adhesive plaster. Hell! And, in every spare inch of the paper, she'd printed encouragement in big, black letters. Things like "Don't panic!" and "Remember, I'm right next door!"

As if he were likely to forget.

He was quite convinced that, somehow, it was entirely her fault. If he'd run the other direction, to old Mrs. Seligman instead, he was sure that *she* would have done the right thing and taken the infant right off his incompetent hands. He ignored completely the fact that he'd never even considered such a thing. Now, his pride wouldn't allow it—not to mention the fact that Mrs. Seligman probably couldn't hear the baby cry, even if his pounding on her door in the middle of the night didn't cause her weak heart to give out.

He was also bound and determined that—since it *was* all Katherine's fault—he wasn't going to give her the satisfaction of running to her when he failed. He would manage, damn it, even without all her insulting instructions. How hard could it be—although he supposed the knowledge that, in his entire life, he'd never been alone with a child of any age, much less an infant, was not terribly encouraging. Even at the orphanage he'd kept far away from the nursery. He'd grown early, and been apprenticed out as soon as they could find someone willing to take him.

He'd been aghast when Katherine informed him he would have to feed the child every two hours through the night. Two hours! How was a man supposed to get any sleep? But it hadn't taken long for him to discover that two hours was an optimistic estimate.

For it wasn't only the feeding. There were bottles to prepare and wash. Soaked and smelly diapers to change. And the slight problem that she seemed to much prefer *his* arms to doze in than her nicely padded dishpan bed. Imagine that.

Not to mention that, when he had, at last, gotten her settled in, sleeping peacefully away with a slight, rumbling snore—who ever would have thought such a tiny creature could snore?—he'd snatched no more than fifteen minutes of sleep himself before he came awake with a jerk, his heart pounding, wondering why it was suddenly so quiet. He'd dashed to her side, just to make sure she was still breathing—though this time, thank God, he hadn't woken her when he checked.

And so, just after sunrise, Michael staggered to Katherine's door, the evil, exhausted part of him hoping that he would be dragging her out of a nice snug sleep.

But she was fresh and bright as morning itself, yanking open the door as soon as he knocked to greet him with a big smile and open arms for the baby. *Now* she was happy to take the little girl. She wore a crisp yellow blouse, her gleaming hair tucked neatly into a net bag, and he almost smiled back at her before he caught himself.

"Rough night?" she asked, expertly slipping the infant in the crook of her right arm.

"How could you tell?" He scowled at her; he was certain he did. But she only grinned the more.

"Oh, it shows a bit." She reached up, brushed the hair off his forehead with her warm fingers. He caught a bit of her scent, coffee and vanilla and a hint of rosewater. It felt so good, she smelled so good, that he nearly closed his eyes and gave over to the bliss. Instead, he jerked away and stepped back.

He ran a hand over his head to find his hair sticking up in all directions like a jumble of wind-blown leaves. He'd forgotten to comb it, damn it.

"I'm going to work," he grumbled.

"Would you like to come in for coffee first? You look like you could use some."

How many times had she asked him that, in the months since he'd returned from war? Everyone else in town had long ago learned to stay out of his way, respecting his desire to be left alone. Everyone but Katherine. Katherine stopped to speak to him each time she saw him, asked him for supper or lunch nearly as often, and never seemed the least bit put off when he said no.

He supposed she felt it her duty. She'd been Sarah's closest friend, and probably thought it was her responsibility to look after him. And if he'd started to look forward to seeing her, just a little bit, it hadn't seemed like such a big thing. She had an easy, sunny nature and a quick smile. Who wouldn't be pleased to see her?

But now it seemed entirely too tempting. To feel the warmth of the house creeping out the doorway into the chill dawn, luring him inside; to see the freshness of morning on her skin; to breath in the luscious, yeasty smell of the cinnamon-currant buns that were her specialty. Too easy to begin to believe that there was more for him than what he had, and he'd learned, far too well, that there was not.

"No," he snapped, biting off the "thank you," wondering if, this time, his rudeness would be enough to make her pull back from him, to a distance that would be safer for both of them. He turned on his heel, striding away to the smithy that was his refuge. Work he understood.

"I have a lesson at two o'clock," she called after him, her voice lilting, unperturbed. "We'll see you this afternoon."

When Katherine approached Michael's blacksmith shop at precisely 1:45, he was waiting for them.

Oh, she knew he would never admit it. He made a very good show of looking surprised and unconcerned when she came strolling down the street. But he hardly ever poked his head out the door during working hours; certainly, he never stood out front with his hands tucked behind his back, scanning the sky like he had all the time in the world.

"Look there, sweetheart," she murmured to the baby, just loud enough for him to hear, "Michael's come out to greet us. Isn't that kind of him?"

Michael rocked back on his heels and tipped his head up. "I was just keeping an eye on the weather. The storm blew over from last night well enough, but there are a few clouds out there in the west to worry about. See?"

Katherine spared a glance at the fluffy, innocuous-looking clouds that were just visible over the trees. "I see. Well, here you go." She resisted the urge for one more cuddle and handed over the child. Michael needed to hold her more than she did. "You forgot everything this morning. Luckily, I managed to bring what you'll need along."

"I didn't forget. I was hoping you'd take pity on me and let me have one day to recover."

"Don't be silly." The last thing in the world he needed was pity, Katherine thought. Pity would only serve to remind him that he'd earned it by losing something precious. He'd do much better if everyone in this town would just stop *pitying* him.

"Now then," she went blithely on, "I brought her bed, and plenty of diapers, and one bottle already made up. You shouldn't need more than one, I won't be gone more than an hour. And I brought you something to eat, just a cold beef sandwich and a bit of lemon cake."

"But—"

"Don't you dare say no, Michael. I'm cooking far too much with Mother gone, and you'd be doing me a favor to take some off my hands. And I know full well you never eat enough when you're busy working. I'll be checking when I get back to see that you've finished it."

"Yes ma'am," he agreed, a hint of a bemused smile playing around his lips.

So that was the trick of handling Michael. One simply had to douse him with so many words, so fast, that he didn't have time to frame a refusal before she went on to the next topic.

"We'd best get inside, shouldn't we?"

"The smithy's not really a place for a baby."

"I'm certain it will be fine. At least it will be nice and warm for her, with the fire and all."

She hefted the sack of supplies she'd dragged behind her all the way and slung it over her shoulder. The unbalanced weight of the heavy dishpan in the big bag staggered her, and she stumbled back.

"Is it too heavy for you?"

He was laughing at her; she could hear it in his

voice. When she glanced over her shoulder to check, his face was composed in determinedly sober lines, but amusement glinted in his eyes, and she debated the merits of letting the weight drag her down, just to see if she could get that laughter to break free.

"Of course not," she said airily. "No problem at all. Light as a feather."

"Sorry. My mistake."

Leaning forward to balance the weight, she headed through the big double front doors that were thrown wide.

Inside, every inch of the packed-earth floor held work waiting to be done. Buckets of ax handles in need of blades, stacks of metal bars waiting to be worked into latches, broken wheels, adze heads, rusty hinges, and horseshoes all crowded the small room. A fire blazed in the brick forge in the far corner, a bellows tilted at the ready nearby. Light leaked through the wide gaps in the rough-board walls; old nails jammed into the wood held an assortment of tongs and hammers and other tools.

It was the piece of paper nailed right inside the front door that brought her up short. "What's that?"

Bold black letters asked for information about the family of the baby left on his doorstep.

"Just what it looks like, of course," he said without a flicker of emotion.

She whirled on him. "You can't be serious."

"How else am I to find her parents? I've asked everyone who came in this morning, but no one knew anything."

"But—but—you can't simply hand her off to a *stranger!*"

"And what exactly are we?"

Hard to believe he could just stand there, weight on one hip, looking entirely comfortable with the child tucked in his arms—how easily he'd grown accustomed to holding her—and talk so calmly about giving her away.

Perhaps it had been completely stupid on her part, to think that this could make a difference. To believe that if he finally learned to care about something, anything, again it would lead him to care about life once more, and to hope the baby could do it. A wild, probably futile gamble . . . but then, there'd been little to lose, she'd thought. She'd never have considered it if she'd suspected for one moment that the little one's welfare was in jeopardy. Could she have misjudged so badly?

"With us, at least, we know she's well cared for!"

He ignored her, striding by with that little hitch in his step that was the legacy from the bullet in his hip, and contemplated the cluttered interior of his shop.

"Where do you think I should put her?"

What did it matter where he put her now, if he were willing to surrender her to anyone who wandered in? "Michael, *anyone* could walk in and say she's that child's mother. Anyone!"

"Maybe in there?" He gestured to an old wagon bed tilting in one corner of the shop, awaiting new fittings and wheels. "She'd be sheltered there, at least." He walked over to the wagon and peered over the side.

"Michael, you simply cannot do this, I will not allow it—"

"Hand me the dishpan, will you? This looks good enough—"

"Michael!" she shouted. "Stop it! This is a child, not an unwanted puppy! I will not let you simply consign that baby to heaven knows what fate because you can't be bothered!"

He stilled. His shoulders rose and fell in a deep breath, and he turned slowly, as if finally surrendering to having this discussion with her.

"And what, exactly, are the alternatives here?"

She opened her mouth, closed it again when she realized she had few good options to offer. It was easy enough to think about what would happen to the baby for the next few months; a lifetime was an entirely different matter.

"You were the one who talked me into this in the first place," he said.

"I did not! I—"

The baby stirred, and Michael shifted his grip, snugging her up against his chest, her tiny head cradled in the hollow of his neck. "Katherine, I have every intention of making absolutely certain, before I give her over, that it is her family I'm giving her to."

She understood, then. He was only determined to give the child what he had never had: her family. She chose her next words carefully, wondering how to make him understand that simply being blood wasn't always enough. "Even if they *are* family . . . if the mother chose to leave her on the doorstep of a stranger, rather than with her own family, she probably had a very good reason."

"Katherine, is that really what you believe of me? That I would simply pass her on without making absolutely certain that she was safe?" He watched her intently, as if her answer were very important to him.

Odd, when he'd never much seemed to care what her opinion of him was before. "Why did you ever let me keep her in the first place, then?"

Her mother had always bemoaned her tongue, so prone to babbling out words before her brain had a chance to consider them. And now, it seemed, she'd hurt him, and that was the very last thing in the world she ever wanted to do. "I'm sorry, I spoke too quickly. I do trust you, Michael. I always have." More than he would ever know.

He cupped the back of the baby's head in his big palm, holding it steady, the weathered back of his hand dark against the pale skin and silver-blond down of the infant's scalp, and, just for one sweet instant, she allowed herself to think what that gentle touch might feel like against her own skin.

"Thank you, Katherine."

Michael blamed it on exhaustion.

For certainly, that must be the reason the next week passed so contentedly. He was simply too *tired* for anything else. That had to be why he found himself toting the child around with him even when she wasn't fussing. Certainly it had to be the reason he didn't mind Katherine popping in and out without warning, even though he knew good and well he preferred to be left alone. And it *had* to be to blame for why he kept having disturbing fantasies, every time Katherine came within arm's length, of tugging her to him, just to see if she'd pull away or if she'd sink into his embrace. And why he was half convinced she'd come right into his arms.

It was harder for Katherine. Harder to keep from spending every second with Michael and the baby—not because they needed her help anymore, but because this mirage of the dream was as close as she was ever going to get to the real thing. Harder, too, to wonder whether she'd set this whole thing in motion not, as she'd tried to convince herself, to help Michael heal, but as a good excuse to get closer to him, and suspect that it just might be the latter. She'd always been honest with herself about her feelings for him—it had been the only way to deal with them, to acknowledge them and their futility, and then put them safely away. It disturbed her greatly to think that she might have been deluding herself all along.

And harder still—oh, so impossibly hard—to walk into his smithy on a bright spring afternoon, to see him sitting on a stool holding the baby with that heartrendingly besotted expression on his face, and not lose her own heart. Completely, irrevocably, and, she knew, hopelessly.

"Get much work done this afternoon?" she asked.

He glanced up, hair shining with the rich color and gloss of the finish on her Chickering piano, and smiled. Darn it, he looked happy to see her. Why'd he have to go and do that? There was a time when she would have sold her playing fingers to have him look at her like that.

Maybe she still would.

"I got all kinds of work done."

"Of course you did." She appraised the room with its jumble of half-finished projects, the same ones that had been there two hours ago when she'd dropped the child off; the fire in the forge, long faded to smoldering embers; and him, without his leather apron.

"Tons of work."

"Perfectly obvious," she agreed.

He caught her staring at the boxes piled in front of the advertisement asking for information. He'd added a keg of nails today, and now only a small corner of the paper peeked out from behind the stack.

"I didn't have anyplace else to put that stuff," he said.

"I can see that."

"So . . . how were the lessons today?"

"Excuse me?"

"What?" He frowned. "You ask me how my work went every day. You didn't think I knew how to make polite conversation?"

"You've never tried it before."

"First time for everything. So, how was it?"

"I've had better."

"What happened?"

"Nothing in particular."

His eyes narrowed. "Why don't you want to tell me, Katherine?"

"I was at the Wilcoxes'." She watched carefully for his reaction to the mention of his former in-laws. Though she'd hoped for something else, she got about what she expected: tight mouth, blank eyes, determinedly neutral voice.

"How are they?"

"Fine."

"The lesson didn't go well? I always liked Elizabeth."

"It wasn't Elizabeth that was the problem. It's her mother."

"Now that I can believe."

It was no secret in Mooretown that Audrey Wilcox was a woman with plans. Her plans for her eldest daughter had most definitely *not* included Sarah returning from a brief visit to her aunt's with a fiancé in tow. Certainly not a fiancé with no family, no background, and worse yet, no prospects.

Katherine debated for a moment. It was none of her business. But, where Michael was concerned, it seemed that whether something was her business or not had ceased to matter long ago.

"Has she . . . have you spoken with her since you returned?"

"No." He stood up abruptly. "Time for you to take her and get out of here. I've got work to do."

"Katherine!" Michael pounded once again on her front door, hoping she wasn't a sound sleeper. "Get up and let me in!"

It must be nearing two, the moon a sliver of cold light. He'd wrapped the baby in a soft cotton blanket and held her tucked against his chest, under the coat he'd thrown on. He prayed she was warm enough, and that taking her out into the night hadn't been the worst thing he could do. The stone steps were cold as well-water beneath his bare feet, and he shifted, debating whether he should go around back, toss a few rocks at Katherine's window, and try to wake her that way.

Finally the door flew open. The interior of the house was dark; only a splinter of moonlight revealed a sleepy-eyed Katherine, swathed in a baggy robe with her tangled hair loose around her shoulders. "What is it? Did you run out of clean diapers again?"

"She— The sound woke me up. I didn't even know what it was at first, I guess it's some sort of cough, but—"

Her drowsiness vanished, replaced by instant alertness. "Is she having trouble breathing?"

"It seems a little labored, I think."

She tugged the door open wider. "Bring her on in. It's cold out there."

As he ducked his head and stepped over the threshold, the baby again made the sound that startled him so much, a hollow, papery bark.

"Croup," Katherine said. "I thought perhaps that was it. Come back to the kitchen and we'll get started on treatment."

"Treatment? Is it . . . dangerous?"

"Not usually," she said lightly.

Not usually? That was not what he wanted to hear. He wanted to hear that it was just an annoyance, that there was no threat at all, that it sounded a hundred times worse than it was. Panic coiled low in his stomach.

"And we'll just make sure of it, won't we?" she continued, her voice already far ahead of him down the hall. She had the advantage of familiarity, and it was far too dark in the house for him to find his way quickly.

Up ahead, a rectangle of light flared to life; she must have lit a lantern.

"Hurry up," she called.

When he entered the shadowed kitchen, Katherine was bent over the stove, poking to life the banked remnants of yesterday's fire, adding lumps of coal. The baby coughed again, her whole body shuddering, and he tightened his grip, wishing that, somehow, his arms could give her some comfort, a bit of strength, hating his uselessness.

"What should I do?"

"You should sit down," she said, plopping a big iron kettle on the stove with a *clank*.

"But—"

"Michael, it's going to be all right, I promise, but I'm trying to remember everything right now and you distract me when you talk to me."

And so he sat, feeling helpless and inept, while the baby coughed and squirmed in his arms and Katherine scurried around the kitchen, dipping water from the reservoir into the pot, collecting bottles and spoons. How did she manage it? he wondered. She was so calm and efficient, and he was so scared. This was the one thing he'd spent two years doing every-thing he could to avoid—being terrified of losing someone who mattered—and he'd found himself right in the middle of it again, without even trying. Just for an instant, he imagined walking right out the door and leaving it all behind, back to his empty, emotionless safety, and knew he couldn't do it. It was too late for him; he was already caught.

But please, God, it was not too late for the baby girl he held.

"Here now, I think the water's starting to boil."

Katherine positioned him over the pot and handed him an umbrella, to capture the pungent steam col-lecting around them.

"What's in there?" he asked.

"Just a little lime, a spoonful of turpentine. The steam will ease her breathing."

He asked no more questions, just took up his station, the umbrella in one hand, baby in the other. Hot, moist air swirled around him, and, if his arms started to ache, it seemed irrelevant. Katherine administered her remedies, rubbing warm sweet oil into the child's feet and chest, dribbling beet juice into her mouth, which made her grimace and turn her face away. She cried weakly and coughed, he sweated and worried, and Katherine worked, finally slicing up a few onions and setting them to frying in sizzling lard.

"Really, I know you do seem to have a fondness for feeding me, but I'm not sure now is the time—"

She laughed, and, for the first time, looked up from the baby, now quieter and on the verge of sleep, to him. "I'm making a poultice, for her chest."

"Oh."

"I didn't realize you still had your coat on, you must be ready to burst from the heat. Here, let me."

"No, I—"

She stripped the coat from his shoulders before he could form his protest, before he could warn her that he'd dashed from his house without taking time to dress and there was nothing beneath the coat but the long drawers he'd worn to bed.

"Oh my." Her hand went to her mouth. "You must have been, um, *cold* out there."

Was that *laughter* she was hiding behind her hand? Disrespectful wench. "Here, now, I know I lost a bit of flesh in the war, but that's no reason to—"

"No!" she said quickly. "You look just fine to me."

Her gaze dropped to his bare chest, and a softness came into her eyes, an expression he hadn't seen in the eyes of a woman for so long that he almost didn't recognize it.

She was scarcely any better dressed, he realized. Her bare toes peeked out beneath the hem of her thin robe, and her hair tumbled down her back. This was how a husband would see her, late at night, early in the morning, and the unsought, unexpected intimacy of it hit him with the force of his blacksmith's hammer.

He could lose it all, every shred of the detachment and sanity he'd earned at such terrible cost. Surrender it without a struggle to the promise of having a woman waiting for him beside their bed with her hair loose and feet bare.

Dear God, what was he thinking? He'd believed in the dream once, and it had nearly destroyed him. Surely he knew better than to be tempted by it again.

"I—" He cleared his throat, hoping his voice didn't sound nearly as odd to her as it did to him. "I think she's better. She hasn't coughed for a while."

"Yes, I think so. Her breathing is easier, too." Katherine brushed the baby's nose with the tip of her forefinger. "You had me worried, sweetheart."

"You were worried? It didn't show."

"It did on you." Keep your eyes on her, Katherine warned herself. It wasn't safe—oh, not safe at all—to look at him, the solid muscle formed by years of work, steam-dampened skin gleaming in the faint lamplight.

"I thought you said croup wasn't dangerous."

"It isn't, usually." She considered for a moment

what to tell him. It was the last thing she'd originally intended when she'd hatched this plan, to put him through a night like this, when the life of someone he cared about was endangered, even remotely.

But she couldn't bring herself to lie to him about this. She'd hoped to make him *feel* again. It seemed she'd succeeded. But she could not promise him that there was no potential for pain. She could only hope he would remember that it was worth the risk.

"Sometimes, though, there's a chance that the throat will swell, and the air passage could be blocked," she said.

"What!"

"It's very rare."

He sagged, the air expelling from him in a whoosh. "I'm glad I didn't know about that before."

"Me too. You're almost dropping the umbrella in the pot as it is, and it's the only one my mother left me with."

"Sorry." He snapped up. "How did you know what to do? Did your father teach you? I had no idea."

"No. It's just not an uncommon illness, you know. I've heard my sisters arguing treatments many a time."

"And whose remedy was this one? It seemed to work."

"All of them."

He threw back his head and laughed, and she smiled, relieved to have their relationship back on a more normal footing. If he'd noticed her staring at his chest, it seemed he was quite content to ignore it. The worst of it was, she couldn't quite decide if she was relieved or disappointed.

"I should have known. I suppose she caught your cold after all, and that's where it came from."

"My co— Oh, no, of course not. They're two entirely different things. And I've been *extremely* careful."

"You're sure? I—"

"She's dozing off," Katherine interrupted. "And the onions are just about right, I think. Once I get them on her, why don't the two of you go on into the parlor and rest? I think you've both earned it."

"That we have."

"Not to mention you probably won't get much sleep the next few nights, either."

"I always know I'm in trouble when you say things like that," he said. "What do you mean this time?"

"It's not all over, you know. This was surely the worst of it, but it'll take another couple of days to run its course. And the nights are always worse than the days."

"I can't wait." He set the umbrella aside and held the baby slightly out from him, giving Katherine better access. "Hurry up and get those onions on, then. I've gotten good at snatching a moment of sleep when I can. I want to take full advantage of it."

She bent over the child and peeled back the layers of cloth that covered her. Working like this, she was too close to Michael, the top of her head brushing his bare chest. And far too conscious of the heat from his big, male, barely covered body. If her mother had come in right at that moment, she probably would have fainted dead away at the impropriety of it, but all Katherine could think of was how much she wanted to be decidedly more improper.

"I always thought she was one of the best-smelling things I ever got a whiff of," Michael said. "Most of the time, at least. But, even though I like fried onions, this isn't exactly what I had in mind."

Michael's prosaic comments jerked her right out of her fantasies, and she smiled at her own foolishness. Surely she should have learned by now that there was no point in indulging in fruitless dreams about him.

"There. All done."

She sent them off down the hallway and cleaned up the worst of the mess. Perhaps this once, she thought, she'd keep the baby and let Michael have a few hours of uninterrupted rest. She'd been awfully hard on him, making him take all of the nights, and he could probably use a break.

The small oval of light from the lantern danced wildly as she scooped it up and made her way down the hall. "Michael, I—"

They were both fast asleep. Michael sprawled on the couch, one bare foot propped up on a cushion, the other resting on the floor. The baby curled on his chest, snuggled up under his chin, even in sleep held safe in Michael's strong hands.

Katherine carefully set the lantern down on a side table and simply stood there and watched them, her heart wonderfully, painfully full.

Her plan had succeeded better than she'd hoped, but there'd been a price of her own to pay.

She'd thought she'd come to terms long ago with her feelings for Michael, but she'd badly underestimated their power. Before, her resistance had been bolstered by knowing the acute impossibility of anything between them. That, and the fact that no other woman in the world existed for him but Sarah, had protected Katherine, muted the insistent, hurtful edge. It had been safe to want him then, a distant, pleasant daydream that was nothing like this desperate, growing need.

Then, too, that was before she'd seen his naked chest.

She hadn't the heart to disturb him. She eased the baby from his grip, and his fingers flexed, hold tightening automatically before she gently loosened his grip.

Let him sleep, she decided. She'd take night duty. Just as well, for it was unlikely she'd sleep much, anyway. How could she, when she knew, all too temptingly well, that Michael would be only a few steps away?

3

Two days later, the first day he'd felt comfortable enough to leave the baby in Katherine's care and go off to his own work, Michael found himself hurrying home through air that breathed of spring.

It was stupid, he knew. He *never* left the smithy early. He liked his work, the metal and the fire that had never failed him, even when so much else had. But still, he couldn't seem to help it, to be wise enough and strong enough to detach himself the way he knew that he should.

Katherine had propped the front door wide to catch the warmth of the day, and her music greeted him long before he reached her house, floating through the air as if it danced with the breeze.

Quietly, he stepped into the parlor. She was seated at the piano, her back to the door, the dishpan bed on the bench beside her hip. Her fingers glided over keys the color of cream. The baby let out a yelp, and Katherine tilted her head to her, murmuring something soothing, letting the music go slow and sweet. The lines of her profile were clean, her shining hair swept low on her neck, and her wide smile glowed with maternal love.

And for one pure, dangerous instant, he believed in the dream. It could only be for that one moment. Anything else would be tempting fate, a fate that had showed him well that the dream was never to be his. But, God, right then, he would have sold his soul to be able to capture it for just a little while.

She must have caught a glimpse of him out of the corner of her eye, for she stopped playing and twisted on the bench.

"Hello! I wasn't expecting you yet."

"I finished early." He leaned against the doorway and gestured toward the piano. "That was nice. What you were playing. Very pretty."

"Oh." Was she blushing? The high color suited her well, and she slid her fingers quickly over the keys. She was always touching things, he'd noticed; fingering the baby's hair, running her fingers over the rim of a china cup, smoothing the edge of a ribbon. He had a vague, unsettling notion that he'd been seeing those hands in his dreams far too often . . . only they were stroking him instead.

"Would you like me to play something else?" she asked.

"Maybe later," he said, and cursed himself taking for granted there would be a *later*. Would he never learn?

The baby squawked, and Katherine lifted her up to her level, brushing noses, smiling.

"You are so good with her," he said softly. "Why did you never have any of your own?"

"Oh well." A smile twitched the corners of her

mouth. "I really didn't want my mother to have a fit of apoplexy."

"You *might* have gotten a husband first. She probably would have survived then."

How was she to answer him? Katherine wondered. Afraid that something she didn't want him to see would show in her expression, she buried her face against the baby's neck. "There aren't too many to pick from now. The war has rather limited my choices."

"That's true. But before . . . surely there was someone?"

She couldn't tell him that she'd never found a man to equal her best friend's husband. Even when she'd gotten over Michael himself—or thought she had—she'd wanted what he represented to her, a man who could look at his wife with his soul in his eyes. "It just never happened, I guess. Never the right man." *Liar,* her conscience screamed. "At the right time," she added hastily.

"But—"

"Would you like to stay for supper?" she put in, unwilling to answer any more questions, especially when he was watching her so intently.

"What *is* your obsession with stuffing food down my throat?"

"I'm not sure." Though he still had the thick musculature his work had formed, he'd come home from the war with deep hollows carved beneath his blunt cheekbones and his pants loose around his waist. She didn't know whether to blame the fighting, his injury, or his grief. Either way, it was clearly her duty to fatten him up a little. So what if he'd refused her a hundred times or so already? Sooner or later she'd wear him down.

"Maybe I just have an incurable weakness for helpless strays," she suggested, peering at him over the baby's head.

His eyes narrowed, his smile vanished. "You never had a cold, did you?"

"What?" She coughed, gave a loud and most unbecoming snuffle. "What do you mean? Of course I have a cold."

"And you certainly never had any intention of letting her go to an orphanage."

What was that in his forest-shadow eyes? Pain, anger, resentment? Impossible for her to tell.

Enough then, she decided. She'd lied to him enough. Either he'd taken those first irrevocable steps back to life already or he'd stay in his protective shell. There was nothing else she could do.

"No," she admitted. "I never would have let her go."

"But why?" he burst out, so loudly the child in her arms jumped and Katherine had to shush her. "Why would you lie to me about that?" he continued more softly.

"I . . ." Inadequate words, all of them. "You . . . when you looked at her, Michael, there was something in your eyes, something that I hadn't seen there for a very long time."

"I don't understand."

"I know, it's just that . . . I thought that maybe if you could just feel something, care about *something*, you'd remember why life was worth the trouble of breathing."

His eyes, dark, unreadable, distant, met hers.

"Was I wrong?" she asked slowly. "Are you sorry?"

"No," he said at last, his expression softening, the way it always did when he looked at the babe. "I'm not sorry."

"Will you stay and eat, then?" she asked, expecting him to say no, certain she had pushed him as far as she could for one day—but old habits died hard.

He looked so good, slouched comfortably in her doorway. Familiar, like he belonged there. Too easy to believe that he did.

"You know, Katherine, I think I just might."

If there was one thing Michael learned in the next two weeks, it was that Katherine Williams was a very sneaky woman. She had to be. How else to explain it?

How else could it be that he ended up eating supper at her house every single night? He was always hungry by the time he showed up at her door, and it was hard to cook for himself with the baby in one arm. Plus there was always something wonderful-smelling already prepared when he arrived—something she'd "made too much of," and, well, staying just seemed to be the sensible thing to do.

And what other reason was there that he talked to her so much—*him*, for whom three sentences used to be a long conversation. But the words just kept coming out of his mouth in defense against all the ones that spilled out of hers.

Certainly, there was no other explanation for finding himself, on a particularly warm day in May, sitting on a plaid wool blanket right in the middle of the town square, having, of all things, a picnic.

"There now," Katherine was saying as she waggled a leg of fried chicken at him, "aren't you glad you came?"

"Thrilled."

She pulled a face at his tone, and he had to fight to keep his own expression sober. It wouldn't do to give in to her too quickly.

"Oh, come on, tell the truth. It's a gorgeous day, and I promised you the best custard tarts in town. And I was right, wasn't I?"

"You're just happy because I'm eating."

"You only had two. Here, have another." She dropped one in his hands.

It wouldn't be polite to refuse her, he reasoned. And they really were very good tarts, so he sank his teeth into creamy custard and flaky crust while Katherine beamed in approval.

"See now? This was a good idea, even if you won't admit it. And the baby likes it out here."

"She does at that," he agreed. She lay beside him on the blanket, wiggling in the gentle sun, and he plucked a long blade of grass and tickled her little pink toes with it. "Look there, she smiled at me!"

"Michael," Katherine said in that tone that clearly conveyed she considered him a poor, deluded male. "She's not old enough to smile yet."

"Really?" He brought his face within a foot of the baby's and mugged shamelessly, scrunching his features, sticking out his tongue, and was rewarded by a gummy, lopsided grin. "See?" he said smugly.

"I see."

Because, oddly, Katherine made no further comment, he glanced at her from the corner of his eye to find her studying him with what he'd come to think of as *The Look*—the look that said that, very soon, he'd be doing something he hadn't even considered two minutes ago.

"What?" he asked warily.

"I think we should name her."

"Name her." Though it was awkward with nothing to call her—except the "sweetheart" he whispered when he was certain no one was listening—he'd never thought to name her. It seemed like such a big assumption. What right did he have to give the child a name? Being the one to make the choice implied permanence, responsibility, family, and a dozen other things he'd sworn to avoid.

"Mmm hmm." Katherine sat back on her heels, looking fresh and innocent as the day in her pale blue dress, and he could almost see the wheels turning in her devious mind. "We can't go on calling her 'the baby' for the rest of her life, can we?"

The rest of her life. His chest went hollow. It wasn't that he was stupid . . . he had just never thought that far ahead. But what else could it be, really? He tried to imagine giving her up to a stranger and knew, absolutely, that he would never be able to do it.

"I suppose you have a name in mind?"

"Yes," she said softly. "I think we should name her after Sarah."

"Sarah." He looked down at her, all pink and small and vibrantly, vividly alive, her pale, fuzzy hair blowing in the light breeze, little fingers curling and uncurling like she was trying to capture the sunshine. "Sarah would have liked that, wouldn't she?"

"I think so."

"All right, then." He nodded decisively, surprised at how little it hurt—just a small pang in his heart, not too much, easily soothed by how very *right* it felt. "Sarah it is." *My Sarah.*

"Good. I—" Something over his shoulder caught her attention, and her eyes widened. "Uh-oh."

"What is it?" Twisting, he looked over his shoulder. "Uh-oh," he echoed, having nothing better to say.

Audrey Wilcox bore down on them like an overloaded frigate, her heavy skirts flapping around her black-booted ankles as she took the most direct route to their picnic, with Reverend Hartman in tow behind her.

Guilty as disobedient schoolchildren, they jumped to their feet, Katherine trying to smooth out the messy wrinkles of her skirt. Michael picked up Sarah and tucked her in his arms in self-defense—surely his mother-in-law wouldn't do anything *too* terrible to him if he held an infant in his arms.

"There!" Audrey was ten yards out and closing fast. "You see, Reverend? I *told* you he had a baby!"

Reverend Hartman's mouth was working like a landed fish. He skidded to a stop beside Audrey, who seemed to have plenty of wind left. Clearly, he wasn't up to the pace a thoroughly aggravated Audrey could set. "I see that, Mrs. Wilcox, but, truly, I don't see what the problem is."

"You don't see what the problem is?" If she kept that tone up, Michael was certain, Sarah was going to start screaming any minute, and he wouldn't blame her a bit.

"The problem is," Audrey continued, "that *he*, of all people, is the last person in the world who is fit to raise an impressionable child. And a female one at that!"

"How nice to see you, Mrs. Wilcox," Katherine said in her most placating tone. Michael could have told her it wouldn't do any good. "I understand that you have some concerns, of course, but I assure you, Michael's perfectly capable. I've made absolutely certain of it."

Audrey ignored her. "Reverend Hartman! Certainly you agree with me. Something must be done at once, before the damage is permanent."

The Reverend gathered enough air to sigh wearily. Audrey Wilcox was not only one of his wealthiest parishioners, she was possessed of far more determination than he ever hoped to own. He was not a man who was fond of confrontation, and he'd learned long ago that it was a great deal easier to simply give in to her demands.

"My dear Michael, surely you do not wish to be burdened with the care of a helpless child. It was truly noble of you to attempt it for so long, but I'm quite positive we can take over from here and relieve you of your little problem."

"No," Michael said flatly.

Turning to Audrey, hope lighting his rheumy eyes, Reverend Hartman made a hopeless gesture. "There now, Mrs. Wilcox, we tried."

Audrey closed her eyes briefly, as if she could not bear the sight of the weakness before her. "I know my responsibilities, even if you do not, and I have known it since the instant I heard that Michael harbored an innocent child. It was my duty to investigate, just as it is now our duty to remove it to more appropriate care."

"Appropriate care?"

"Yes," Reverend Hartman put in eagerly, anxious to redeem himself. "Our denomination has a perfectly decent orphanage in St. Paul. They are experts in the care of abandoned children. Undoubtedly they can find adequate placement for this one."

"Audrey," Michael said, his throat painfully dry, unconsciously tightening his hold around Sarah. "I know you think you have a grievance against me, and maybe you do. But, please, don't make her suffer for it."

"I am only doing what is best." Triumph threaded her words. She'd finally found a way to punish him, first for marrying her daughter, then for giving her the child that killed her. If it were only him, Michael would have accepted her revenge. He probably deserved it. But he could not allow her to hurt Sarah—and Katherine—in the process.

"Come now," Reverend Hartman said. "Hand over the child, or I will be forced to go for the authorities.

"I will not."

"Really." Katherine rushed forward, placing herself firmly at his side. "I can personally vouch for Michael. He's quite wonderful with the baby. There's no need for concern."

Jowls in full flap, Audrey pulled herself to her imposing height. "And you, Katherine Williams! I had hoped not to say anything, out of deference to your poor mother. But I have it on very good authority that *he*—" she threw out a pale, chubby hand, "was seen leaving your house extremely early one morning, wearing nothing more than a pair of . . . of . . ." Her lips pinched, as if it was painful to try and force out the word. "A pair of drawers! And I must say, I am *appalled* that you would sink so low, and fall for such , an unprincipled lecher!"

Katherine shot him a look. Her ears were bright pink, but her eyes were lit with unholy amusement. *Darn it*, he thought, *what trouble was that woman's mouth going to get her into this time?* Her clean and loving life had left her with no inkling of the kind of lengths someone would go to for revenge, and he doubted she had the faintest clue what sort of trouble they were actually in. No, she'd assume that, in the end, Audrey and the Reverend would go along with what was best for Sarah.

Not to mention that she was prone to tease him at every turn.

"I swear," he began, ready to explain, to insist they were nothing more than friends—but he was too late. Katherine had sidled between him and their accusers, her eyes downcast, hands linked, and scuffed the earth with her toe.

"I'm so sorry," she said, and Michael wondered if the Reverend and Audrey suspected that the emotion underlying her words was not contrition but budding laughter. "But what's a weak girl to do? You of all people, Audrey, should know what he's like. That glib tongue, his flirtatious ways, that roguish charm . . . How could I possibly be strong against such expert seduction? He's so . . . ." Her deep, longing sigh was nothing short of truly theatrical.

Damn it! He should have known she would be

unable to resist an opening like that, and the opportunity to prod Audrey in the bargain. Why hadn't he jumped in more quickly to stop her? And just who the hell was she describing? He knew darn well that he was none of those things, and he was not—no, he was not—insulted by the fact that she was vastly amused just by saying them.

Audrey gasped and staggered back, her hand clutched to her impressive bosom. "Katherine! How *could* you!"

"Mrs. Wilcox!" The Reverend grabbed her arm to steady her and patted her hand consolingly. "There, now, we'll take care of everything." His lean face now fired with righteous resolution, he turned to address Michael. "Certainly you can see why this is an impossible situation. It would simply be unthinkable to leave an innocent child in the care of an unmarried couple committing Lord-only-knows-what depraved and immoral acts. I simply must insist you turn over the child to someone better able to care for it."

Hell! He knew Audrey, knew she would no more let go of this issue than a starving dog would release a greasy soup bone. Katherine, her wide, disbelieving eyes focused on Sarah, was clearly not ready to accept that this was happening. Why should she? Katherine was not used to the kind of tricks fate liked to play on him.

A strand of hair had worked free of its anchor, lying loose against her neck. Deliberately, he reached up to tuck it away—a lover's gesture, and one he'd been wanting to do for weeks, though he hadn't admitted it until now. Her hair slid through his fingers like corn silk, smooth, warm from the sun, exactly as he'd imagined it would, and she looked up at him, surprised. But she didn't step away, either.

"Well then, Reverend Hartman," he said slowly. "I guess it's a good thing we're getting married, isn't it?"

4

How many times had she fantasized this? A hundred? A thousand? More? In all the times Katherine had dreamed of her wedding night, she'd never even come close to imagining this.

Glumly, she rearranged the little cubes of boiled ham on her plate, sneaking a peek at her new husband across the table. Michael was silent, remote, eyes fixed on his own plate, faint evening light carving deep, bruise-colored shadows under his eyes and cheekbones, and silence weighed as heavily in her stomach as guilt did.

She stabbed at a creamed potato, sending it scooting. Her sister Mary had brought the food right after the wedding. Insisting that the newly married pair deserved at least one uninterrupted night, she'd also whisked Sarah away with her, leaving Michael and Katherine alone—in *his* house, the one he'd shared with his wife.

Was this what it was to be, then? Without the baby between them, was there nothing but silence and guilt? For Katherine was acutely, uncomfortably aware that this was entirely her fault. Hers, and her well-intentioned, impulsive schemes and her runaway mouth. After all, in the end she'd gotten precisely what she wanted, even if it wasn't the way she had intended. But Michael . . . Michael, who she knew full well had never wanted another wife at all, had been saddled with *her*.

The fork dropped from her fingers, ringing against the plate, clattering on wood, and, at the sound, Michael finally lifted his eyes from his unwavering contemplation of his watermelon preserves.

"I'm sorry," they said together, and smiled weakly, awkwardly, like ill-met strangers, at the coincidence.

"You first," he offered.

She traced the edge of her coffee cup with her thumb. "I . . . I don't know what I was thinking, saying that to Mrs. Wilcox. I guess I thought that anybody who mattered, anybody who knew me, would believe me over her, and I couldn't resist rattling the self-righteous old snoop. I never dreamed—"

"I know you didn't. It wouldn't have made any difference anyway."

"You don't think so?"

"No. She'd finally found a way to get to me. You just happened to be in the way."

Silence reigned again, broken only by the hiss and pop of the fire in the stove, the whistle of the wind around the back corner of the house.

"And . . . you?" Katherine prompted at last.

"What am I sorry about, you mean?"

"Yes."

Michael stared down at his hands, his cracked and scarred and rough hands. It was safer than looking at her over his dish-cluttered table and thinking *wife*, thinking he could put those hands on her, where he hadn't earned the right to put them, and knowing she wouldn't refuse him.

He'd robbed her of so much. Things that every woman wanted, things that Katherine—especially Katherine—deserved. A slow, sweet courtship; a wedding ceremony anticipated and planned for months, attended by her entire family; most of all, a husband of her own choosing, one she loved and who could love her back.

Worst of all was the lurking, painful suspicion that he hadn't tried very hard to stop it. He should have thought of something, anything, rather than drag her into this. He'd left her no way out when he'd suggested marriage in front of Reverend Hartman. She would no more be able to give up Sarah than he would, and he'd known it.

Why hadn't he tried harder? He wanted her; it was no use pretending any longer. And now he had her, without any of the guilt that would have come with pursuing her, with *deciding* to marry her—he'd married her because he'd had no other choice . . . or had he? God, was he really such a selfish bastard?

"Michael?"

"I'm . . . sorry." He spoke haltingly, searching for words. "I . . . know this isn't what you wanted."

Her tongue slid across her bottom lip, leaving a slick gleam in the lamplight. "It's not what I intended, no."

"I will not . . ." *Damn it! Say it, man. You have to give her this much, at least, even if it will be the hardest thing you've done yet.* "You married me only for Sarah's sake.

I realize that. You . . . don't have to consider me your husband in any other way. I won't ask you to . . . not tonight. Or any night, unless you . . ." Unless you want to, he'd almost said. Idiot! Why would she want him? She was nearly shaking, her hands trembling, the sheen of tears in her eyes. Had just the mention of it frightened her so much? He rushed to allay her fears. "The second bedroom, upstairs, at the end of the hall. You can use it."

The pain in her chest nearly doubled her over, and Katherine was faintly surprised that she still breathed. Was that to be her life, then, to sleep in his house, to raise a child with him, but never to touch him, never to know him as a wife knows a husband? Impossible. She could not live like that.

She rose to her feet, leaning on the table until she was certain that her knees would hold her, and made her way around to him, stopping only a foot away.

"Michael." She couldn't do this; she didn't have the courage. But there weren't any other choices, none that she could bear. "I know that you don't love me."

He stared at her mutely, eyes dark as firs at midnight, while she waited for him to speak. There, she'd given him time, and he'd said nothing. She hadn't realized she was still so foolish, that she'd harbored some glimmer of hope that he'd dispute her claim. He didn't love her; the worst was behind her.

"But I want this night, Michael." She took his hand—the big, flawed hands she loved so well—and let her fingers explore, search out all the scars and patches, find all the changing textures it held. "If this is to be my marriage, my life, I want as much as I can have, no matter what that is."

Dear Lord, if only he would say something! But he only watched her, as the silence echoed with the sounds of their breathing—his harsh, labored; hers rapid and fluttery. She brought his hand to her face, settling her cheek into the rough abrasion of his palm, and closed her eyes.

"I know you do not love me," she whispered again. "But, please, Michael, let me love you."

He moved with startling, violent swiftness, surging to his feet, sweeping her into his arms, striding across the kitchen floor.

"You don't have to carry me."

"Let me, Katherine." His voice was dark, intent. "Let me get this much right, at least."

It should have hurt her, that he had nothing else to give her—only his body, nothing of his heart. Maybe tomorrow it would. But for now the burgeoning excitement flickered within her, grew, overwhelmed the concerns of her heart with the much more insistent demands of her body.

"I wouldn't want you to hurt yourself, though. I have plans for you later, you see."

His smile was wicked and roguish and filled with promise. "So do I, Katherine. So do I."

With that, she gave in, laid her head against the hard plane of his chest where his heart thundered heavily in her ear. He carried her easily down the hallway, and Katherine was both surprised and relieved to find that they went right past the ground floor bedroom. How thoughtful of him to realize that she would not want to have this night in the room that he'd shared with his first wife.

The stairway creaked beneath their weight. He

shouldered open the nearest door, not pausing until he'd crossed the room and laid her on the quilt-covered bed.

The dove-gray light of late evening filled the room, shadowing the corners, softening the harsh lines of his face. He sat beside her, the mattress bowing beneath his weight.

"I find," he said, "that I'm not sure where to begin."

"I'm afraid I won't be of much help there."

"No?" He reached out, searched for the pins in her hair and removed them one by one, combing the rumpled strands out with his fingers again and again. "You got us this far."

"I know the theory," she said, conscious of the solid feel of his hip against her side, keenly aware that that small contact was more than they'd ever touched before, and knowing that there was far more to come. "But I'm a little short on the practical side of things."

"Ah." He wound a strand of hair around his forefinger and rubbed it with his thumb, savoring the texture. "And I'm more than a little out of practice."

"It's been . . . a long time?"

He nodded. "That surprises you?"

"I guess I— Maybe."

"After—" He stopped, swallowed.

"After Sarah, you mean? You can say her name, you know."

"It seemed in sort of bad taste to mention my first wife's name on our wedding night."

"She was my friend, too, Michael."

"Yes. Yes, she was." He slid his hand down, framed her collarbone. Her pulse fluttered beneath his fingers, her skin beating with life. "After her, Katherine, anybody else . . . it just felt all wrong."

Katherine drew a deep, shuddering breath. "And . . . now? Does it feel wrong now?"

Michael paused, searching for reluctance, for anger, for recriminations. Instead, he found nothing but anticipation, nothing but heat and the steady, insistent thrum of desire only leashed with a fierce struggle.

"No," he said at last. "It feels . . . right." His hand skimmed down her, whisking over her collarbone, her breast, her ribs, just enough to give her a hint of warmth, to make her arch into his touch, not nearly enough to sate her, coming to rest on her waist, squeezing lightly. "Of course, I haven't felt *much*, yet."

Her smile was all the reward he needed. And all the encouragement necessary to cause him to lower his head and, at last, find her mouth with his own.

How many people ever got what they most wanted? Katherine wondered. And how many fewer, having gotten it, found it to be even more than they'd imagined? But so it was for her, for not even a thousand dreams had prepared her for this, for the vivid pleasure of Michael's kiss, for the dark seduction of his tongue stroking hers and the taste of his warm breath mingling with her own.

He pulled back reluctantly and came to his feet beside the bed, working the buttons at the neck of his shirt. "I'd better do this now; who knows what shape I'll be in later."

"Michael?" She sat up to see him better, intending to ask what he meant, but he was stripping off his shirt, exposing rugged muscle and smooth skin that gleamed in the misty evening light, and she couldn't seem to form the words.

No matter. He understood, and reached out a hand to show her. "I might not be able to undo the buttons later. I'm shaking already."

"For . . . me?"

"You never guessed? What I said at supper—it was so foolish of me, to think that I could sleep down the hall from you, know that you are mine, and not come to you. I never would have lasted the night."

That he could want her so much filled her with wonder. That he would tell her, *show* her, sweeping away any last doubts that he might regret this, that she was wrong to be so forward, touched her almost unbearably. She cupped his hand and brought it to her mouth, letting her lips and tongue learn its surface, rough and smooth, the feel of hard bone and sinew under work-battered skin, and it drew out his groan.

When she released his hand, he tore off the rest of his clothes with such speed that she might have laughed, if she'd had any breath left. It seemed incredibly decadent somehow, that he would be naked, fully bare for her eyes and her hands, while she was still covered from neck to toe.

But not for long.

He joined her on the bed and set himself to work on her own fastenings, taking longer than it should because he kept stopping to brush his fingers over the lobe of ear, to stroke along her collarbone, to skim over a newly exposed shoulder, as if he couldn't wait to touch each bit of her he uncovered.

Part of Katherine was grateful for the muted but

strong evening light, delighted for the chance to see him clearly, to learn each line and plane with her eyes. The rest of her . . . the rest worried, that he would see her so clearly, too, and that he would be disappointed.

Michael left her little time to fret. His hands dusted over her skin, leaving little spangled bursts of heat behind. His mouth, too, a wicked, wooing mouth that glided over her, sought out curves and shadows and made them his. And her deepest fear, the one she hadn't even admitted to herself—that Michael would take her to his bed remembering another—turned out to be no concern at all, for he breathed her name with each kiss and permitted no doubt that it was she he wanted beneath him.

She'd dreamed about lovemaking. Even, once or twice—perhaps a few times more—thought about sex. But she hadn't known the two would be one, that the sweet tenderness could combine so powerfully with the grinding good ache that was acutely physical.

Michael thought he knew her. Believed that, over the last few weeks, he'd imprinted her form on his mind, he'd been so aware of her, even as he'd tried to convince himself he shouldn't be. Elegant Katherine: narrow shoulders, delicate breasts, graceful hands. And so it surprised him to find that beneath her crinolines was a surprising abundance of flesh— deeply curved hips, ripe belly, lush soft thighs that a man could sink in between and lose himself in the pleasure of it. Even big, sturdy feet!

It made him feel like he knew a secret about her, one no other man knew, or ever would, and the thought made his blood beat thick and hot. He wondered if he would ever again be able to walk down a street behind her, to see the subtle sway of her hips under her skirts and know what lay beneath and not have his thoughts become all too obvious.

This was what he wanted, so much so that he could not believe he had denied himself so long. To lose himself in her, utterly, wonderfully. So that there was nothing else in his life, his world, than the feel of her silky flesh going damp with heat beneath his palm. Than the sight of her pale skin flushing pink with the passion he knew he had caused. Than the sound of her heart, thundering beneath his ear when he laid his head on her chest, his open mouth only inches from her nipple, washing it with hot, moist breath, and seeing it tighten abruptly, waiting for his stroke.

"Katherine," he mumbled again, reeling, sex-drunk, at last coming to lie beside her, his naked body tucked along her side. He cupped her chin, brushing his thumb back and forth across her lower lip, color-stained and wet and plumped from his kisses. "I want to . . . it is better, for a woman, if the act lasts a while. But this time—it's been too long, for me, and I don't think I can hold off long enough to make it good for you. So, if you're willing, I want to pleasure you first."

"P-pleasure?" she stuttered, lids sweeping down to shield her eyes.

"Surely you know that there is pleasure."

"Yes." She gulped. "I had heard something about that, maybe."

He brushed his fingers over her rose-streaked

cheeks, charmed and aroused in equal measures. "Are you embarrassed?"

"Who me? Uh-uh. Never a bit."

"I never would have thought it of you. Your cheeks are red."

"And you're not blushing?"

"No." Indulging himself, he flexed once against her hip, wondering if the unfamiliar feel of his hard length would make her pull away. Instead, she shifted a bit, pressing closer, and he knew that, though her mind might be a little shy, her body was not. "Of course, I doubt that there's any blood left over to rush to my face, anyway."

A smile, just a little one, barely tipped the corner of her mouth. "There we go," he said. "That's what I wanted." He kissed each lid, lightly, fragile skin and the flutter of soft lashes against his lips. "Open your eyes, Katherine, and look at me."

He needed to see her, to watch her pupils darken and look into her eyes as passion made them go wide, then sleepy, with feelings he had nurtured. Wanted to see the subtle reflection of every touch, every stroke, and know that only he had ever witnessed how beautiful Katherine was when the stun of pleasure first burst over her senses.

"Please?" He gently turned her face toward his. "It's only me, Katherine. Only Michael."

"No!" Her eyes flew open. "Not *only* you," she whispered fiercely. "It is you, Michael. It *is* you."

His gaze held hers as his hand glided down, lazily, easily, pausing to polish a shoulder, cup a breast, curve over her hip. He nudged her thighs apart, big hand settling into her damp heat, and she gasped.

"Look at me."

"I think I—"

"Don't think. Not now. Just look at me, and feel."

He probed carefully, circling, gauging her response. Her hips pulsed, and his strokes echoed the rhythm. The evening light dimmed, fading the rest of the room into darkness, smudging edges, so nothing else existed but the two of them and the vivid pleasure that flowed between them. Her lips parted on a ragged breath, and her body arched against his hand, a keening cry breaking from her throat.

"Michael . . ."

"Yes," he urged her, drinking in with all his senses, sight and touch and smell and sound, as she shuddered in his arms, the sweetest gift, shock and ecstasy and emotion radiant on her face.

She relaxed slowly, sinking against him, burrowing her face in the hollow of his neck, murmuring. "That was pleasure? That seems much too . . . mild a word for it."

He laughed, and her hand drifted down his side, coming to rest on his hip, her thumb angling along the joint of his torso and his leg, barely rubbing an inch from his sex. Heat shot through his body, blurred his vision, thrummed in his veins.

"Your turn," she whispered.

He levered over her, pausing to run his gaze over her once more. Rumpled hair, flushed face, shadowed curves, nipples relaxed and deep-colored from her release, pale thighs spread wide for him: a sex-pleased woman, and need surged.

"I don't know," he said hoarsely, dimly shocked he managed to form the words, "how much it's going to hurt you."

She smiled, sleepy, satisfied. "I don't think anything could hurt me right now."

Clamping his teeth together, he entered her slowly, fighting instinct, body warring with emotion. He craved release . . . but he wanted to make it last, to stay deep within her, where there was nothing of pain and loss, only the wondrous, wicked pleasure of having her hot flesh close around him, tighten, pulling him closer, sensation rippling from the base of his spine.

She winced, once, a quick intake of breath, her fingers digging—almost pain, all pleasure—into his back.

He eased out, slowly, back in, groaning, balanced on the edge. Again, so good . . . He pulled out abruptly, pressed himself against the softness of her thigh, liquid heat spurting from him even as the ripping loss of withdrawing from her tore at his senses.

Shaking, raw throat gasping for air, he fell to her side and pulled her close, using the only bit of strength that remained to gently rub her hip—an apology, gratitude, and regret, all in one caress.

Katherine swept the jumbled hair from her face, lifting herself up on one elbow to look at him. "Why did you do that?"

Hurt settled into her eyes, rapidly replacing the confusion. Damn it, he didn't want to do this, to ruin all the warmth and sweetness and pleasure with reality. He wanted to sink into the things they could have, instead of dwelling on what couldn't be.

Too late. His action, leaving her when he did, had already reminded them.

He touched her cheek, silk under his fingers, and

wondered if, when tonight was all over, he'd ever get to feel her skin again, and how he would ever survive it if he didn't.

But he found himself wanting to put it off, to delay telling her the things he must.

"You must want to clean up. I'll get you some water."

"Michael, I—"

But he was already gone.

He dipped water from the reservoir on the side of the stove, checking first too make sure it was the right temperature. He searched through piles of cloths before he found one he deemed soft enough for her. Pitiful services, he knew, but they were the only ones he could do her now.

The bedroom, when he returned, was too dark for him to see her. But he felt the weight of her eyes, the bewilderment, the heavy accusation. He lit a small candle, enough to guide him, not enough that he must clearly see her face and know the hurt he'd caused her. He carefully sponged his seed from her thighs, wondering as he did so if he'd also wiped away any chance at the life he'd hoped they'd have together—friendship, physical compatibility, a shared concern for the child, and knew that minimal, businesslike marriage would never be enough for Katherine. She deserved so much more, but he had nothing else to give her. Nothing else he *dared* give her.

Silence lay heavy between them, broken only by the lap of water as he dunked the cloth, the quick intake of her breath as he cleansed her. Finally, she laid her hand on his biceps.

"Why, Michael?"

Still clutching the wet towel, he dropped his hand to his naked lap and raised his head to face her. To look her in her night-shadowed eyes and tell her; she deserved that much, at least. He only wished he had better reasons to give her, something logical and sensible. Something that she could understand, that didn't sound so weak.

"I . . . can't," he said haltingly. "To get you with child . . . I just can't take that chance."

"Look at me." The candle enclosed them in a small oval of light, warming her skin to pale apricot. "I'm not Sarah, Michael." She gestured to the full roundness of her hips. "The women in my family . . . we're built to have children; we could practically repopulate a city all on our own. Nothing would happen to me, I promise you."

He groped for words that seemed beyond his reach, a way to explain that it had nothing to do with her, and everything to do with a fate that snatched away everything he cared about, almost the instant he let himself believe in it. To describe the sheer impossibility of risking her like that.

"It wasn't your fault, Michael," she said softly.

The room spun around him, her perception slicing painfully close to his guarded heart. But if she could see this much, didn't she understand the rest, too?

"She didn't want me to go, you know. Begged me not to."

"No. I didn't know."

"She didn't tell you?" It was so wrong, to drag regrets and pain and loss into a night that should have been about newness and pleasure. But he knew no other way to show her the way things had to be, to make certain she wouldn't expect impossibilities. "I figured, every time we fought, you had to hear all about what a stubborn fool I was."

"You . . . disagreed?"

"Of course we disagreed. It was a marriage."

Katherine's perceptions shuffled, readjusted. They'd had a marriage then, not the perfection she'd always thought it. It helped, somehow, to know that; made her hope that perhaps something begun even under these flawed circumstances might grow to something solid and real, too.

"She didn't want me to go. But I— A man served his country. I never questioned it. Figured they'd take me anyway, and I'd rather go on my own terms. Told her I had a skill that was needed, and that I'd be far away from danger, making horseshoes, and promised her I'd come home safe."

He swallowed hard, candlelight reflecting wetly in his dark eyes. "Never thought that I'd march off to war, and she'd be the one who wouldn't survive it."

She wanted to hold him, to wrap her arms around him and absorb some of his hurt for her own, to share it with him as she longed to share everything else. They should have been close, two naked people in the bed they'd loved in no more than a half hour before. Instead, the strip of bleached white sheet that separated them seemed like so much more, a cold barrier she had no idea how to breach.

"She shouldn't have been alone."

"She wasn't alone," Katherine said.

"What?"

"I was with her, Michael. And there was nothing

you could have done that would have made any difference. I swear it." *Please, God, let him believe me. Hasn't he suffered enough?* "She never blamed you."

Hope warred with disbelief in his eyes. And then Katherine watched in despair as his expression shut down completely, as remote as the frozen man who'd limped home from war to his empty house and empty life.

"I volunteered to transfer to the front lines the day my commanding officer told me I'd lost them."

"You wanted to die."

"Yes." Darkness shadowed his face, his words. "I almost did. But, after I was shot, they transferred me to your father's hospital, and he refused to let me."

"I know." She paused, wondering if she should go on. But if they could have nothing else that she'd hoped for between them, at least they could have honesty. "I was at Audrey's, the day they were notified you were wounded. I telegraphed my father, asking him to take care of you." Though she greatly feared she didn't want to know the answer, she asked anyway. "Are you . . . do you wish I hadn't?"

"Katherine. Always taking care of me." Without touching her skin, he lifted a strand of hair from her shoulder, rubbed it between his fingers. "No," he said, genuinely surprising himself. "Thank you." *I don't want to die.* Despite it all, he no longer wished to die. When had that happened? A month ago? Tonight?

A hopeful smile curved the corners of her mouth. But, even if he wanted to live, that didn't mean he was willing to let his heart be ripped from him once again. And it would be unforgivable of him to mislead her, to give her the impression that simply no longer welcoming death changed anything else and he had something inside him that didn't exist. That choosing to breathe meant he still had the capability to love. He jerked his hand away, a clear rejection of their tentative bond, and her budding smile faded.

"I'm tired of talking," he said, voice shaded with remoteness. "Go to sleep."

She studied him a moment, then nodded. "All right."

And a night that had begun with shattering passion ended with a loneliness all the more unbearable for its unexpectedness, as they lay, carefully separated by a narrow, unbreachable space, and listened to each other's mock-even breathing until the soft rose wash of dawn slipped in.

5

Katherine had honestly believed that it would be enough.
That she would be content with the part of Michael
she could have, with companionship and passion,
with the right to be present in his life. And so, over
the next two weeks, it came as a most unwelcome
surprise that it was not. That being so close to having
everything she'd ever dreamed of, close enough to
almost feel it and not be able to claim it for her own,
was so sharply painful.

She tried to imagine enduring years like this,
watching Michael try to separate strong emotion from
the calmer, safer ones. His visible struggle to detach
himself from both her and Sarah, to keep their rela-
tionships pleasant instead of powerful, was wrench-
ing to witness—and, to Katherine's despair, for the
most part successful. With her in his house, relieving
him of the constant demands of Sarah's care, he
worked more and talked less.

And at night . . . at night he taught her the potent,
overwhelming power of passion, even as he refused to
complete the act fully. It was becoming nearly impos-

sible to bear the piercing sense of loss when he separated from her at the moment she felt closest to him. Even harder to continue to find a way to hide her tears from him when he did so.

She'd quickly learned that it was not sensitivity to her feelings that had prompted Michael to bring her upstairs on their wedding night. He no longer used the bedroom he'd shared with his wife. In fact, the door was kept firmly closed, and she'd never seen him go near it. Perhaps it was only her imagination that had him shading over a bit to the far side of the hallway when he walked past it.

Or perhaps not.

After a rousing morning outside in the shade of the big old tree, playing with her toes, Sarah had settled in for a much-needed nap. Katherine took the opportunity to attack the neglected floors, which desperately needed a good scrubbing. Now, she stood outside the closed bedroom door, hands on her hips, and argued with herself.

She had no right to go in there. If Michael wanted it shut up, that was his choice. It wasn't as if the room didn't hold painful memories for her, too, for it was where she'd sat for hours by Sarah's bedside, holding her hand, until her strength gave out. Not to mention that, after everything that had happened, Katherine should have learned to leave well enough alone.

On the other hand, every other floor in the house was glassy-clean. Certainly this one could use it, too—housekeeping was obviously not one of Michael's talents. It might be hours before he was home to give her permission, were she to wait to ask it. He hadn't come home for lunch either of the last two days. And it somehow irritated her, this closed-off room, a symbol of the parts of himself Michael barricaded from her.

All right, then, she decided. The knob turned easily in her hand, and she gave a slight push. Creaking on its little-used hinges, the door yawned open.

Katherine stood, stock still, in the doorway and stared.

Nothing had changed.

The room looked precisely as she remembered it. The big four-poster bed that Sarah had labored and died in still stood in the center of the room, covered with the lace spread she had crocheted when she was sixteen and put away for her marriage. The starched white doilies still sprawled on top of the dresser, topped with the milk-glass lamp. Faded pictures of roses decorated the walls. And the night table beside the bed still held the cut-glass vase that Katherine had filled with wildflowers and brought to Sarah when she'd felt her first pains. Katherine had emptied it of the withered blooms herself, the day after Sarah's funeral when she'd set the room to rights.

That was the last time she'd been in here, and it looked as if no one had entered since. Powder gray dust drifted over the furniture; the sun had bleached and streaked the yellow cotton curtains drawn over the windows. The room was musty, neglected, abandoned . . . a shrine?

Her heart heavy, Katherine stepped back, out of the room, leaving it as she found it. What good would it do to clean it? She could no more bring that room back to full life than she'd been able to do with

Michael. She could scour a good finish on the place, but she couldn't touch the heart of it.

"*What are you doing?*" The sudden, harsh words startled her, and she jumped, turning to find Michael striding down the hallway toward her.

"I . . . I was just cleaning up. I thought this room could probably use it, too." Her smile was a little wobbly. "I didn't expect you back yet."

"I was hungry."

"Oh." She searched for some clue to his emotions. Was he angry at her? Hurting from the memories she'd stirred? His lids were lowered, lashes veiling his eyes, face utterly expressionless. "I'm sorry, Michael, I'll stay out of the room from now on," she ventured.

"Do whatever you want." He shrugged, but she noticed his careful positioning, at an angle to her, his back to the open doorway, so there was no chance he had to look into the bedroom. "It's your house, too."

"But if you want me to—"

"Do whatever you want," he repeated.

In for a penny, in for a pound, she thought, and plunged ahead. What more did she have to lose? "Michael, it's time to heal."

His jaw clenched, mouth going tight and hard. "You don't think I would if I could?" he said, voice carefully, fiercely even. "You think I *choose* it to be this way?"

"Yes." Katherine sucked in a shaky breath. "I think you do. Because it's easier, easier than risking loving something that you might lose. But, if that's how you live, what's the point? And what if you're wrong? What if you could have had it all, if you'd only taken the chance?"

He glared at her, and for a moment she wondered if she'd finally gone too far, pushed too hard, and he would thrust her out of his house and life in one quick shove.

Abruptly turning on his heel, he headed for the kitchen. "I'm going to eat. Are you coming?"

She watched his rigid back disappear down the hallway. Would he always walk away from her, when she got too close? Then she reached out and gently, softly, shut the door to the untouched room.

Michael had spent nearly a year in battle, in mud holes and blood-spattered fields and scorched forests, bullets winging past his ears and cannonballs roaring over his head.

But that was nothing compared to the battle he fought over the next few weeks.

Dear God, how am I to resist them? That was the question he fired at an unresponsive Heaven a dozen times a day. How was he to protect himself and them? For there was no getting around it: what Michael Collins loved, he lost.

And yet . . . and yet, he was weakening. Falling into the wonder and rhythm of having a family.

How was a man to watch the wide, delighted smile of a baby and not lose his heart? To see the wonder and delight in Sarah's fresh eyes and not want to witness every new expression that would come into them over the years?

And how was a man to steel himself against coming home to the soft, welcoming kiss of an extraordinary woman? To resist the love, patient and powerful and amazing, simmering just beneath his surface, waiting, waiting, for his armor to crack?

God, how was he to control this passion that held him in its unbreakable grip? It would probably be better if he never touched her at all, he knew. But he was weak and, each night, as he heard the regular sighs of her breathing, felt the warmed sheets in his bed, he reached for her. And every night he drew closer to that line, to surrendering completely, to not finding the strength to pull back when he neared the sharp, seductive edge of his control.

Dear Lord, he was to do this for months? A year? A lifetime? Impossible. Still, he couldn't shake the fear, couldn't bring himself to take the last, irrevocable step he'd denied for so long and had been so convinced he must forever resist.

Summer bloomed. Sun-heated air, ripe with growing crops, billowed through his open front door. From the kitchen drifted the scent of the orange cake Katherine was baking for Sunday supper.

Michael crouched on the floor. Propped up on her chubby forearms, Sarah lay on her tummy on a butter-colored cotton blanket, blinking at him. He was convinced she was going to learn to roll over at any moment.

A brisk knock interrupted them. Perhaps it was one of Katherine's sisters; since her mother still hadn't returned from Anne's, they'd all made a habit of dropping in now and then. Checking up on him, he supposed. But then, they rarely bothered to knock.

He rolled to his feet and strolled over to the door, still looking over his shoulder at Sarah. It would be just like a female to flip over when he wasn't watching.

The couple who waited outside were strangers. Middle-aged, both of them. The man, with big, meaty hands and flat, dark eyes, stood with his burly chest thrown belligerently forward, as if daring Michael to toss him off his front porch. The woman, demurely two steps behind, might have once been pretty, with her delicate features and pale coloring. Now, she simply looked worn.

"Can I help you?"

Jamming his heavy chin forward, the man scowled. "We come to fetch our grandchild."

"Katherine! I'd think you'd better get in here, please."

Michael's shout came just as she was checking the not-quite-finished cake. She'd never heard that tone from him before, an undercurrent of anger and dark emotion, and a creeping dread worked its way through her limbs. She shut the oven door with a bang and hurried to the front room.

Katherine didn't like it. Didn't like the two people who stood stiffly just inside the door, a cold, determined-looking man and a long-suffering woman. Didn't like, either, the grim set to Michael's mouth or the hunched posture of his shoulders, as if he'd just taken a heavy blow.

She quickly checked to make certain Sarah was all right. She was, still gurgling happily in a patch of sunlight. It couldn't be so terrible, then; as long as Sarah was well, they'd manage anything else. "What's going on?"

Seconds crawled by. Finally the man shot an impatient, near-contemptuous look at Michael. "You gonna tell her, or should I?"

"These . . . *people*," he said, his intent gaze never wavering from them, "claim that Sarah is theirs."

Dear God. Her knees threatened to crumple beneath her, and she groped for the back of a nearby chair for support. "She is not," she managed to gasp out.

"We been lookin' for months, off and on, ever since our daughter done run off. Finally heard that someone left a baby on your doorstep. Figured she abandoned her responsibility just like everything else and took herself off to Lord knows where."

Desperate for reassurance, her gaze sought Michael's, but he didn't look her way, merely continued studying the couple as if weighing their claim.

He could *not* be considering this. She refused to believe it. But, please no, this would be such an obvious way out for him. This was his chance. Turn Sarah back over to her family, and he could go back to his guarded, safe life and never again have to struggle with things such as emotion and loss.

Katherine scooped Sarah up, holding her so tight she whimpered in protest, and rushed to Michael's side. Needing any connection with him, with the family she'd thought they might grow into, she reached for his hand. "Michael?"

His fingers closed around hers, warm, tight, reassuring, betraying all the intense feeling that wasn't visible on his face. *Thank God*, she thought. They were in this together, at least.

"Let me get this straight," Michael said. "Your daughter ran away when she was close to term, and you believe she delivered this baby and left it on my doorstep?"

"That's right."

"Why would she do a thing like that?"

"Hard to say. She's a sinful girl, no way to know why she does anythin'." The man shrugged, dismissing his daughter. "Don't know why she didn't stay at home, if she was gonna give it away anyway. We had a perfectly respectable home all lined up for it."

Trembling, Katherine lowered her head to rest her cheek against Sarah's. Dear God, they intended to take the child, and they didn't even want to keep it?

"And what makes you certain that this child is yours, then?" Michael asked, clipping off each word.

"What else can it be? Can't be that many babies without mothers flopping around this area at the same time, could there?"

"It would be unusual," Michael agreed.

The man bared his teeth in what was obviously meant to be a smile. "Hand it over, then, and we'll be on our way."

"I'm afraid I'm going to have to ask for some proof."

"Proof?" the man said, as if he'd never heard of the word. It had clearly never occurred to him that they wouldn't be happy to be well rid of an abandoned baby.

"She . . ." The woman spoke hesitantly, as if uncertain whether she would be allowed to, and pointed at Sarah. "She looked just like Davinda did, when she was that age."

"I'm sorry," Michael said reasonably, shaking his head as though he regretted making it so difficult, all the while his desperate grip nearly crushed Katherine's fingers. "But it would be irresponsible of

me to simply take your word on this. Perhaps someone saw your daughter in Mooretown? Or near my
house?"

Hot color crept up the man's thick neck. "No.
There's a farmer name of Schmidt, north o' town, that
someone thought he saw her with the night she run
off. But the man wouldn't talk to us. Still won't." His
hands flexed, forming brutal fists as if he longed to
use much more forceful measures to make the farmer
talk.

"You haven't got any proof, then. Is there anybody
who can even vouch for your daughter's pregnancy?"

Katherine held her breath, certain the man was
going to launch himself at Michael. But Michael
merely looked at him calmly, one eyebrow raised,
waiting for his answer.

"You must understand," Michael said, "I'm just trying to make sure we've got all the facts straight."

"No one knew!" he shouted.

"Please," his wife said. "We're decent, God-fearing
people. We kept her shame hidden, and we're just
trying to do our duty now so we can put this disgrace
behind us."

"Then you have nothing to worry about, for, you
see, this baby's not yours." His rigid control broke.
"*She's mine.*"

"But . . . but . . ." The man's eyes narrowed angrily.
"What do you mean? The whole town knows some-
body just dumped it on your doorstep!"

"Really?" Michael voice was once again cool and
composed. "I didn't realize that story worked so well."

"That *story*?"

"Mmm hmm."

"But . . . why? Why would you lie about a thing like that?"

"Oh well." He forced a chuckle. "The true story is a little embarrassing, you might say. This one was a whole lot simpler for everybody concerned."

"You're saying she's *yours*?" Hostile suspicion edged the man's words. "Why'd you ask us all those questions, then?"

"I just wanted to make sure there wouldn't be any future questions." He tugged Katherine to his side, his solid length against her body comforting and strong. "But make no mistake. Sarah is ours, and we plan on taking very good care of her. You don't have to worry about it any longer."

The man stared at Michael, jaw working. *Please,* Katherine prayed, *just drop it and go away. You don't want her, anyway, and we love her so much.*

Finally his face cleared. "Come on." He jerked a thumb at his wife. "Let's get out of here."

The door had no more banged shut behind him before relieved tears flooded Katherine. She threw herself against Michael's chest, the baby wedged between them, and his arms came around her, familiar, secure.

"Careful now," he said. "You don't want to squish her, now that we've got her for good."

Katherine gave a watery laugh and pulled back— not enough to step out of his embrace, just enough to look up into his beloved face. *He did it!* she thought jubilantly. He'd taken the chance, protected Sarah, chose to have a child in his life, forever.

Surely now he was ready to hear her news.

"Michael," she said softly, unaccountably shy, "I

suspect I'm . . . I think we're going to have another child."

His eyes chilled. He dropped his arms and stepped away.

It's only shock, she told herself. He wasn't expecting it, and he just needs a little time to get used to the idea.

"I've been very careful."

"I know." Her heart swelled, full of the knowledge that she would always be Sarah's mother, and that soon her belly would grow with a new life to bind the three of them together even further. "But life has a habit of finding a way, Michael."

She waited for an elated smile to spread over his face, for him to pull her close and kiss her with joy. Instead, he stalked past her and rushed out the front door.

"Your cake's burning," he said, the acrid scent of smoke and waste snaking through the room.

He went straight for the swing in the ancient oak, the one he'd put up the last time he'd learned a child of his had been conceived, and that had hung, neglected, abandoned, ever since. He slumped into it, the old rope creaking, a lonely sound.

Katherine stared out the window until she was certain that her shattered heart still pumped blood through her body. Then, clutching her daughter, she ran from the empty house.

Katherine spent three hours at her sister Mary's house, crying, before she decided she'd had enough. She'd chosen her path, she'd made her bed, and now she was damn well going to lie in it. So she grabbed Sarah and headed for home.

She checked the smithy on the way home, just to make certain Michael hadn't gone there to hide. He wasn't still in the swing, or anywhere else in the yard. But she couldn't find the wretched man in their bedroom, the kitchen, or the front room, either.

Well. Frustrated, Katherine slumped in a chair, wondering where to look next, until a thump from the back of the house drew her attention.

She found Michael in the closed-up bedroom. Except it wasn't closed-up anymore. The wood floor was blotched with uneven damp spots from a fresh washing. Broad streaks smeared through the layers of dust where he'd obviously tried to wipe them away. Now, he was pulling Sarah's clothes from drawers, awkwardly folding them, and tucking them into a limp, bulging sack.

She made a small squeak of surprise, and he looked up from his task, grinning broadly. "*There* you are, finally."

"You knew I would come back?"

"Sure." He strolled over to her, unhurried, his steps light. "You're not exactly the kind to duck and run, Katherine. More like the kind to stand and duke it out."

There was something different, beyond his light-hearted words and smile, so completely fresh that it took her a stunned moment to register it. And a full minute to believe it.

His soul was back in his eyes.

And he was looking at her.

"I'll tell you a secret, though." He leaned forward, a

conspiratorial twinkle in his Christmas tree-colored irises. "Another hour, and I was gonna come looking for you."

"You were?" She knew she sounded stupid and slow, but she couldn't seem to make her tongue work right, couldn't get her brain to catch up with her racing, celebrating heart.

"Mmm hmm." He rocked back, tucking his thumb into the waistband of his pants. "Where's Sarah?"

"She was tired. I put her down in her room." Too many questions. Katherine didn't know where to begin. "What are you doing?"

"I'm packing up Sarah's clothes. Could Reverend Hartman find someone who could put them to good use, do you think?"

"I'm sure he could." She struggled to make sense of it, began to believe, even as she dared not. "But, Michael . . . *why?*"

"Oh." His head tilted as he appraised the room with its curtains thrown wide, bright summer sunlight spilling through. "Thought it was time to get the place cleaned up, since it seems like we're going to be needing a real nursery. With two babies in the house and all."

"A nursery?"

"Yeah." His smile softened, filled with tenderness. "Katherine." His rough palms cradled her chin gently. And then he kissed her, soft as goose down, sweet as a homecoming after a long, difficult trip. "My Katherine," he whispered when he finally lifted his head.

"Michael?" Her eyes stung, blurring his handsome, familiar features.

"You know what happened when you left? For five minutes—until I realized you'd come storming back—it hurt. It hurt like hell, Katherine."

"That's . . . good?"

"Damn right it's good." His thumbs stroked lightly over her cheekbones, cherishing. "Because I realized something. If I ever lose you, no matter how much I try and hold back, no matter how hard I try not to love you, it's still gonna hurt."

His voice went low, warm, so rich she felt it deep inside. "If you go out in the street and get hit by a wagon—or if I do—whether it's next week or next year or six decades from now, I can't change it, and I can't make it hurt any less."

His lips quirked. "I don't think it's going to happen, mind you. But I couldn't change it if it did." He stepped closer, hips brushing her belly, and everything inside her softened, yearning. "All I can do—the only thing I can do, all any of us can do—is grab every little bit of time and live it, to cherish every second we get with the people we love. 'Cause it's a gift, every single moment of it. And, no matter what happens, I'll never be sorry I had this time with you. I'll only be sorry if I waste it."

"Michael, I lo—"

"Shh." He pressed his thumb against her lips. "I'm not finished yet, and it's for sure, once you get started, who knows when I'll have another chance."

She smiled against his finger, more than willing to wait her turn.

"I've got no right to ask this, I know. And I wouldn't blame you a bit if you said no, considering everything that's happened. But I'm going to ask it anyway." She felt the slight tremble of his fingers and was awed that she could stir so much emotion in him. "I know I haven't shown it so far, but I know how to love a woman. I'm good at it. And so, Katherine, please." It was all there in his eyes for her to see, everything she'd thought she'd never find, as he echoed her own words back to her. "Let me love you."

Her heart nearly burst. Maybe it did, becoming something new and whole and free. She hurled herself into his arms, pressing her lips against his—a celebration, a vow, sparking a heady, rapidly growing passion.

Gasping, needing a breath, he reluctantly pulled back at last. "I take it that was a yes?"

"I'm not sure. Better try it again and see."

"You're sure you're feeling all right? Your condition, and all? I wouldn't want to—"

"If you don't hurry up and kiss me, I can guarantee that, in a few minutes, I'm not going to be feeling very good at all. And, if that happens, neither will you. I'll make sure of it."

His tongue was doing something wicked and enticing, his hand sliding tantalizingly close to her breast, when the shriek of a very unhappy baby pierced the air. Resigned, they laughed against each other's mouths.

"This is going to be our life from now on, isn't it? Getting interrupted?" he asked.

"Not for more than a couple of decades or so."

He sighed deeply and released her.

"I'll make it up to you," she said. Made bold by love, she reached down and cupped his hard length through the loose canvas of his pants, rewarded by his quick intake of breath.

"Disgraceful wench." Placing his hand on her shoulders, he spun her around and gave her a gentle nudge toward the door. "Better go, quick, before our daughter starts to waste away from having to wait hours and hours for her next meal."

At the doorway, she paused to glance over her shoulder at him. "Later?"

His smile was full of love and hunger and wicked expectation.

"Later," he promised.

SUSAN KAY LAW is the author of six novels, from *Journey Home*, which won the romance Writers of America Golden Heart Award, to *One Lonely Night*, available this summer. She currently lives in Minnesota with her husband and two sons.

PART 2

Tomorrow's Promises

1

Grew up like the prairie lilies,
Grew a tall and slender maiden,
With the beauty of the moonlight,
With the beauty of the starlight.

—Longfellow, "The Song of Hiawatha"

Montana Territory, 1865

Davinda had been in the Montana Territory for a while and she was still in awe of its loveliness. It was a wilderness of steep, wooded slopes and flowery mountain meadows, where streams tumbled over the waterfalls, and blue lakes lay in peaceful valleys. Along the wooded river valleys and on the pine-clad slopes of the mountains, elk, deer, and wild longhorn sheep fed in great numbers.

Her blond hair loose and flowing over her shoulders, Davinda rode her gentle mare through the wind-blown buffalo grass, the crystal clear water of a river rippling and splashing over the rocks at her side.

"The Yellowstone River," she murmured to herself, thinking of her journey up the Missouri River. It had taken her three months to reach the Montana Territory, where she had started anew after having left the most precious part of her life behind on a doorstep.

Tears filled her eyes at the memory of gazing down at her baby daughter's tiny face just before leaving her for someone else to raise. She remembered how trustingly her daughter had looked up at her.

That trust in her daughter's eyes had been what had made it easier for Davinda to say her final good-bye, for Davinda knew in her heart that she had done what was best for her child. She would have never had a normal life with Davinda. She would have been raised in the shadow of shame.

Knowing without a doubt that she *had* done the best thing possible for her daughter, Davinda snapped her reins and rode in a faster gallop along the river that ran snake-like through the territory. Davinda had the rest of the afternoon to enjoy these leisurely moments alone. She had completed her chores back at the ranch and had anxiously slipped on a riding skirt and white blouse for her outing.

It was at times like this that she felt the total freedom she had sought the day she had fled from her father's farm to make a life elsewhere.

She smiled when she thought of Clarence and Elaine Masters, the couple with whom she shared the two-bedroom cabin at the small ranch where she now lived. They had found her on the steamboat *Yellowstone*, where she had stowed away for the journey to the Montana Territory. Clarence and Elaine had seen that she was weak and half-starved, and had understood her loneliness. They took her under their wing and shared their riverboat cabin with her for the entire journey. And when they reached the Montana Territory, where Clarence had already established a ranch before bringing his wife from St. Louis, they had invited Davinda to live with them.

She had only accepted their offer after they agreed to let her work for her keep. They were getting on in age and he could be a great help to them.

Clarence and Elaine made her feel as though she belonged. They made her feel like someone worthy of love, whereas her father had tormented her so much after having discovered her pregnancy, she had begun to feel totally worthless.

Yes, she was glad that she had left her daughter for someone else to raise, so that her child could have a chance in this world of heartache. A world Davinda had become acquainted with after learning of her betrothed's death in the Civil War.

She despaired at the thought of how different it would have been had he lived. They had planned to marry as soon as he returned from the war.

But they had not waited for those exchanged vows before making love. While saying their good-byes before he left, they had shared a passionate night together. Until then, they had only exchanged embraces and sweet kisses.

But that one evening, when they knew they would not see each other for many months, perhaps years, things had gone further.

Because of her pregnancy, she had become an object of embarrassment to her father. Her mother couldn't even shame him into accepting Davinda and the child out of love, instead of despising them.

Unable to bear such tormented thoughts any longer, Davinda pushed them aside. She slowed her horse to a canter. When she spied sprays of colorful wildflowers along the riverbank, she drew a tight rein and stopped. Elaine loved flowers. She always enjoyed having a bouquet for the dining table. Davinda would pick a few flowers, then return home. She remembered Clarence's warnings of the dangers of traveling too far while on her outings. Although they had never been confronted by Indians, Davinda was aware that several tribes lived in the area.

Thus far, she had never come face to face with any Indians—and hoped she never would. The tiny pearl-handled pistol that she carried in her skirt pocket whenever she left the safety of the ranch might not be enough to save her against a renegade Indian.

Securing her reins on a low tree limb, Davinda started to walk toward the flowers, then stopped abruptly when she heard a low moan coming from behind a thick stand of bushes a short distance away.

Turning around slowly, Davinda slid her hand inside her pocket for her pistol, then withdrew her hand quickly when she heard another low, painful groan. This time she could tell that it was a woman.

Forgetting the danger she might be in, and the pistol that might help ward off that danger, Davinda hurried toward the sound that had turned into a continuous whimper.

When she stepped behind the bushes and saw who was there, she gasped. It was a very pregnant Indian woman. She was in hard labor, and it was obvious that she was having trouble giving birth to her child. Her eyes were filled with pain. Her brow and her long, black hair were wet with perspiration. And blood pooled between her outspread legs, where she had drawn up the skirt of her buckskin dress.

Davinda was momentarily too stunned to move. In her mind's eye she was remembering feeling alone herself while having her child. The Schmidts had been kind, but they'd also been strangers. Giving birth on that long awful night, on the run from her father, in a strange house—nothing familiar to ease her fear while she struggled with that completely new, powerful, undreamed-of pain—it had been lonely and frightening and exhausting. She's despaired over her parents' harsh betrayal, over Johnny's death, over so many things while lying there waiting for her child to be born!

Her thoughts returned to the present when the Indian woman's eyes locked with hers. In them there was no fear, but instead a silent plea for help. Davinda forgot the barrier between their two worlds. She would not leave this woman to have her child alone. It would be a heartless thing to do.

And having survived a difficult birth herself without a doctor's help, Davinda knew what was required here. The difference was that the child seemed lodged inside the woman's birth canal. This baby needed some encouraging, and all that Davinda could think to do was to reach up inside the woman and help lead the baby.

Sweat beaded on Davinda's brow and she winced as she slid her hands slowly up inside the woman. She came close to losing her courage to complete the task when the woman let out a loud scream of pain.

But knowing that both the mother and child's lives were in jeopardy, Davinda continued until the child, a tiny copper-skinned baby boy, lay in her arms, crying.

Davinda stared at the umbilical cord. Mrs. Schmidt had used sewing scissors when Davinda finally delivered. But Davinda had no scissors with her today.

How then . . . ?

She stared in disbelief when the Indian woman reached down and took the child, lay him across her breasts up close to her face, then separated the child from her body by biting the cord in half. With trembling hands, she tied it.

Davinda forgot her wonder when the Indian maiden closed her eyes and drifted off into an unconscious state. Panic filled Davinda and she thought the woman was dying. If she was, what would happen to the child? Davinda was certain that if the Indian woman died, she could not leave the child there to die with her.

Was it meant for Davinda to give up her own child to raise someone else's?

Davinda started to reach for the child, then stopped when the woman's eyes opened again. Davinda scarcely breathed as she watched the woman slide the bodice of her dress down to expose a breast, and placed the nipple to the baby's lips.

The woman's eyes drifted shut once more as the child hungrily nursed from the breast. Davinda was torn as to what to do.

If the woman survived the trauma of giving birth, Davinda would have to take her to safety. Certainly she could not abandon this woman and newborn child. Yet it was obvious that the woman was in no condition to travel. She had lost much blood. And she surely would not want to be taken into the lodge of white people when she had family out there somewhere, who were concerned about her welfare.

Davinda started to reach for the child, then drew her hand quickly away when she heard movement behind her. She stiffened, then turned her head around to see who was there.

Her eyes grew wide with fear. She saw a tall, frowning Indian warrior standing in the clearing, so close that she could reach out and touch him. She stumbled to her feet and took a clumsy step backward.

She was shaken not only by his presence and her fear of him, but also by his handsomeness. He was a tall, spare-built man of sinewy limb. His sculpted features and his cheeks were well pronounced. His eyes, which were large and dark as midnight, gazed at her from a copper face. His waist-length black hair, darker than charcoal, hung free of braids, a beaded headband holding it in place. He wore a vest of puma skin, fringed buckskin trousers, and black moccasins. She knew from their color that he was a Blackfoot Indian, for they were the only Indians known for their black moccasins.

Walking Thunder stared back at the white woman who radiated such a natural, enchanted beauty. Her eyes were the color of violets that dotted the mountainsides in spring and summer. Her hair was the color of sunshine. Her face was expressive, with a strong passion lying just beneath the surface. Yet there was sadness in her eyes that seemed to outweigh her fear as she gazed up at him in mute silence.

But Walking Thunder had no time to think further about the white woman. His gaze shifted to his sister, and then the child which lay in her arms, suckling at the breast.

His gaze then went to the pool of blood that lay beneath his sister. His insides tightened and he realized that the birth of her child had not come easily.

He looked again at the white woman. The blood on her hands proved that she had helped Summer Hope in her time of trouble.

Again he knew that this was not the time to be in awe of a white woman for whatever reason. His sister was drifting in and out of consciousness. He feared for her life.

Davinda watched the Indian warrior drop to his knees beside the woman. She felt his despair when he spoke something to her in his Blackfoot tongue. She could see the devotion he felt for her when he placed a gentle hand to her cheek.

When the warrior spoke to the woman again, her dark eyes fluttered open.

He encircled the woman with his arms and held both her and her child against his powerful chest.

While the warrior concentrated on the woman and child, Davinda saw her chance to escape. She turned and ran toward her horse. When she reached it she quickly untied the reins and swung herself into her saddle.

Davinda rode off, following the path of the Yellowstone River, which would lead her back home. She felt safe enough, for the warrior surely would not abandon the woman to come after her. And he must realize that she had helped the maiden. There would be no reason for him to come after her.

Yet she still did not feel comfortable with the situation. If this Indian did not like the interference of whites on land that he might still see as his, he would not have to look far to find Davinda.

As she rode in a harder gallop, Davinda could not get the newborn child out of her mind. The pangs of heartache rose anew within her. Holding the infant a moment ago had made her remember too much all over again. Would she ever be able to forget the child she had left behind? Would she ever feel free to love again?

She was glad when the cabin came into view in the clearing up ahead. She had found a new life there. She would not allow memories to ruin it.

Davinda thought back to the Indian woman. She wondered if all Blackfoot women went away to have their children in the forest alone. If so, just how many of them died? How many babies died with them?

"Davinda!" Elaine shouted from the door of the cabin as Davinda rode up. "Child, you've been gone again for too long!"

Davinda drew a tight rein beside the door. Elaine saw the blood on her hands and clothes and paled. "Good Lord, Davinda, you're hurt!" she cried, rushing to Davinda as she slid from the saddle.

Elaine grabbed Davinda's hands and stared at them, then looked up at her questioningly. "What happened, child?" she murmured. "Where did this blood come from? I don't see any injuries."

Davinda slipped her hands from Elaine's. She gazed down at them, then slowly looked up at Elaine and told her everything.

Afterward, Elaine hugged Davinda. "Lordie, lordie," she said. "You could have been scalped by that warrior."

Davinda looked toward the dark shadows of the forest. She wondered if she had come across the Blackfoot warrior under different circumstances how he might have treated her. Was he the sort who hated "white eyes," as Indians were known to call white people? Would she see him again?

Elaine put her arm around Davinda. "Honey, come inside," she said. Elaine looked over her shoulder, her eyes searching through the forest. "And let's make sure our door is bolted tonight."

Clarence was bald, tall, and slender, and a narrow mustache shadowed his upper lip. He stood sullenly beside the stone fireplace inside the cabin, filling his pipe with tobacco as Davinda entered. "And so you had a confrontation with Indians on your outing today, did you?" he grumbled. He gazed down at her bloody hands, then squinted his eyes as he nodded toward her. "I told you plenty of times that you shouldn't go horseback ridin' alone. From here on out, I insist that you ride with me, do you hear?"

"You worry too much about me," Davinda said softly, not committing herself one way or another by agreeing with Clarence.

It was true, though, that she was glad to be safe in the lovely cabin. She looked around her at things that had, of late, become familiar. Everything contrasted so much with the wilds outside where Indians roamed free, as one with nature. Here in the safety of her home she realized just how lucky she was. The walls were mellow with flickering light from the fire that caressed the large logs in the great stone fireplace. Elaine's collection of salt and pepper shakers glinted in the sunshine that poured through the window opposite the fireplace. The old mahogany dinner table that Davinda had rubbed with beeswax this morning shone so much that she could see her image in it.

Along another wall stood a wonderful walnut cupboard for which Clarence had traded a load of corn. It was filled with Elaine's china, which was hand-painted with colorful wildlife scenes.

Their pantry was crammed with tangy smelling apples, bumpy yams, and dried figs and dates.

"Davinda, I had expected you home before now," Elaine said, drawing Davinda from her thoughts. "I had Clarence drag the tub into your room. I already have it filled with bath water." She frowned at Davinda. "It was hot when I first poured it. Now I imagine it's scarcely warm."

"It will be just fine," Davinda said, giving Elaine a soft hug. "Thank you for preparing it for me. I truly do need a good soaking." She stepped away from Elaine and placed a gentle hand on her cheek, looking past the wrinkles that ran across it. "You go and relax by the fire. There's a chill in from the mountains, cold for June."

Davinda went to the privacy of her room and closed the door. And after she settled into the tub and felt warm and secure, she thought back to her experience today. She could not help but feel lucky to have lived through her first encounter with Indians, especially the Indian warrior! She shuddered at the thought of how it might have been under different circumstances.

2

It was almost night. The sun had disappeared behind the sharp-pointed gray peaks of the distant mountains. In a valley sparsely timbered with quaking aspens, white birches, and cottonwoods, smoke from several Blackfoot lodges rose heavenward in slow spirals. Tom-toms beat out a steady rhythm into the fading light of dusk. Voices lifted in song.

A fire sent off soft, golden rays inside the large council lodge where Chief Walking Thunder's beloved sister lay, battling for her life. Walking Thunder stood in the shadows of the buckskin-covered tepee, his gaze intent on his sister.

His heart ached as he slid a slow gaze over to a woman who sat in an even darker corner, whose breast was offering nourishment to Walking Thunder's nephew. When Summer Hope's body had become hot with a raging temperature, her tiny son had been taken from her limp arms and placed in another's.

Walking Thunder again looked at his sister, whose body was surrounded by those who were singing over her. He had already offered his prayers to Old Man, Napi the creator, pleading with Old Man for his sister's recovery.

Stiffly, his hands doubled into tight fists at his sides, Walking Thunder watched as the healing ceremony progressed into something more dramatic. Those who had been standing near his sister now sat down in a wide circle around her and the roaring fire. Two elderly men who knew well the art of healing went to the back of the lodge and faced each other. They had spears, which they held above their heads, thrusting them back and forth at each other in time to the singing.

Near the doorway, two old women also stood facing each other. Each one held a *puk-sah-tchis*, maul, which they swung at their sides while keeping time with the drumming and singing.

A big roll of belly fat hung close over the fire and dripped its hot grease into the flames. As the grease sputtered and spattered in the fire, the singing continued, and the tom-toms beat out their steady, droning rhythm.

"*Ahk-sa-ke-wah, ahk-sa-ke-wah,*" the women sang. The two old men jabbed their spears at one another as the two old women began to pretend to hit each other with their mauls.

This continued for some time, then the singing ceased. The mauls and spears were lowered to the sides of those who held them.

Even the tom-toms were silenced.

Everyone watched as Shadow Claw, the village Shaman, entered the lodge, his black hair glistening in thick folds down his back, his buckskin robe dragging on the floor behind him.

Walking Thunder met his approach.

Together they went and stood over Summer Hope.

For a long time Shadow Claw shook his large rattle ornamented with beaver claws and bright feathers over Summer Hope, his chants filling the air with a steady, solemn drone.

Everyone held their breath in anticipation when Shadow Claw took the belly fat from the fire. Turning and facing everyone, he gave the slab of dripping fat a mighty swing around the circle of people so that the grease just barely missed the faces of those who were participating in the ceremony.

Once this part of the ceremony was over, everyone except Walking Thunder and Shadow Claw walked past Summer Hope. Each of them gave her a last, lingering look, then left the lodge in single file.

Shadow Claw placed a gentle hand on Walking Thunder's shoulder. "I leave you now to be alone with Summer Hope," he said, his voice drawn. "All that can be done for her has been done. The rest is left up to Old Man who makes the final decision as to who lives or dies. Treasure these moments with Summer Hope, for I feel they will be your last."

Shadow Claw gave Walking Thunder a tender embrace, then left the lodge.

Walking Thunder wiped the tears from his eyes and knelt down beside his sister's sickbed. His eyes wavered as he saw just how frail she looked on the thick pallet of furs and blankets. His heart felt as though it might break into tiny pieces when he recognized the death rattles that were now surfacing from his precious sister's lungs.

The hideous sound that came with death could not

even be drowned out by the mournful howling of wolves on the nearby bluffs, nor by the bellowing of the buffalo that roamed this mighty land of the Blackfoot.

"*Ni-sis-ah*, *ni-sis-ah*, sister, sister," Walking Thunder cried.

He leaned over her and held her in his arms. Cheek to cheek he held her, the heat of her face scorching his flesh.

"Why, why?" he said, his voice breaking. "You are all I have left of this earth! Our parents are gone. So are most of our close relations."

"I am . . . not . . . leaving you . . . alone," Summer Hope said in a raspy whisper. "There is *no-ko-i*, my son, your *nephew*. I . . . leave . . . my son with you." Suddenly, memories flooded through her mind of her beloved husband, who had died only recently in a skirmish with the Blackfoot enemy, the Crow.

Hearing her voice, realizing that she had emerged from that black dread of unconsciousness, Walking Thunder leaned back and gazed at her. "*Ni-sis-ah*, my sister, you are going to be all right," he said thickly. "The songs. The prayers. The curing ceremony! They will help you!"

"*Nis-ah*, my brother, the songs and prayers were heard by Old Man," Summer Hope said, gasping for breath. "He even witnessed the curing ceremony. But in response, what Old Man has given me is not a longer life. Old Man has blessed us, *nis-ah*, with these last moments together so that I can speak of things to you that are important to me. Then, *nis-ah*, I shall close my eyes and welcome death. I shall then be met with opened arms by all those loved ones who have gone to the Sand Hills before us."

"Do not speak of death as though it is something blessed," Walking Thunder said, his voice breaking. "If it takes you from me, it is wretched!"

"*Nis-ah, nis-ah*, please . . ." Summer Hope whispered, her eyes fluttering slowly closed, then open. "Please raise Little Fox as though he were your son. Let him learn from you. Teach him how to ride and shoot. Teach him the secrets of the hunt . ... the magic of being Blackfoot."

"Yes, I will do all those things," Walking Thunder said, nodding. "This child will be raised in the tradition of all Blackfoot warriors. He will be admired by all who will know him."

"Also, my brother, teach my son the morals that have made you into such a wonderful, adored man," Summer Hope said.

Weakly she clung to Walking Thunder as she took gasping swallows of air.

"There . . . is . . . something more I wish of you," she said, so softly that Walking Thunder could barely hear her.

"Whatever you ask, I shall do," Walking Thunder said, realizing by the shallowness of her breath that the end was near. He lay his ear close to her lips and listened.

"In my lodge, among my cherished belongings, you will find a special necklace of bear claws," she said, her chest heaving. "Go and find the white woman who came to my rescue. If not for her, my child would have died within my womb! Because of her, Little Fox breathes. *Nis-ah*, brother, find her. Reward her with my bear claw necklace. Tell her it is the only way I have of . . . thanking . . . her."

Walking Thunder's eyes widened. His sister mentioning the white woman and wanting to thank her in such a special way seemed ironic to Walking Thunder. He had also been thinking about the woman and felt a need to thank her for what she had done for a stranger . . . an *Indian*.

Yes, the white woman had been on his mind, but he had fought against searching for her. There had been too much about her that had disturbed him in ways he wished to forget. He had seen in her beauty . . . gentleness . . . caring.

He kept forcing himself to look past her intrigue and remind himself that she was white. It was not wise to enjoy looking at a woman whose skin did not match his own. He was a great Blackfoot leader. He should at all times be thinking of women within his own tribe!

Yet he found it impossible to ignore his feelings. Suddenly the skin coloring did not matter.

"*Nis-ah*, will you do that for me?" Summer Hope whispered, drawing his attention back to her.

"Yes, I will find her," Walking Thunder said thickly. "I will take her your necklace."

Walking Thunder was thrown into a whirlpool of despair when Summer Hope's body went limp in his arms.

When he realized that she no longer breathed, he stared at her, then cried despairingly to the heavens.

"*Ki-yo!*" he cried. "*Ni-sis-ah*, my sister, oh, my beloved sister!"

Little Fox began to wail.

Walking Thunder looked past his own despair, realizing that his duties to his nephew began *now*.

Meditatively, Walking Thunder gave Summer Hope one last kiss on her cheek, then wrapped her in a number of robes. Her body would soon be prepared for the burial rites.

Walking Thunder knew where he would take her. He would place her on a platform of lodge poles amid the branches of her favorite tree, a birch that stood tall and white on a bluff that overlooked the village. There she would always be a part of her people's lives. She would forever hear their songs and their laughter. There she would always be near her son.

Walking Thunder lifted Little Fox into his arms. "My sister is never gone from me as long as I have you to love," he whispered to the child. "And from this day forth, you will be my *no-ko-i*, my son."

3

Davinda groaned as she slowly awakened to the strong smell of scorched wood. The back of her head throbbed and the stench burned her throat and lungs. She coughed and leaned up on an elbow to look around her.

Tears blurred her vision as she looked for Clarence and Elaine. She found them with their hands still intertwined, stretched out on their stomachs several feet away from Davinda.

Dried blood stained their clothes where they had been shot in the back as they had fled from the cabin. Fiery torches thrown on the roof and through the windows had started the blaze.

Davinda saw that everything had been destroyed! The livestock that was not stolen, including her beautiful mare, had perished in the fire.

She closed her eyes as memories flooded her mind in vivid, white flashes. She had been in the barn gathering eggs when she had heard the arrival of many horsemen.

Mortified, Davinda had looked through a crack in

the wall and watched a mixture of red- and white-skinned men circle the cabin. She saw them toss the torches toward the cabin, and had felt totally helpless as she watched her friends flee, then fall victims of gunfire.

Davinda had escaped the barn just before it was, also, set ablaze. She had stumbled over a rock and fell to the ground in full view of one of the assailants. When she realized it was an Indian, she had expected to be shot.

When the renegade rode toward her, she scrambled to her feet to run away. Unfortunately, she hadn't been quick enough. Sitting hunched over on his saddle, the Indian had laughed and circled his horse around her. His pock-marked face had been twisted grotesquely into an ugly picture of hate as he continued to stare down at her.

Too proud, too frightened to plead for mercy, Davinda had stood her ground and waited for the bullet that would end her life.

While standing there, so helpless, so tremblingly weak with fear, her past had flashed before her eyes . . .

She had seen her beloved mother, whose violet eyes had mirrored Davinda's, and whose arms were once warm and welcoming.

She had seen her father, whom she had adored as a young girl. Later he had turned into a tyrant when she confessed to him that she was with child.

Finally, she saw her tiny baby, whose precious face she would never forget.

The Indian screeching a loud war cry wrenched Davinda back to reality. She gasped with pain at the blow to her head when the Indian's rifle butt sent her into a quick, black void of unconsciousness.

She reached her hand up to the back of her head now and found a huge knot through the dried, caked blood in her hair. "Lord, he thought he had left me to die!"

Davinda was thankful that the Indian hadn't used a bullet on her. She tried to rise to her feet, but soon discovered that her knees were too wobbly to hold her full weight.

Again she gazed at Clarence and Elaine, but only for a moment. She could not bear the sight. She buried her face in her hands as tears ran from her eyes in torrents. "Why?" she cried. "Why? They were so kind . . . so caring."

She cried until she had no more strength or tears left in her. After trying to get up again, only to crumple again back down on the ground, she inhaled a deep, quavering breath and shut her eyes.

But her eyes did not stay closed for long. They snapped open in desperate fear when she heard the sound of an approaching horseman. She could not help but wonder if those who had been here earlier might have decided to come back. Perhaps the pock-marked Indian, whose face she would never forget, had realized she might have survived his blow.

Oh Lord, she despaired to herself, had he returned to finish her off?

Or had she been purposely spared long enough to endure the torment of seeing her beloved friends lying there dead? Yes, the Indian who had laughed and jeered at her while circling her with his horse could be that cruel, she concluded.

Or perhaps this was someone else who might make it a habit to profit by the misfortune of others? Perhaps he had waited for the fire to die down and for the ashes to cool. Then he could pilfer through the remains for whatever he might find that might be useful to him.

Davinda was afraid of *all* of these possibilities and knew that she was at the mercy of whoever it was. She felt that her only chance for survival was to pretend that she was still unconscious.

Her heart pounding, her throat dry, Davinda lay as lifelessly as possible on her side. She closed her eyes tightly, as she heard the horse stop only a short distance away.

She waited.

And silently prayed . . .

Abhorred by what he had found on this beautiful June day, Walking Thunder stared blankly at the devastation that lay before him. The house . . . the outbuildings . . . the dead animals!

He had left his village only this morning, after several days of mourning his sister, to search for the white woman. He carried Summer Hope's bear claw necklace in the buckskin bag that hung at the right side of his saddle.

And he also carried something else today. Inside his heart he brought with him warm feelings for the kind white woman. It was his deepest desire to approach her as a friend, and hope that she would welcome such advances. She was as mysterious to him as the stars that brightened the heavens at night.

He wondered if those who lived in this cabin might have survived this attack by evil-minded assailants. Walking Thunder slid out of his saddle and secured his horse's reins to a low tree limb. He moved stealthily toward the dwelling's charred remains. Not sure what he might find, he placed his hand on the knife that was sheathed at his right side. His black moccasins made no sound as he continued walking.

Suddenly he stopped dead in his tracks. His breath caught in his throat when he saw the body of a woman lying a short distance away. She was close to what he thought might have once been a dwelling that white men called a barn.

Spirals of dread moved through Walking Thunder as he studied the color of the woman's hair. His heart felt as though someone's fingers were painfully squeezing it as he realized there were too many similarities between this woman and the one he sought today. Not only was her hair the same color of gold, but her figure was equally delicate.

His pulse racing, Walking Thunder went to the woman and knelt down on one knee. Slowly he reached his hand out to smooth back the locks of her golden hair so that he could see her face.

Davinda found it harder and harder to lie there so quietly when she could hear the breathing of the person who was kneeling beside her. She expected at any moment to feel the cold steel of a knife enter her heart, ending her days on this earth forever.

Or was she soon to feel a knife at her throat?

Or perhaps a gun was pointed down at her, ready to fire!

She fought hard not to flinch when she felt warm fingers on her cheek.

She held her breath as she felt someone touch her hair.

Then some scent on the stranger's clothes, a herb smell of some sort, wafted up Davinda's nose.

She panicked, for she knew that she was going to . . .

She sneezed once, twice, three times . . .

Walking Thunder jumped with alarm, then stared at her when she turned her face toward him.

Their gazes met and locked.

Davinda recognized the Indian. He was the very one who had been on her mind since their encounter in the forest, after she had helped the woman with the child. She could not help but be afraid of him. She could not know that he had not been a part of the initial raid that had taken the lives of Clarence and Elaine. Was this the thanks she got for helping the woman? If so, she would never understand, but she knew that if it were true she would hate him forever!

"Get away from me," Davinda managed to say through her rage and fear. She tried to wriggle farther away from him, but found that each movement caused her head to throb that much more.

Walking Thunder ignored her pleas and stayed where he was. He watched her try to rise to her feet, but she was too weak.

"I am glad that you are alive," Walking Thunder finally said in English. He had learned the white man's tongue from trappers, traders, and the pony soldiers while he had been in council with them.

He gazed at her blood-soaked hair. Gently he turned her so that he could see the huge knot on her head. "*Hai-yah*! You are injured," he exclaimed. "Walking Thunder will take you to his lodge. Your injury will be treated."

Davinda paled, then squared her shoulders and tried to look brave. "I am going nowhere with you," she said. She nodded toward the bodies of Clarence and Elaine. "And stop trying to pretend that you are a friend. But of course you will deny knowing anything about the deaths of those who were so dear to me."

She looked at all the destruction around her. "And of course you will deny having given orders to set fire to everything," she said, swallowing hard.

She turned her gleaming gaze up at Walking Thunder. "I hate you, you . . . you . . . sav—," she stopped just short of saying savage. That word alone could cause him to forget that he wanted her alive. The term was hated by all Indians.

Davinda had never in the past referred to Indians as savages. She had always tried to understand their plight after they had been forced to give up so much to white people. But at this moment she felt nothing but a deep hate and loathing toward them. She had watched helplessly as one had pulled the trigger that had taken the lives of Elaine and Clarence. An Indian had left *her* to die.

"Why do you hate Walking Thunder?" he asked, cocking an eyebrow. "As you helped a Blackfoot maiden in her time of trouble, I now earnestly offer *you* help."

"Why would you? Because you wish to make me your captive?" Davinda spat back. "You know that I have no choice but to do as you say. I am at your mercy, aren't I?"

Davinda lowered her eyes when she felt compelled to cry again. She tried to will the tears away as she did not want him to see her cry. She wanted to continue to look strong. She wanted to continue being defiant.

Yet she was filled with so much sadness and an utter helplessness over everything that was taken from her this day, she could not stop the tears as they spilled from her eyes and flowed down her cheeks.

Walking Thunder saw her flood of tears and looked toward the charred remains of the cabin. He saw two bodies—a man and a woman.

"Your parents died today?" he asked. He gently lifted Davinda's chin with a finger so that their eyes could meet. "That is why you are filled with such remorse? With such hate and anger for those who came and killed today?"

"They weren't my parents," Davinda sobbed. "They were my dear friends." An angry defiance filled her eyes again. "Please quit pretending you care! Don't you understand that makes me hate you even more?"

"*Wo-ka-hit, wo-ka-hit*, listen. I do not deserve your hate, for I am not guilty of this atrocity," Walking Thunder said thickly. He took her into his arms and rose to his feet. "But I see now that only time will prove the truth to you. Until then, I will show you through my deeds that I am a friend, not an enemy. I am of the *Sik-si-kau*, Blackfoot tribe. I am of the *Mas-to-pah-ta-kiks*, the Raven Carriers band of Blackfoot. Raven Carriers are known to keep peace with the white eyes, not war."

Davinda tried desperately to free herself as he turned and carried her away from the carnage. "No! I don't believe anything you say!" she cried, her head aching even more fiercely as she fought against his hold on her. "Please let me down!"

"It is best that you leave this place of death," Walking Thunder said. His horse whinnied as he approached. "*Ok-yi*, come. The wound on your head will be medicated today. In time, your wounded heart will also be healed. I will make both happen for you."

"You have already made enough happen, and it is all *wretched*," Davinda said. She felt weak and her head hurt so badly she could hardly concentrate on what she was saying or doing.

"I see that it is a waste of my voice to argue with you about what has happened today," Walking Thunder said as he stopped beside his horse. "And it is a waste of your voice to continue accusing me. Tomorrow things will look brighter for you. It will be the beginning of a new life. And you will find it a much better life than the one you are leaving today."

"I found much happiness living with Clarence and Elaine," Davinda said, wincing with pain when he lifted her to his saddle. Each time she moved, her head throbbed like dozens of hornets had stung her scalp. "I had almost put my painful past behind me. Now I have lost my only friends. I will miss them dearly."

Walking Thunder gazed up at her questioningly, but he did not inquire about her painful past. This was not the time to delve into her history, or into the mystery of why he felt so compelled to befriend her. But he and the woman both had much to learn about each other, and they would learn together.

Walking Thunder swung himself up into the saddle behind Davinda. Possessively, as though Davinda already belonged to him, he slid an arm around her waist. He held her as he rode toward the forest.

Suddenly Davinda turned and gazed over his shoulder. "No," she cried. "I can't leave like this. I must give them a Christian burial." She looked at Walking Thunder. "Please take me back. Help me bury them!"

"It is best not to linger any longer here today," Walking Thunder said, sending his horse into a harder gallop. "Yet I, too, understand your feelings toward those you have lost to death. I have lost many loved ones in my lifetime, more than I wish to think about."

She was stunned by how gently he spoke and treated her, yet she still could not help but think he had a part in the massacre today. He must have realized that whites lived near after he saw her help the woman. Since that day, she had worried what his knowledge might lead to.

If he had taken part in today's massacre, surely he had second thoughts about having left her there to die. Guilt must have sent him back to check on her— guilt over knowing that she did not deserve to die. Davinda had helped bring a Blackfoot child into the world. Was it for that reason that he had decided to save her?

But what could she expect from him now? she wondered in despair.

4

As they approached the Blackfoot village, Davinda gazed at it with apprehension. She was afraid that the Blackfoot people would resent her presence. She would never forget that first meeting with Walking Thunder . . . how he had glared at her as she had stood over the beautiful Indian maiden. In his eyes she had seen many emotions, among them a deeply imbedded resentment.

"We will soon be in my lodge," Walking Thunder said, drawing Davinda out of her reverie. "You will be safe there."

Davinda turned and gave him a look of disbelief. She was in awe of what he had just said about being safe with him. How could he possibly think that she trusted him? After what had happened to her friends, how could he expect her to feel safe anywhere ever again, especially among Indians who had cause to hate all white people!

"Safe?" she said mockingly. "Ha! As safe as I would be in a den of wolves!"

"You are wrong," Walking Thunder said thickly.

132

"Soon you will take back words that wrong this Blackfoot chief."

Davinda's lips parted with wonder. "You . . . are . . . a Blackfoot chief?" she managed to say, wishing she could erase the amazement in her voice.

"Yes, Walking Thunder is head chief," he said. He lifted his chin proudly when he realized that his true identity was impressive to the white woman. "Head chief leads. All others follow."

Now Davinda was more apprehensive than before. She was certain that she was in the presence of a powerful man whose word was stronger than that of others among his people. Surely he had the power to command a death sentence on those he saw as his enemy.

"Your name?" Walking Thunder asked guardedly. He watched her eyes as her troubled emotions caused their violet color to darken into something even more beautiful.

"You need not know my name," Davinda said, stubbornly turning her face away from him, though she knew that her attitude could get her into even more trouble. She still felt the need to look strong in the eyes of this Indian chief.

Again she looked over her shoulder at him. "As soon as I am well enough, I plan to escape. I will go to Fort Chance and ask for help in securing myself passage away from this wretched land of Montana," she blurted out.

With that, Walking Thunder said no more. He pursed his lips tightly together. He saw now that he had much persuading to do in a little span of time. This woman who would not share her name with him was not all that ill. In a matter of days she would be well enough to travel.

And he did not make a practice of keeping captives. If at the end of their time together she wished to leave, he would have to allow it.

But Walking Thunder believed that his powers of persuasion would prevent that from happening. He saw this woman as someone in need of so much. Not only had she lost loved ones today, it was apparent that somewhere in her past she had been terribly wronged. Otherwise she would have been living with members of her family instead of with those she referred to only as "friends." He would make the Blackfoot people *her* people so that she would never get that lost, sad look in her eyes again.

Although her head was throbbing unmercifully, Davinda gazed around her, memorizing the lay of the land for that moment she would escape. She planned to steal a Blackfoot horse and leave under the cover of darkness for the nearest fort. She was not quite sure how far she was from Fort Chance, where Clarence and Elaine had always gone for their supplies. If she followed the Yellowstone River, however, it would eventually lead her to the fort, which had been established at the junction of the Missouri and Yellowstone Rivers.

Yes, she would find her way there. By then she would know whether or not to condemn this Blackfoot chief for what had happened today.

If she could get over her uneasiness over him possibly having been one of those who came and killed today, she could see just how handsome and gentle he was. His eyes were so dark and mystical, they had come close to mesmerizing her more than once. And it was hard for her to look past the absolute mystery of him being an Indian chief.

As they drew closer to the outskirts of the Indian village, she could not help but be fascinated by it. She had never seen one before and was in awe of the hundreds of smoke-blackened, cone-shaped lodges. Their peaks released drifting, lazy smoke into the breeze.

A tree-fringed stream, fresh from the distant mountains, flowed by the camp that was pitched upon four table-lands. Here the enemy, red or white, could not pass by without being seen. Behind the tepees, the hills were dotted with many horses.

As Davinda entered the village, she saw that the dwellings were very large and handsome. They were colorfully designed with paintings depicting the sun, lightning, and the various seasons of the year.

The people had formed a line to greet Walking Thunder's return to the village. She noticed they stepped aside and made way for their chief as he rode toward a large tepee at the end of the line.

Children reached up and touched him on the leg adoringly. Adult men and women nodded at him, their smiles waning as they looked past him to gaze at the woman he brought among them.

Davinda was afraid to look at their faces. She didn't want to see the hate they might feel for her. All she wanted now was to get inside the large tepee and lie down. Davinda was totally exhausted. It was difficult to hold her head up another minute. It felt as though it weighed a ton on her shoulders.

Yet she also knew that once she was inside that larger lodge, she would be alone with the Indian chief.

A thought sprang to mind. Through her own personal traumas today, through her sorrow over having lost two special friends, she had not thought once about the Indian woman whose child she had helped deliver. Had she survived? Had the child?

So bone-weary, her head aching, Davinda went limp in Walking Thunder's arms as he lifted her from the saddle. The fight momentarily gone from her, only wanting to sleep, Davinda lay her cheek against Walking Thunder's chest as he carried her inside his spacious tepee.

She welcomed the warmth of the lodge fire as Walking Thunder lay her on a pallet of plush robes made of fur. During her ride to the village, the sun had slid beneath the distant hills and the evening chill had begun to sweep down from the mountains.

Only wanting to sleep and escape the reality of her situation, Davinda snuggled beneath the robes. Walking Thunder slipped another pelt over her. She could feel his presence as he stayed on his haunches for a while longer to gaze at her. She ignored him.

Sleep.

All that she could think about was sleep.

In that void of blackness she could escape all of her hurts, all of her pains, all of her losses.

But when a baby started wailing from somewhere within the lodge, Davinda's eyes opened. The crying stopped and she heard Walking Thunder speaking softly. Davinda sat up and studied the dark shadows at the back of the lodge.

The fire's glow cast enough light for her to see Walking Thunder holding and rocking a child slowly back and forth in his arms. Her heart skipped a beat at the sight, knowing that the child must be the one she had helped deliver. Davinda was relieved to see that it was alive and well.

She could not help being moved by the beautiful sight of Walking Thunder and the child. She could tell by the expression on Walking Thunder's face that he adored the child.

A woman's voice spoke up and drew Davinda's searching gaze farther into the dark recesses of the tepee.

She found the woman who was holding out her arms for the child, and whose thick, heavy breasts were exposed, awaiting the child's tiny lips to suckle from one of them. Davinda's insides tightened. This was not the child's mother! Davinda would never forget that lovely face . . . the youthfulness of it.

This was a much older woman. She was not petite. Her breasts were so large, they hung down against her chest like huge melons. And, Davinda concluded, the woman seemed to be much older than Walking Thunder, which had to mean that she was not his wife.

Then why was she there? Davinda asked herself. *Where was the child's mother?*

Dread grabbed Davinda at the pit of her stomach when she realized what the answer to her question had to be.

Surely the child's mother had died.

After Walking Thunder placed the child in the arms of the woman, he turned and saw that Davinda was watching. He returned to her and sat down .

"The child's mother is dead," he said, staring sadly into the flames of the fire. "She has gone to the Sand Hills. It is the shadow land and place of ghosts, the Blackfoot's future world. But she continues to live on here on this earth in her son."

"I'm sorry," Davinda said, truly regretful, for she knew too well the despair of losing loved ones. Her own loss was too fresh in her heart not to understand this man's grief.

Walking Thunder turned quickly to Davinda. "She was not my wife," he said. "She was my beloved *ni-sis-ah*, younger sister. She walks today with our parents in the Sand Hills. I have no wife. I have no parents. All that I have is my nephew, Little Fox."

Davinda was taken aback by her reaction to learning that this man was not married. She was actually glad!

Afraid of her feelings, and drawn into the mystique of this man, she had an urgent need to flee.

She started to rise, but fell back down to the blankets when pain shot through her head in heated flashes.

"I will send for Shadow Claw, our village shaman," Walking Thunder said, having seen her agony. "With Shadow Claw's hands purified by the smoke of burning sweetgrass, he will speak words of curing over you."

"Don't you dare!" Davinda found the strength to say. "I don't want any hocus pocus spoken over me! Just leave me alone! Let me rest! I . . . need . . . rest."

Sobbing, she crumpled down onto her side. She wasn't even aware of the Indian woman leaving. All that she knew was that she felt a deep need to sleep. She hoped that tomorrow she would awaken and discover that this was all a horrible mistake. A nightmare!

Again she welcomed the dark void of sleep. She fought off dreams that ate away at her heart—dreams of discovering her friends' bodies, of leaving her child on the doorstep, of her father's loud accusations when he had discovered that she was with child.

A soft noise drew her awake. She looked around the tepee. The fire had died down to burning embers. Across the fire she saw Walking Thunder asleep on a pallet of furs. He looked so peaceful, so beautifully handsome in his sleep, as though he was an innocent child instead of a powerful Blackfoot Indian chief.

The sound that had awakened her came from the cradle at the far end of the tepee. The child had awakened. He cried softly one moment, then made sweet cooing sounds the next.

The noises tore at Davinda's heart. They reminded her too much of her daughter. And that someone else was there to comfort the girl if she awakened in the middle of the night. Someone else would hold her . . . would sing to her . . .

Little Fox's voice grew stronger as he began to cry louder.

Davinda looked over at Walking Thunder again. It was obvious that the child's cries had still not awakened him. And the older woman was not there. She must sleep in her own lodge at night. Davinda looked at the cradle again. Slowly she shoved the robes and pelts away from herself and rose to her knees.

Her heart was racing. She ignored a warning that came to her in flashes, that it was best not to take even one look at the child. She feared that if she saw him she would remember the day she had left her child behind on a stranger's doorstep. The guilt and the pain of missing her child so much might worsen.

But she could not help herself. She was drawn to the Blackfoot Indian baby and the need to see him.

Without any more hesitation, she crawled back to the cradle and gazed down at the tiny bundle. She sighed when she saw him. Comfortably wrapped in a white rabbit-fur blanket, all that was exposed of Little Fox was his face. But that was enough for her to see his sweetness and fall in love with him.

When the child caught Davinda gazing down at him, his cries waned into soft purring sounds that touched her heart.

Davinda's arms had ached to hold a child since that dreadful night when she had given up her baby to be raised by someone other than herself. She couldn't help it when she reached down inside the cradle and eased the child into her arms. She began to rock the child slowly back and forth, softly singing a song her mother had always sung to her as a child whenever she had needed comforting.

All the emotions that Davinda had tried so hard to push to the back of her consciousness resurfaced. She realized how much of her heart and soul were missing by having forfeited those special moments with her own child to someone else.

Tears streaming from her eyes, she gently touched the small babe's cheek, feeling its utter softness. "Precious . . . precious . . ." she whispered.

5

Walking Thunder awakened with a start. He had not meant to sleep so soundly through the entire night. The white woman! If her strength had returned, she might have slipped away into the night and no one would be the wiser.

His gaze swept across the dying embers of the lodge fire. Walking Thunder's heart skipped a beat inside his chest and his throat instantly went dry when he saw that the white woman was not there. She *had* left his lodge while he was foolishly sleeping!

The soft sounds of Little Fox waking drew Walking Thunder's gaze back to the darker shadows of the lodge.

His heart began an anxious thudding inside his chest, and a smile fluttered on his lips when the muted light of morning came through the smoke hole opening and revealed to him that the child was not in his crib, nor was he alone.

The white woman had not left his dwelling. She was in the back lying on a white bear robe beside Little Fox's cradle, sleeping. Nestled comfortably against her bosom, Little Fox lay in the curve of her arms. Walking Thunder could tell that he was content. The child sweetly cooed amidst his rabbit-fur blanket.

Dressed in only his brief breechcloth and no moccasins, Walking Thunder crept silently to the back of the lodge. Taking in the beautiful sight of the woman and child together, he realized it was something natural . . . something right. Walking Thunder settled on his haunches beside them.

His feelings for Davinda were building. He so badly wanted to reach out and touch her pink cheeks, or run his fingers through her golden hair.

But he did not want to startle her awake.

He even wished that she would sleep a while longer so that he could just sit there and watch her. His thoughts strayed, and he wondered how it would feel to blanket this woman with his body and make love with her.

Her kisses would taste like the sweet wine of grapes.

Her hands caressing his body would be like nothing else he had ever felt in his lifetime.

While imagining himself with her he could almost feel the warmth of pleasure as it swept through his loins and up into his soundly beating heart.

"Where am I?"

A voice . . . *her* voice, brought Walking Thunder out of his reverie. He gazed into Davinda's violet eyes as she looked at him questioningly.

Davinda could not believe that she had actually held the child through the entire night. She had awakened and found that her fitful dreams had been true, that she *was* in an Indian's lodge, that Clarence and Elaine *had* been murdered in the most vicious way.

Tears came to her eyes as she looked away from Walking Thunder. "It truly did happen," she whispered. "Oh Lord, I didn't dream it."

Walking Thunder saw that her sorrowful remembrances were flooding her thoughts and he understood how it had to be eating away at her heart to think back to how her friends had died. He reached a hand out to touch her cheek, then thought better of it. He had to give her time to accept all that fate had handed her.

Hopefully the pain inside her heart would be less today than it was yesterday. Each day it would soften until eventually she could live with her loss.

He had learned how to accept his own misfortunes after the deaths of his loved ones. He knew, by having experienced it far too often, that it was not an easy task to put the trauma behind you.

When Little Fox began to whimper, Walking Thunder gently slipped him from Davinda's arms. "I will take Little Fox to Flower Woman for his morning bath and feeding," he said. "Then I will return. Food will be brought to us, and if you wish, you can go down to the river for a bath."

"I don't want food and I don't want a bath," Davinda cried, giving him a look of total defiance. "I just want things back the way they were!"

"That can never be," Walking Thunder said, gently rocking Little Fox back and forth in his arms. "You must begin today reaching for new tomorrows, new alliances . . . an entirely new life."

Davinda wiped tears from her eyes as she watched him leave the lodge with the child.

When her head began to throb, she remembered her injury. Reaching up and touching the lump, she winced. Yet she was relieved to know that the pain was not as severe as it had been yesterday.

She grimaced when she felt the dried blood on her hair. It was no wonder that Walking Thunder had suggested a bath. She did need one. Perhaps it might make her feel better.

Remembering how weak her legs had been yesterday, she stretched them out before her. Would they carry her to the river today? Would they carry her back to the lodge?

She was amazed to realize that she had matter-of-factly thought about returning to the lodge instead of stealing a horse and leaving the Blackfoot village!

Then she sighed, knowing that it was too soon to think of getting on a horse. She was still too weak to travel far enough to reach the fort. Yes, she would wait one more day, then surely she would be strong enough to endure the horse ride that would take her away from this place.

Her knees trembled as she rose slowly to her full height. She steadied herself and reached for her head when its throbbing worsened. Again she felt the dried blood.

"I *must* get to the river for a bath," she whispered.

Not wanting to put on the same clothes that she now wore, which carried not only the blood from her wound, but also the stench of the fire, she looked around her slowly, hoping to find something to wear somewhere in the tepee.

She took time to study the interior of the dwelling since Walking Thunder wasn't there to watch her. She was amazed at how clean and neat everything was. Mats made of peeled willow twigs covered the floor. Gourds, baskets, and clay pots sat neatly in place along the walls.

She stared at an impressive exhibit of warring attire and weapons—bows and arrows, lances decorated with many colorful feathers, and Walking Thunder's shield and headdress.

It was hard to envision Walking Thunder in a long, trailing feather headdress. He seemed too young and modern to be an Indian chief.

Davinda wanted to get her bath over with before the entire village wandered down to the river for their morning bath. Realizing that time was passing quickly, Davinda rummaged through Walking Thunder's belongings until she found a buckskin robe. She held it out and frowned. It was huge and very long, yet at least it was something that she could change into.

A familiar scent made her draw the garment to her nose. She closed her eyes as she sniffed it. Her insides grew warm with desire when she smelled Walking Thunder's scent on the buckskin fabric. She slowly rubbed the fabric against her cheek, imagining that it was his flesh against hers.

She could not deny the feelings she felt for the Blackfoot chief. This morning when she had seen him attired in only a breech clout that left little of his anatomy to her imagination it had been hard to act defiant.

In truth she wondered how it would feel to be

kissed by him. When he had held her on his horse with him, his muscled arm had felt so powerful . . . so natural, as though it belonged there.

Confused by her foolish— by her *improper* thoughts about the Indian, Davinda shook them from her mind. She went to the entrance flap, slowly moved it aside, and gazed out.

She saw only a few people wandering about and felt secure that she would have the privacy she sought for her bath. She crept on outside and went down to the river.

The water was so cold it stung Davinda's flesh. Yet she found it invigorating. She swam up one side of the river and down the other, then rubbed her skin briskly to get it as clean as she could without the aid of soap.

It felt wonderful to lower her head into the water. The lump did not throb as much anymore. She gently scrubbed around the wound until the blood was removed, then she hurried from the river and pulled on the robe.

She giggled when she looked down at herself and saw how comical she looked in the huge robe. It was so large it could have swallowed her whole. Several times she almost tripped on the fringed hem of the robe as she walked back to Walking Thunder's lodge.

Upon entering his lodge, she found him waiting for her. His intense eyes were dark as he watched her come closer and sit down across from him on the other side of the fire. She could see a quiet amusement in his eyes as his gaze swept slowly over her and the attire that she had chosen from his selection of clothes.

She ignored how her appearance in his robe seemed to amuse him. At least he wasn't angry that she had taken liberties with his wardrobe.

"You knew where I was?" she asked softly. "You trusted that I would return? You did not feel the need to come and escort me back to your lodge?"

"I knew where you were and I knew that you would go no farther," Walking Thunder said, laying another piece of wood on the fire. "Your heart tells you that you are wrong to accuse Walking Thunder of murdering your friends. Your heart tells you to apologize to Walking Thunder for such accusations."

"My heart tells me none of those things," Davinda snapped back. "I . . . I . . . just needed a bath. That's all. And . . . and . . . I was too weak to escape. I *had* to return to your lodge."

"The gown fits you well," Walking Thunder said, a smile quavering on his lips.

"Oh hush," Davinda said. She folded her arms over her chest. "I know how I look. But at least I am clean."

"You can wear one of my breech clouts after your next bath, if you wish," Walking Thunder further teased, hoping to create a lighthearted mood in his lodge this morning.

Davinda's face grew hot as she gazed over at him in his scanty attire. His copper chest was so well-muscled! His shoulders were so broad! His stomach was so flat!

She dared not look any lower. Her mind had already been filled with too many foolish thoughts this morning about the handsome Blackfoot chief.

When she did not respond to his teasing remark

about the breech clout, and he saw her blush of embarrassment, he felt that he had gone just a mite too far with his comments. The last thing he wanted was to make her any more uncomfortable than she already was in these new surroundings.

"Today I shall have one of our women who is of your same size bring you a dress to wear and moccasins," he said.

He soon saw that that comment did not seem to please her any more than anything else that he had said today. He had to go slow and easy with her.

Yet he felt as though he had made some progress with her. She *had* taken a bath as per his suggestion. And she *had* returned of her own volition to his lodge, as though it was a natural thing for her to do—as though he were someone she could trust, perhaps even have feelings for.

But he knew now that he wanted much more from her.

And in time, he would have it.

Davinda became aware of the smell of roasting meat wafting in through the open entrance flaps from the nearby lodges. She was aware of children's laughter, dogs barking, and horses neighing. She could also hear the chatter of women and men outside as the day's activities began.

Her eyes widened when a maiden who was perhaps Davinda's age came into the lodge carrying a huge wooden tray of food. Davinda could not deny how good the food looked to her or just how hungry she was. And she knew that she would eat as much as possible, for that was one way to get her strength back for her escape.

Davinda eyed the tray of food more closely when Walking Thunder came and offered it out to her.

"Eat," he said softly. "Long Skirt's mother is a good cook. Many Cooks Fire spends her day cooking while Long Skirt does the other chores for her mother and her people."

"Long Skirt?" Davinda said, looking quickly at the woman as she quietly left the lodge. "What a strange name for a woman."

"As she would perhaps think your name was as strange if she knew it," Walking Thunder softly defended. "You have yet to speak it. Is that because you would rather I call you by a name I assign you? Perhaps you would like to be called Woman With Lump On Head, or Woman Who Is Spoiled?"

Davinda's lips parted in a gasp. She glared up at him. "What horrible names," she said. "But of course you would think of the most horrible name for me, wouldn't you? You just want to torment me since I haven't bowed down to you as I am sure you are used to, being a powerful Blackfoot chief and all."

Walking Thunder's jaw tightened. "And did you see Long Skirt, as you say, bow down to me?" he asked, his eyes narrowing angrily. "You are wrong again about this Blackfoot chief and what he expects of his people and friends."

"Yes, I know," Davinda said with a sigh. "You are just an ordinary Indian who expects nothing from his subjects."

Walking Thunder inhaled a quick, agitated breath. "I am losing my patience with you and your bitter tongue," he said. "I know this is not the real you saying such things. I watched you with Little Fox. I saw your gentle side. I know there is a side of you that is good."

He leaned down closer to her face as he knelt before her. "I am known for my good judge of character," he said smoothly. "I know that I am not wrong about *yours*."

He thrust the tray of food into her hands. "Now eat and say nothing more to me that will cause me to doubt my judgment of you."

Davinda's lips parted, yet she suddenly felt no more urge to be spiteful to him. She held the tray of food and he sat down next to her and took a huge piece of meat and began to eat. She wanted to apologize, to tell him that she only behaved this way because she was still not certain whether or not he was in part responsible for Clarence and Elaine's deaths.

Would she truly ever know? she wondered despairingly.

Her stomach growled, reminding her of how long it had been since she had last eaten. She gazed down at the variety of meats that lay on the platter and at the strange looking cakes.

"What kind of meat is this?" she blurted out. "Which kind did you choose to eat?"

Walking Thunder slowly slid his gaze her way. He smiled devilishly. "I am eating skunk meat," he said slyly. "It has the best taste and *smell*."

Davinda paled. She quickly placed the platter on the floor. "Lord," she gasped, "I'm not eating *skunk*."

Walking Thunder finished eating his piece of meat, then took another piece from the tray. He held it up close to Davinda's lips. "I lied," he said softly. "None of this meat is skunk. What I offer you now is rabbit."

She looked into his eyes. "Please quit teasing me," she said, her voice breaking. "I . . . I . . . am hungry. Please be truthful about what you are offering."

"Rabbit," Walking Thunder said, his voice serious. "I offer you rabbit. But if that does not please you, there is also boiled boss ribs on the plate, and sarvis berry pemmican cakes. Eat. Enjoy."

Famished, her stomach aching, Davinda took the meat he offered and ate it in quick gulps.

Ignoring the fact that he was watching her, she grabbed more food and ate and ate until she was finally comfortably full. She then welcomed a cup of water, which she gulped down in long, deep swallows.

Her heart suddenly stopped when someone outside of the lodge shouted to Walking Thunder that many horsemen were approaching the village. Soldiers from Fort Chance!

Davinda and Walking Thunder's eyes quickly met in a silent questioning.

6

The spell between Walking Thunder and Davinda was broken when they heard the horses stopping just outside Walking Thunder's lodge. He placed gentle hands to Davinda's cheeks. "You will stay inside my lodge?" he questioned softly.

When she didn't answer him, he gave her a final lingering look, then left.

Davinda wasn't quite sure why, but something told her not to step outside just yet. There had been something in the way that Walking Thunder had asked her to stay in the lodge, and the soft look in his eyes, that had persuaded her not to do anything too hasty right now. If she was wrong about Walking Thunder, and he was not guilty of Clarence and Elaine's deaths, she didn't want to be the cause of his wrongful arrest. Each moment she passed with him, she found it harder and harder to believe that he could be guilty of any savage crimes!

Needing to know so many answers to so many things, she inched closer to the entrance flap and listened. Colonel Brady, the commander in charge at

153

Fort Chance, was telling Walking Thunder about having found the charred remains of Clarence and Elaine's home. They had also found other settlers' homes burned and destroyed.

Scarcely breathing, Davinda listened closely to what Colonel Brady was saying, stunned to know that there had been so many raids on innocent people. No, it did not seem possible that Walking Thunder could be responsible. Whoever could kill so easily as those who were spilling blood across the land had to be filled with much rage. In her presence Walking Thunder had never shown any signs of being capable of such rage.

And those who killed so easily could not be capable of changing personalities as quickly as Walking Thunder would have needed to in order to kill heartlessly one minute and then generously befriend her the next!

Hope of Walking Thunder's innocence filling her, she continued listening . . .

"Yes, I know that there are more than Blackfoot living in the Montana Territory, but, Chief Walking Thunder, you are under the most suspicion because your village lies close to all of the settlers' homes that have been burned," Colonel Brady said icily. "I see how you might think that scaring some whites might send the rest fleeing from this land that you might feel is still yours."

"Yes, it is true that in the past my forefathers gave battle to all people who came to cross boundary lines of land given to us by Old Man to keep them out," Walking Thunder responded, his voice void of emotion. "But in time, things changed. The Blackfoot saw advantages to making friends with the white eyes. The Blackfoot let our friends, the white people, come in, and you know the results. Because we, Old Man's children, disobeyed the law by allowing whites to live on land given to us by Old Man, we are losing, inch by inch, the land that has been ours since the beginning of time. It does eat away at my heart to see the land being swallowed almost whole by whites. But long ago I made peace with the situation and have accepted life as it is handed to me. Walking Thunder, a Raven Carrier Blackfoot, *never* kills innocent whites for what others have done to lure them to this land that offers so much. You are looking at the wrong man when you speak of such accusations that only renegades who carry vengeance inside their hearts would do."

When a sudden silence fell between Walking Thunder and the colonel, Davinda could not help but wonder what the cause was.

She slid the flap aside and peered outside. The hair at the nape of her neck bristled in fear when she recognized the Indian scout who sat at the colonel's right side on a black mustang. How could she ever forget his pock-marked face? It was the man who had tormentingly circled her with his horse right after she had seen her dear friends shot in the back.

This very Indian had hit her over the head with the butt end of his rifle!

Davinda suddenly realized that it was obvious that this murdering, thieving scout who rode with the soldiers had no alliance whatsoever with Walking Thunder, or he would not be there with those who came to accuse the chief of such savage crimes.

A river of sensations washed through her at the knowledge that Walking Thunder was innocent. She had been so wrong to treat him so coldly. All along, when she had defied him, he had been innocent.

Davinda's heart skipped a beat when the Indian scout saw her standing there staring at him. It was the sudden shock in his eyes that told her that *he* also recognized her.

Davinda knew the danger she was in. She remembered him leaving her to die on the ground during the massacre. She had no choice but to speak up in Walking Thunder's defense. She had to do everything within her power to save him, especially now that she was certain that he was an innocent man.

But she would not point an accusing finger at the Indian scout just yet. She must find the perfect time. She didn't want to cause a confrontation in the Blackfoot village among the scout, Walking Thunder's people, and the cavalry.

Her insides trembling, the scout still glaring at her, Davinda left the lodge and stood tall beside Walking Thunder. She held her chin high as she saw surprise leap into the colonel's eyes, not only because of her presence there, but surely because of the way she was dressed. She still wore the huge, loose Indian robe.

"Davinda Norris?" Colonel Brady asked in shock. "You're alive?"

He raised an eyebrow as he continued to stare at her. "What are you doing here?" he asked warily. "Are you aware of what happened at your friends' ranch? Do you know that they are dead?"

"Yes, I know," Davinda said. She swallowed hard as

she pushed the death scene out of her mind's eye. "I was there. I . . . lived . . . through the massacre." She slid the scout a sidelong glance, then looked quickly at the colonel again. "I was left for dead."

She smiled up at Walking Thunder. "If not for Walking Thunder, perhaps I *would* be dead by now," she felt proud to announce, now that she knew of his innocence. "He brought me here. He cared for me."

"Then you can speak up in his behalf?" Colonel Brady asked, placing his hand on the handle of the saber sheathed at his right side. "Can you tell me that he was not responsible for the recent massacres?"

"He is not responsible for what happened to me . . . and Clarence and Elaine," Davinda said softly. "And I am certain that he is innocent of any of the other crimes you have discovered in the area."

She could feel Walking Thunder's eyes on her. Davinda had heard his slight intake of breath when she stood there vouching for him.

Of course he would be surprised, she thought to herself. Until now, she had not shown any signs of having believed him.

"Chief Walking Thunder, it seems I owe you an apology," Colonel Brady said, extending a hand toward him. "Can we shake on it? As you know, I'm new in command at Fort Chance. I have not had the opportunity to get to know you well."

Walking Thunder hesitated, then reached out and shook hands. "Your apology is accepted," he said thickly. "Come again when we can share a smoke and more pleasant talk."

"I would like that," Colonel Brady said, nodding.

He turned around and nodded to his soldiers.

"Retreat!" he shouted. "Head back to the fort! There is no more to be said or done here!"

The soldiers wheeled their horses around and all but the Indian scout and the colonel rode in single file out of the village. The colonel turned and gazed down at Davinda. "I'm sorry about what happened to Elaine and Clarence," he said solemnly. "Davinda, there is no need now for you to stay with the Blackfoot." He offered her a hand. "Come and ride with me back to the fort. I can help you in any way you wish. If you need money for travel out of the Montana Territory, I will oblige."

Davinda took a step away from him. Her eyes wavered as she gazed up at him. She knew that it was going to look strange for her to stay with the Blackfoot when she had been generously offered help by the colonel. But she knew she must stay with Walking Thunder. She was afraid of the Indian scout who realized she knew enough to get him hanged!

She felt that she would be much safer with the Blackfoot than in the custody of the colonel. Surely, as soon as she left the fort for parts unknown, the scout would follow and kill her.

"Thank you, but for now I think I shall remain awhile with the Blackfoot," Davinda said, avoiding the scout's steady glare. "I . . . I . . . am not well enough just yet to travel." She reached her hand to the lump on her head. "The ride to the fort would be too uncomfortable for me. My head has not yet healed."

The colonel's gaze went to Walking Thunder. "By damn, chief, as I see it, this woman wanting to stay with your people is absolute proof of your inno-

cence," he said. "Yes, I truly believe you are an innocent man."

Davinda looked over at Walking Thunder. She saw
him as a man of great pride and restraint. When the
colonel had shown his distrust of Walking Thunder,
he had stood in leather-faced silence.

Walking Thunder suddenly spoke his mind and
wonderfully, magnificently defended himself. "You
should have never doubted me," he said. "The
friendship of my Blackfoot people toward whites
has been fostered by decades of commerce with
beaver hunters who roamed our mountain home-
land. All those who have commanded at the fort
before you knew that Walking Thunder and his
people walk the white man's road of peace. Were
you not told that by the colonel who only recently
left to command elsewhere? Perhaps your ears were
closed to the truth because you did not wish to hear
him, out of bad feelings you might have for all
Indians."

The colonel's round face turned crimson. "I am not
a man of prejudice," he said stiffly. "I have always felt
moved by the plight of the Indians. When I came
today to accuse you of the atrocities in this area, it was
at the urging of others who thought you might be
responsible."

"And who might have wrongly sent you here?"
Walking Thunder asked, his voice tight.

The colonel glanced at the Indian scout accusingly,
then sighed deeply and refused to answer.

Davinda saw this as a possible time to tell the
colonel the truth, herself, but the scout's glare kept
her silent.

But she vowed that soon he would pay for what he had done. After she told Walking Thunder everything in the privacy of his lodge, she knew that it would not be long before the Indian scout got his comeuppance.

"I must catch up with my regiment," Colonel Brady said, wheeling his horse around. He gave Davinda and Walking Thunder a slow stare over his shoulder before riding away with the scout at his right side.

Walking Thunder turned to Davinda. "We came close to blows," he said. "If not for you, we may have. You spoke up on my behalf. Although I am unsure why you did it, I thank you."

He held the flap open for Davinda, then walked into the lodge behind her. Walking Thunder stood over the fire beside her, He gently placed his hands on her shoulders, and turned her to face him. Their eyes met. Then he drew Davinda into his gentle embrace and kissed her.

Davinda's knees almost buckled from the passionate feelings that suddenly enveloped her. His lips were so warm, so masterful, yet so sweet. It felt wonderful to be held by him, to feel how much he adored her by the way he kissed her.

Realizing now just how much she wanted Walking Thunder, Davinda twined her arms around his neck and openly returned his kiss. For the first time since she had lost her betrothed in the war, she felt needed . . . desired!

When Walking Thunder slid a hand between them and cupped one of her breasts through the buckskin fabric of the robe, Davinda felt faint from the rapture it stirred within her.

But the voice of Flower Woman just outside the lodge drew them apart. She was asking for permission to enter with Little Fox, saying that he was bathed and fed.

Walking Thunder could not find it in his heart to move away from Davinda just yet, though. He gazed down at her. He had denied himself the pleasure of a woman for so long, it stirred his very soul to be close to one he was developing such strong feelings for. For too long now he had placed his loyalty to his people before his need to choose one special woman to call his very own.

Yes, there had been plenty who had warmed his blankets at night. That had been enough, till now. Now he wanted more. He wanted a wife.

And he would not let the color of Davinda's skin alter his decision to have her. It was what was in both their hearts that mattered. And he would not allow himself to feel disloyal to his people because of this woman whose very eyes even now mesmerized him!

"Flower Woman is calling your name again," Davinda said, bringing Walking Thunder out of his thoughts. She had felt so many things as he had stared down at her. She could tell that he was battling his feelings over her inside his heart, almost the same as she had fought her own feelings for him . . . until now. Her heart had won over everything else. She could not help but give in to her feelings of wanting . . . of needing him.

Walking Thunder gave her a soft smile and gently reached up to touch her cheek. He went outside, got Little Fox, and brought him back inside the lodge.

"Can I hold him for awhile?" Davinda asked, gazing down at the child wrapped in a soft rabbit-fur blanket. "He is so sweet."

Walking Thunder gingerly placed the infant in her arms. He stood beside her and listened as she spoke to him.

His heart warmed at the sight of this wonderful woman holding the child he adored. They were perfect together and seemed naturally drawn to one another.

Davinda slowly rocked Little Fox back and forth as she walked toward the cradle. She saw Little Fox's eyes drift closed and gently lay him in his crib. As she drew a soft buckskin blanket over him Walking Thunder spoke.

"You will stay longer with Walking Thunder? You will fill my lodge with your sunshine?"

"Yes, I shall stay awhile longer," she murmured.

When they heard horses pass by outside, Walking Thunder looked toward the front of the lodge and frowned. "The colonel knew who urged him to come and accuse Walking Thunder of the crimes being committed in the area," he said, his voice drawn. "Yet he would not tell me."

He gazed down at Davinda. "If he knows who sent him to my village, surely he knows that this person might be in cahoots with those who are killing and maiming across the countryside," he added through clenched teeth.

Davinda recalled how guardedly the colonel had looked over at the Indian scout. "Yes, he knows," she blurted out. "And now so do I."

Walking Thunder took a step away from her. "Are you saying that you still believe I am guilty?" he asked, his jaw tightening.

"No, I was not speaking of you," Davinda said

quickly. "Walking Thunder, it was the Indian scout with the colonel. *He* is the very man who knocked me unconscious. He rode with those who killed my friends. Some were Indians. Some were white!"

"And so Black Cloud is in on the havoc!" Walking Thunder said, a sudden bitterness in his eyes.

"Black Cloud?" Davinda asked softly.

"The scout who rides with the colonel is called Black Cloud. He was once a part of our village until he was banished for wrongful deeds. Not knowing the black heart he carries inside his chest, the whites took him in. I even believe he might be responsible for the raid on our village which took the lives of my father and mother. It was shortly after he was banished that it happened. But I had no proof."

He placed his hands on her shoulders. "Why did you not speak up and tell this truth to the colonel when he was here?" he asked softly.

"I was afraid to," Davinda said, swallowing hard. "I thought it was best to tell you later, in private. I thought you might know how to deal with someone like him better than the white officers would. And I did not want to start a possible confrontation in your village that could endanger your people, especially the children." She paused and then added, "I did not want to place you in danger."

"I thank you for worrying about my people," Walking Thunder said. "And about their chief."

He went to stand by the fire and stared into the dancing flames. "I will find a way to deal with Black Cloud," he murmured.

"How?" Davinda asked, moving next to him. "What are you going to do?"

"I will send a warrior out to follow his each and every movement," he said. "If Black Cloud is leader of a band of renegade Indians, he will soon die."

"There were also white men with the Indians," Davinda said.

"Those are outlaws who have come to this land to search for yellow rocks called gold," Walking Thunder grumbled. "Those who have not been successful in that venture join parties of renegades and prey on those white eye settlers who have been successful at making their lives better on this land."

"They are vicious killers," Davinda said, trembling at the thought of how heartlessly they had gunned down Clarence and Elaine.

Walking Thunder saw that she was being overtaken again with thoughts of what had happened to her friends. He reached out and drew her into his arms. "Remember that you are safe now," he said, holding her close.

"I know," Davinda whispered. "I know . . ."

7

The days had passed with Davinda hardly noticing. She had become immersed in the daily lives of the Blackfoot and found their way of living so different from her own, so much more difficult. On the other hand, the customs were so interesting, it was easy to look past the hardships of Indian life.

Davinda was dressed in a lovely beaded dress and black moccasins. She was caught up in a Blackfoot celebration called the Camas Feast. As she sat among Walking Thunder's people near a great outdoor fire, Davinda became mesmerized by dancers circling around the fire. Their feet stamped out the same rhythm as the tom-toms played by drummers at the outer edge of the crowd.

As she continued to watch the dancers perform, her hands went to the bear claw necklace that Walking Thunder had given to her. She was deeply touched that it was from Walking Thunder's sister.

He had explained to Davinda that Summer Hope had sent him to look for her with this gift of thanks for having saved her son's life. That was why he had been there that day, right after the massacre of her friends. He had been searching for her to deliver the necklace. Destiny had led him to her for another purpose. They were meant to be together!

A warm hand slid into hers, and as the fingers intertwined with her own, Davinda's heart leapt in ecstasy. She turned her passion-heavy eyes to Walking Thunder as he scooted closer to her. They both sat away from the others on a high platform covered with expensive pelts.

"You are intrigued by the celebration?" Walking Thunder asked, smiling at Davinda. She looked beautiful. Her hair was braided with flowers and a flower belt looped around the waist of her doeskin dress.

"Yes, it's very interesting," Davinda murmured, returning the smile. She was in awe of how Walking Thunder was magically sweeping away all of the past pains from her heart.

She found so much love and warmth in him. His caring nature meant he was always there to make sure that she didn't slip back into the moods that had troubled her so often since she had said good-bye to her child.

Tomorrow he was escorting her to the small cemetery that sat on a slope of land a short distance from the fort. She wanted to pray over Clarence and Elaine's graves. Davinda had been relieved when she had received word that the soldiers had given them Christian burials.

After spending time at the graves, she was going to ask Walking Thunder to take her back to the ranch. Although she hated seeing the devastation, she had something important to do there nonetheless.

"In those Blackfoot clothes you look like sunshine," Walking Thunder said. "Do you feel comfortable wearing them?"

"I cannot help but feel beautiful in this lovely dress," Davinda said, turning to face Walking Thunder. He looked breathlessly handsome in his fringed buckskin outfit with beaded vine work running along the outer seam. A headband made of otter fur held his long, flowing hair back from his face. Around his neck he wore a necklace made out of bear claws that matched the one that she wore. His black moccasins had the same beaded design that were on her own. Long Skirt had made them the moccasins for this special occasion.

Walking Thunder shifted his gaze back to the dancers. "Did you understand my explanation of today's ceremony?" he asked.

"Yes," Davinda answered, beaming, as she too again watched the dancers. "And I find it so exciting to be with your people like this, sharing." She swallowed hard. "I'm so glad they do not see me as an intruder in their lives."

"There are some who do carry resentment of your presence inside their hearts but they will not ever reveal it to you or me," Walking Thunder said. He gave her a stern look. "They do not defy their chief by questioning his judgment on anything."

"I'm sorry about having doubted you when you said that you were not guilty of murdering Clarence and Elaine," Davinda said.

"Speak of it no more," Walking Thunder said. He placed a finger to her chin and lifted it so that her eyes could meet his. "All of that belongs to the past. Leave it there."

"Yes, in the past," she murmured. "Tell me something, Walking Thunder?"

"What do you wish to question me about?" he asked. "I will give you answers."

"Why is your band of Blackfoot called Raven Carriers?"

"Of all the flyers in the sky, there are none as smart as the raven," he said, gesturing skyward, as though the birds he spoke of were there. "The raven's eyes are sharp. Their wings are strong. They are great hunters and never go hungry."

He smiled. "Far, far off on the prairie, the raven always sees his food," he said. "Even hidden deep in the pines it does not escape his eyes!"

Walking Thunder removed a slender stick from a long parfleche sack at his side and showed it to Davinda. It was beautifully dressed with many colorful feathers. On the end of it was fastened the skin of a raven, its head, wings, and feet.

"This, made of everything raven, was my father's guardian spirit medicine," he said solemnly. "It is now Walking Thunder's."

Their attention was drawn back to the dance when the Blackfoot people suddenly began to sing loudly and clap.

They soon understood why. The excitement was building into something more dramatic. Dancing in a lively, jerky manner, the male performers were now weaving in and out around the fire wearing animal-head masks. They also wore breech clouts, revealing bodies that were brightly painted.

"The performances of our 'Animal-Head Mask' dancers are dear to the Blackfoot's heart," Walking Thunder said.

His eyes gleamed as he watched the performers dancing to the double-beat of the Indian tom-toms, while listening to the voices singing "*Hai-yah, Hai-yah*" in a high pitch.

He pointed to the men playing the tom-toms. "And do you hear how the drums are vibrating and speaking to the spirits?" he asked, nodding his head in rhythm with the steady beats.

"Yes and I find it all so fascinating," Davinda said, also nodding in time with the music. As she continued to watch the colorful performance, she began thinking about the Camas Feast Ceremony.

Since her arrival in the Montana Territory, she had familiarized herself with many plants of the area. The camas plant was one of them. It was a yellow, sweet, sticky bulb that grew abundantly in certain localities on the mountain slopes. She knew that they were delicious roasted.

But not until the day that Davinda had seen several women returning from the mountains with huge bundles of camas bulbs had she realized the importance of this plant to the Blackfoot people. She had gone immediately to Walking Thunder and asked him what the women were going to do with so many of the plants.

Walking Thunder had explained to her that there would be a celebration of the camas plant. He had explained it to her as she had watched the women dig a large pit in the center of the village, which was then lined with flat stones.

A huge fire had been built deep into the pit, and after several hours the stones and earth were thoroughly heated and the coals and ashes were removed.

The women then lined the pit with grass and filled it to the top with camas bulbs. More grass, twigs, and earth was added. On top of this a fire was built, which burned for two days.

"It is almost time now for the pit to be opened," Walking Thunder said, bringing Davinda out of her thoughts. "That is the main part of the ceremony, when everyone will enjoy their first taste of this year's freshly roasted plants."

Suddenly the dancers stepped away from the fire, and the drums and rattles ceased playing. The circle of people broke up into small groups as the women gathered around the huge pit.

Walking Thunder took Davinda's hand and led her from the platform. They walked to the pit and watched. When the pit was opened, the small children ran up to it and sucked the syrup that had collected on the twigs and grass that had been used to cover the camas plants.

"The syrup is very sweet," Walking Thunder explained to Davinda. "It is quite a treat for our children, who do not have great supplies of candy like white children."

Davinda gave him a questioning look, then smiled. Yes, he might think that all whites were rich and always had candy on hand for their children. In truth, most people she knew could only afford to buy their children an occasional stick of penny candy.

She watched as the fresh-roasted camas plants were taken from the pit and placed on huge platters. Everyone sat down and began to enjoy the feast.

Davinda joined Walking Thunder on the ground and ate heartily. The camas plants tasted heavenly.

They reminded her of the chestnuts her parents had roasted over the fire on Christmas day, oh so many years ago.

When everyone had eaten their fill, the rest of the roots were gathered and spread out on huge sheets of buckskin to dry in the sun over the next several days. Then the roots would be put in sacks and stored away. Some were to be pounded up with sarvis berries and dried.

The special day was over and everyone drifted off to their lodges. Walking Thunder walked Davinda back to his, where Flower Woman was holding Little Fox and awaiting their return.

"And so my little brave is still awake?" Walking Thunder asked, lifting Little Fox into his arms. He gazed down at the dark eyes that were studying his face. "*No-ko-i,* my son, one day you, also, will dance and sing around the fire with the others your same age. I shall make you a special animal mask for the dance."

Davinda gazed over at Walking Thunder and smiled to herself as she watched him with Little Fox. She felt blessed to have been brought into their lives. It was wonderful to see them together. And when she held the child, she no longer was filled with painful remembrances of her own. There were things in life one had to accept. She was finally accepting the loss of her daughter.

She watched Flower Woman leave, then grew warm inside when Walking Thunder placed Little Fox in her arms. She laughed softly when the baby yawned and stretched his arms high over his head. "I think he's trying to tell us something," she said, smiling over at Walking Thunder.

"I do not see how he would welcome his cradle

over your arms, but if I am to hold you in *my* arms, we must place Little Fox in his bed," Walking Thunder said, chuckling.

Davinda brushed a soft kiss across Little Fox's brow, then handed him to Walking Thunder. She watched him rock Little Fox for a moment in his arms before placing him in the cradle.

He then turned to Davinda and drew her into his arms. "My woman, I need you," he said huskily. "My body aches for you. Does your body not send messages to your heart of its needs? Of its hungers?"

Davinda tensed. She leaned away from him, her eyes searching his.

"Is it too soon?" he asked, placing a gentle hand to her cheek.

"Everything has happened so quickly with us," she answered, her pulse racing.

"Life is too short to wait for what might seem a proper time for certain things," he said huskily.

"Yes . . . I . . . know," Davinda said, forcing thoughts of so many painful memories from her mind.

He drew her into his arms again. "Now is the moment for us," he whispered against her lips. "Now, Davinda. Now. Put aside everything and everyone from your mind. There is only you and me."

Another time, another night, and another man tried to push into her consciousness. She remembered what had once transpired in the throes of passion. But this was now. This was Walking Thunder. Oh Lord, she loved him much more than she had ever loved any other man, so much that she would risk the world to have this night of lovemaking with him.

He stole her breath away with the suddenness in which he swept her up into his arms and carried her to his bed at the far side of the lodge.

She clung to him when he spread her out beneath him on the thick pallet of furs and blankets. His lips smothered her cry of passion with a fiery kiss as his hand moved inside the skirt of her dress and found her throbbing woman's center. As his fingers caressed her, her head began to swim. She sighed with pleasure as he slipped a finger up inside her.

As he nudged her knees apart and he slid her dress up past her waist, she feverishly undid his buckskin breeches and slid them down past his thighs. She closed her eyes and moaned when she felt the heat of his manhood probing where she was wet and ready for him. She opened her legs more fully to him and gasped with pleasure when he entered her with one wild, insistent thrust.

Ecstasy fully claimed her as he plunged more deeply inside her in a dizzying rhythm. She cried out in soft whimpers against his lips when he ripped the front of her dress down the middle, giving him full access to her breasts.

His burning hot lips brushed her cheeks and ears, then moved over one of her breasts, his tongue swirling around the stiff, resilient nipple.

Then he kissed her lips again. He kissed her long and deep this time and moved powerfully within her as her hips gyrated against his.   •

Spasmodic gasps filled the air as they both moved closer to the ultimate pleasure.

Davinda trembled with readiness as Walking

Thunder drove into her swiftly and surely, their bodies straining together hungrily.

He gathered her into his arms, anchoring her against him, then made one last maddening plunge that brought them both to the brink they had been seeking.

Davinda arched and cried out against his lips. Walking Thunder shuddered his seed into her, then rolled onto his back, his breath coming in heaving gasps.

Still caught up in the wonders of the lovemaking, Davinda curled up and lay close to Walking Thunder. She reached a hand out and caressed his manhood.

"It was wonderful," she whispered. Then she giggled as she gazed down at the dress that had been a gift from Long Skirt. She was still in awe of Walking Thunder having ripped it. "But what am I to tell Long Skirt when she asks why I never wear her dress anymore?"

He turned toward her and cupped her breast with his hand. "Tell her nothing," he said, chuckling. "Just smile. It will be our secret."

She sat up on the bed and slowly undressed. "Are you always that passionate while making love?" she asked, her cheeks warming with desire.

"Always," he said, chuckling as he slid his breeches off. He sat up and drew his shirt over his head, then tossed it aside. "Shall I show you again?"

Davinda crawled over next to him. Gently she shoved him down onto his back, then straddled him. "Let *me* show you *my* way," she said huskily, hardly believing this was her saying and doing these lustful acts.

But she could not help herself. Being with this man she loved so deeply seemed to have brought out the passionate side to her nature.

Walking Thunder had no chance to reply. Davinda's hair lay around his head in golden, silky strands as she leaned low and kissed him. One of her hands guided him inside her.

Whatever Walking Thunder had planned to say slipped from his mind as he was lost again to ecstasy, to his Davinda.

8

The next morning Davinda rode grim-faced on a white mustang, the fringes of her buckskin dress fluttering around her ankles in the wind. Her strength fully regained, she was finally going to visit Elaine's and Clarence's graves. She was going to say her final farewell to them. Walking Thunder rode beside her on his powerful steed. He sat tall and straight-backed in his fringed outfit.

The farther Davinda traveled, the more she saw the pock-marked face of the Indian scout who had been a part of the massacre . . . perhaps even the leader of the heartless heathens!

She quickly looked over at Walking Thunder. "Is the warrior still following Black Cloud?" she asked, drawing Walking Thunder's attention to her. "He surely can't go for too long without riding with the scoundrel renegades and outlaws. It's been several weeks now since . . . since . . ."

"Yes, he is being watched, and not by only one warrior now, by many," Walking Thunder interjected, stopping her just short of having to say the words that he knew tore at her heart each time she said them. "Black Cloud will get caught in his own trap. Be patient. In time, you will see that justice will be done."

"I'm so glad that your warriors are staying close by, keeping an eye on him," Davinda said, sighing. "At least I know that he won't kill or maim anyone else. Not while your warriors are there to stop him."

"He has to make a move toward wrongdoing before we have the proof that will help place a noose around his neck," Walking Thunder said. "And he will, my woman. He will, and soon. Killing is in his blood. It is like the stinking fire-water alcohol that white men crave. Killing is addictive to those whose hearts are black with evil."

Davinda shivered. "Yes, I imagine so," she murmured. "I just wish he could have been stopped earlier."

"He should have been," Walking Thunder said thickly. "When I first suspected he might be guilty of such horrendous crimes, I should have sent my warriors to watch him then. But too often life gets in the way of some of man's best intentions. The needs of my people and my duties as chief after my father's death took precedence over everything else. And when Black Cloud became the white man's scout, I could not help but believe that I had been wrong about him." His jaw tightened. "I was wrong, all right, but about the wrong thing. Black Cloud will be stopped."

"Thank you for coming with me today so that I can speak words over my friends' graves," Davinda murmured, wanting to lead the conversation away from things that made Walking Thunder feel guilty. She knew that he did everything with such passion, and if he felt guilt about *any*thing, that would also be with much conviction . . . such passion.

She was familiar enough with guilt to know that it could linger like a festering sore.

"I so dread seeing the graves of my friends," Davinda said then, her voice breaking.

"Yes, I can understand, but remember that I will be there with you to soften the hurt," Walking Thunder said gently. "My arms will hold and comfort you."

"You are so sweet, so caring," Davinda said, tears burning at the corners of her eyes.

Then her thoughts strayed to something else that gave her cause to be uneasy. She had to find a part of her past today and reclaim it. The locket. It was her only true link to her former life.

She hoped Walking Thunder would understand why she must claim it, and her reason for having it in the first place. Davinda didn't want him to turn his back on her over something that happened in her past. He had said more than once that the past was past. Today and tomorrow were all that mattered.

"Can I not lift some of the sadness from your heart?" Walking Thunder said softly, seeing how she was suddenly so quiet and absorbed in her thoughts. He gestured toward the distant mountains. "Today is the sort that should make all mankind be glad to be alive."

He pointed to a herd of bighorn sheep that grazed peacefully in the sun on the mountainside. "Do you see the bighorn sheep?"

"Yes," she answered. "They have always amazed me

by their grazing on the mountain slopes' more dangerous places."

"There is a reason for their ability to do that," Walking Thunder said, his eyes twinkling. "Old Man put all kinds of animals on the ground. When he made the bighorn sheep, with its big head and horns, he made it out on the prairie. It did not seem to travel easily on the prairie. It was awkward and could not go fast. So Old Man took it by the horns and led it up into the mountains and turned it loose. It skipped about among the rocks and went up fearful places with ease. That was what it was fitted for . . . the rocks and the mountains."

"That's such an interesting story," Davinda said. "I love your way of explaining things. But, Walking Thunder, I'm puzzled by something.'"

"And that is?" he questioned.

"Your reference to Old Man," she said. "I have heard you talk of Old Man before. Who . . . or . . . what is Old Man?"

He laughed softly, then smiled over at Davinda. "Old Man is the Maker . . . the Creator of all things. The Sun is a man, the supreme chief of the world. The flat, circular earth, in fact, is his home, the floor of his lodge, and the overarching sky is its covering. The moon, *ko-ko-mik-e-is*, night light, is the Sun's wife. The pair have had a number of children, all but one of whom were killed by pelicans. The survivor is the morning star, *a-pi-su-ahts*, early riser."

He paused, then reached over and took her hand. "My woman, the sun is the person whom we call Old Man," he said. "Every good thing, success in war, in the chase, health, long life, all happiness comes by the special favor of the Sun."

"Just as I feel that everything on this earth is a blessing from God," Davinda said softly. She swallowed hard. "There is so much for us to sort through to acquaint each other with our separate beliefs."

"It will be an education welcomed by this chief for I will be doing it with you," Walking Thunder said. They rode into a clearing and could see the fort in the distance. He looked over at Davinda and saw that she was staring at the cemetery that was only a short distance away. He drew a tight rein and held back while she rode on. He watched her dismount and kneel down beside the graves.

After a time she rose to her feet and went to her horse. Walking Thunder rode up next to her. "It is done?" he asked thickly. "Have you made peace with your God and friends?"

"Yes, I have made my peace," she said, swallowing hard. "It is just that I . . . I . . . can't believe they are dead."

"It is only their bodies that lie in their graves," Walking Thunder said. He slid from his saddle and drew her into his arms. "Your friends' spirits live on for all eternity."

He glanced heavenward, then smiled at Davinda. "Their spirits are here now. They are whispering in the wind their good-byes to you."

Davinda was touched by Walking Thunder's tender ways and his thoughtfulness to her in her time of sorrow. Overcome with emotion, Davinda flung herself into his arms.

Walking Thunder held her. Easing her away from him, he framed her face between his hands. She lifted her eyes to meet the softness in his. "My woman," he said. "We must move forward now with our lives. Leave this behind you."

"I know," Davinda said, nodding. She backed away from him and flicked tears from her eyes. "Now I would like to go to the cabin," she said guardedly, seeing an immediate look of questioning in his eyes.

"Why?" he asked. "There is nothing left there but charred remains and bad memories."

"There is something more," Davinda said, her heart pounding. She realized that soon she must reveal all of her tormented past to Walking Thunder. The locket. She would have to explain the locket! And she knew that this might cause him to turn his back on her in disgust.

But she also knew that she must take that chance, for she must have the locket! This was a part of her past that she could not let go of.

Walking Thunder studied her thoughtfully. He knew that something was deeply troubling her. He sensed that it was something she did not yet wish to speak about or she would have already told him. He also knew the art of restraint and patience. He would practice it now and trust her judgment and her reasons for wanting to return to the scene of the massacre.

"Let us go now," he said, swinging himself into his saddle.

She gaped up at him, her lips softly parted. "You will not go with me to the cabin?" she asked, surprised that he refused her. Until now he had not refused her anything.

"When I said let us go, I meant to the cabin," Walking Thunder said, seeing the instant relief in her eyes.

Sighing with happiness, and relieved that she had misread him, Davinda mounted her steed and rode off with him.

Soon they arrived at a clearing where the charred remains of the cabin and outbuildings were visible. Davinda shivered as she stared at what lay spread out before her like some evil thing. Everything was black, and the wind occasionally lifted and swirled the ashes into the air.

She gave Walking Thunder a guarded look, then rode away from him and stopped at the very edge of the yard where debris had blown from the cabin. This was where the cabin had once stood. The chimney rose into the air like some tall mighty fortress.

Walking Thunder rode up next to her and drew a tight rein. He followed the line of her vision and saw that she was looking at the chimney.

When she turned to him, and he saw her despair, he wanted to encourage her to leave . . . to leave all of this behind her and never think about it again.

But when she looked up at him pleadingly, he nodded a silent understanding. Inside, however, he was full of questions that would come later, for he wished to know what had brought her here today.

"Give me a moment, then I will be ready to return to your village with you," Davinda murmured. She saw the questioning look in his eyes and was grateful that he was not voicing his concerns aloud.

"Go," Walking Thunder said, nodding. "I will wait."

Her pulse racing, she walked toward the black ashes and knew she would have to walk through them to get to the chimney. But she would walk through hell itself to retrieve the link to someone dear to her forever.

Lifting the hem of her dress, she walked gingerly through the remains of what had been a wonderful life, if only for a short while.

As she moved through the ashes, she saw the charred remains of familiar things . . . the organ, the dining table, the broken china, pieces of the salt and pepper shakers from Elaine's collection, much more that tore at her heart.

At last she reached the chimney. Her fingers trembled as she reached for the small stone she was familiar with. She circled her fingers around the stone and soot flaked away from it.

Then one yank and the stone was free.

Her pulse raced as she dropped the stone, then reached inside and found the locket where she had hidden it only a few days after arriving at the ranch.

Tears filled Davinda's eyes as she gathered it within her fingers and drew it out of its hiding place. When it was in the palm of her hand, she gazed down at it. The sun reflected off the gold into her eyes, momentarily giving her a vision of the face of her baby, as though its picture were there, gazing back at her.

"You have found what you are after?" Walking Thunder asked, standing at her right side.

Walking Thunder's voice drew Davinda back to the present. She held her hand out for him to see the locket, and nodded.

"It is something valuable to you, this thing that shines in the sun?" Walking Thunder asked, staring at the tiny locket.

"Yes, very," Davinda said, circling her fingers around the locket.

She stepped up close to Walking Thunder. "This is only half of what was once a beautiful locket," she said, her voice breaking.

"There is no chain," Walking Thunder said, reaching out for the locket. He studied it closely. "Or is it not to be worn around the neck as most necklaces are worn?"

Davinda grew quiet, not wanting to tell him everything at this time, then sighed. "Yes, it is usually worn about the neck, but . . . but . . . the chain is gone," she murmured. "I guess I will have to find another one, somehow."

Walking Thunder could see that Davinda was very emotional about this personal possession, and he could understand. He, too, had items that had belonged to loved ones who had gone on before him. He would help his woman keep her locket safe from now on. He would, also, make her a special leather thong on which she could place her locket so that she could wear it around her neck on the days she chose to wear it instead of the bear claw necklace.

Clouds suddenly covered the sun. Walking Thunder glanced at the sky, then looked down at Davinda. "*Ok-yi*, come. We should return home," he said thickly. "I sense the approach of a storm."

"Yes, I'm ready," Davinda said softly, going to her horse. She slid the locket into the saddlebag, then swung herself into her saddle.

As she rode off with Walking Thunder, she refused to take another look at what she was leaving behind.

Now she had the task of telling Walking Thunder

the truth about the necklace. Why it was so precious to her. Why it represented a small part of her heart that she had left behind!

Yet still she hesitated. Knowing about her past could make him lose respect and love for her as quickly as she breathed the words across her lips.

But, still, she knew now that she had no choice but to tell him. She could go no further into their relationship with only half-truths.

He deserved better.

She turned to him, to ask him to stop so that they could talk. But she did not get the chance. Rifle shots rang out like thunder on a still night.

A scream froze in Davinda's throat.

9

Walking Thunder started to grab for his rifle in its gun boot, but stopped when he and Davinda were suddenly surrounded by many gunmen. Black Cloud was the leader, a grim smile quivering on his lips.

"Ease your hand away from your rifle or I will shoot you dead at the blink of an eye," Black Cloud said. He edged his horse closer to Davinda's while keeping his gaze leveled on Walking Thunder.

Glowering at Black Cloud, Walking Thunder slowly eased his hand back from the rifle. "*Mah-kah-kan-is-tsi,* you who are not true to the Blackfoot blood that runs through your veins are a disgrace to your Blackfoot brothers," he said with a snarl to Black Cloud.

"When I was banished from the Blackfoot village I proudly set aside anything of me that *was* Blackfoot," Black Cloud said, his eyes angrily flashing back at Walking Thunder. "Your father, your people as a whole, disgraced me. And over a few stolen horses."

"Only because you stole horses?" Walking Thunder

186

asked incredulously. "You think you were right to steal horses from your brothers? This proves that you deserve to live apart from your ancestors in the Sand Hills when you die. Your soul will never rest. Your spirit will forever wander. When people hear the mournful howl of a wolf on the cold nights of winter, it will be, in truth, your spirit crying out for mercy. No one will listen or care."

Enraged, Black Cloud raised the butt end of his rifle into the air and brought it down across the back of Walking Thunder's head, knocking him from his horse.

Davinda screamed, jumped from her horse, and knelt down over Walking Thunder. She studied the head wound and discovered that the rifle butt had only grazed Walking Thunder's flesh, momentarily knocking him unconscious.

Black Cloud dismounted and kicked Davinda away from Walking Thunder with the heel of his boot. "White tramp," he snarled. "You who wear the clothes and shoes of Blackfoot, do you think that makes you Blackfoot? Ha, it only ridicules and mocks the people who once were my reason for living."

He kicked her again, sending her rolling along the ground even farther away from Walking Thunder. "They deserve you, yet today they lose both you and their . . ." His lips curled into a bitter smile. "And their chief."

Davinda held her stomach as pain rocked her. Cold sweat beaded on her brow, and she bit her lower lip to keep from crying out.

Then all hell seemed to break loose as Walking

Thunder's warriors appeared on every side of the gunmen, firing their guns and shooting arrows. Davinda tried to see what was happening, but the dust being stirred up from the horses' hooves blinded her.

Feeling her way along the ground, hoping she wouldn't be crushed beneath a horse, Davinda finally found Walking Thunder. She swept her arms around him and held him close as he awakened, groaning.

"Your warriors have arrived!" Davinda cried through the thundering noise of gunfire, horses, and Blackfoot war cries. "Lord, Walking Thunder, they barely arrived in time! I truly believe that Black Cloud was going to shoot me!"

Walking Thunder reached a hand to her face. "I failed you!" he cried. "My warriors failed you."

"No, never say that," she returned. "Things are going to be all right. Your warriors will be the victors here today!"

"I must get you out of harm's way," Walking Thunder said, pushing himself up from the ground.

He gathered Davinda up into his arms and bent low as he carried her around the fighting men. As he started to set her down behind a huge boulder, the firing ceased.

"What if . . . ?" Davinda said, her spine stiffening in fear as Walking Thunder slid her from his arms.

She was afraid to think of what was going to happen to both her and Walking Thunder if his warriors had not been successful at fighting off the gunmen.

Would they be hanged?

Or shot?

Or would she be raped first, then killed? That thought made her feel ill.

"Walking Thunder!"

It was Wolf Eye. Hearing his favored warrior speak his name through the swirling dust, Walking Thunder knew the battle had been won by his men. He smiled when Wolf Eye stepped into sight, his shoulders proudly squared.

"It is over," Wolf Eye said with relief. "Had we not been delayed by a rattlesnake throwing Swift Turtle from his horse, you would not have been put through that ordeal, believing we had forgotten you. We have dutifully followed Black Cloud for days. Only a short while ago did he meet up with the other renegades and outlaws. We were just about to overtake them when we saw you, riding ahead of them. Then the rattlesnake intervened."

"Do not despair over what you had no control over," Walking Thunder said, placing a gentle hand on his warrior's shoulder. "You have come and done your part. Because of you there will still be a marriage in our village between your chief and the woman of his heart."

Wolf Eye turned to Davinda. "I am sorry that you have been subjected to such ridicule today," he said thickly. "Had you died . . ."

"Don't think anymore about it. And please, don't feel that you owe me an apology," Davinda said, moving over to stand beside Walking Thunder. She slid an arm around his waist. "You are a hero, Wolf Eye, for having saved your chief's life."

Wolf Eye smiled broadly, then turned and looked

down on the ground where Black Cloud lay, his hands tied behind him. "Except for Black Cloud, all of the renegades and outlaws died," he said sourly. He turned to Walking Thunder. "What is Black Cloud's fate to be? Does he die now, by the rope? Or do we take him back to our village and let him die a slow death while everyone watches?"

"Neither," Walking Thunder said, stepping away from Davinda. Glaring, he stood over Black Cloud. "He chose to live in the white man's world over the Blackfoot's. We will let the white man deal with him. That way, our people will be spared the trauma of having to look onto his face of betrayal. They deserve much better than that. There is soon to be a wedding. I will not spoil it for myself, my woman, or my people!"

Walking Thunder turned to Wolf Eye. "But you can still place a rope around his neck," he said. "He will be tied to your horse and be made to walk to Fort Chance."

Walking Thunder's eyes gleamed as he gazed down at Black Cloud again. "Yes, he loses his horse today. He will walk instead of ride to the fort. A Blackfoot who is horseless is an object of reproach and pity!"

He watched Wolf Eye slip a rope around Black Cloud's neck, then he stared at the boots on the renegade's feet. It was an added insult that he had thrown away his Blackfoot moccasins to don the footwear of whites! "Remove his boots," he ordered, his voice low, void of emotion. "He will walk barefoot from now on since he chose to cast away his black moccasins as though they are worthless trash!"

"You will be sorry for this," Black Cloud said with a snarl as his boots were removed and tossed aside. "When I am freed, I will come for you."

"And what makes you think the white man will free you when they realize that you were the one who has killed and robbed from whites?" Walking Thunder asked, leaning into Black Cloud's face as he was yanked to his feet with a jerk of the rope.

"It will be your word against mine," Black Cloud said, laughing throatily. "Who will believe you over someone who has been a trusted scout for the soldiers?"

Walking Thunder's jaw tightened as his eyes battled with Black Cloud's, then he smiled slyly and glanced over at his men. "Place the dead renegades and white outlaws on horses," he shouted. "We will transport them to the fort. They are all the proof we need to show that Black Cloud has wronged not only the Blackfoot, but also the whites. That he was with those who are responsible for atrocities in the past, that he rode as one of them, is proof enough that he deserves to hang with the worst criminals."

As the men were tied to the horses, Davinda stood back with Walking Thunder. "Let me see your head," she said. "I want to check your wound."

"It is all right," he said, holding his chin high. "Your lump from the massacre was twice as big as mine will be."

"We are lucky to be alive," Davinda said as Walking Thunder walked her over to her horse and helped her into her saddle.

"Such are the risks of everyday life while living where there are those who are greedy and bloodthirsty," Walking Thunder said, his eyes locking with hers. "I have learned to take each day, one at a time, and feel blessed when the sun is replaced by the moon once more in the sky."

A low rumble of thunder drew Walking Thunder's attention to the sky. "The storm has passed us," he said. He smiled over at Davinda. "One by one, the storms of life are getting behind us."

She felt a deep inner peace as she rode away with Walking Thunder at her side. She looked past Black Cloud, who was stumbling along behind Wolf Eye's horse as everyone headed toward the fort. She felt no pity for the renegade.

They journeyed to the fort in silence.

The sun was setting in the sky when they arrived at Fort Chance.

After Black Cloud and the dead had been handed over, Davinda saw a huge paddle wheeler make its appearance around the bend in the Missouri River. Its tall smokestacks were blackened with smoke and its decks were lined with people.

Davinda remembered the last time she had been on a paddle wheeler, and why. Swallowing hard, she quickly looked away from it, and turned her horse around. She rode away with Walking Thunder and the others following a short distance behind.

Seeing the paddle wheeler after retrieving her locket, Davinda knew she could not wait any longer to tell Walking Thunder about her past. Each moment that passed made her feel more and more torn with the need to rid herself of the guilt she felt for not having been truthful with him. Once she knew they were to spend their lives together she should have told him. Davinda could not bear to carry this burden around inside her any longer!

Davinda looked at Walking Thunder sheepishly. The fear of telling him everything made her heart race. "Can we stop for a while?" she asked softly. "Can the others go on without us?"

"Do you need to rest?" Walking Thunder asked, seeing her weariness .

"Yes, and . . . and . . . I have something I wish to tell you," she said, heaving a heavy sigh. "It's something I should have told you earlier."

Walking Thunder looked at her questioningly for a moment longer, then turned his horse around and rode back to tell his warriors to go on to the village without them.

Davinda and Walking Thunder rode into the shadows of the forest and stopped at a stream that was surrounded by beautiful, purple violets. Walking Thunder lifted Davinda from her saddle.

He picketed both of their horses beside the water, then took Davinda's hands and sat her amidst the violets.

"Tell me what is on your mind," he said huskily.

Davinda swallowed hard, then began her sad story of heartbreak and rejection. Scarcely breathing, he listened.

"It happened during the war," Davinda began, watching his expression as she continued. "I was involved with a man. I had known him for a long time. We were childhood friends. It seemed only right when he gave me a ring and I . . . I . . . promised myself to him."

She no longer dared to look into Walking Thunder's eyes. She was afraid to know how this was making him feel. She did not want to know if he felt betrayed because she had not told him everything earlier.

Davinda knew that the worst was yet to come. She wanted to get past that quickly, for only then would she know if Walking Thunder could still love her.

"When he was to leave and join the fighting, we . . . we . . . spent a night together like no other," she said, lowering her eyes as she recalled the clumsiness of their approach at lovemaking. "We made love."

She tried to hear whether or not Walking Thunder had gasped at knowing that. But he gave no response.

She heard nothing.

He was still devotedly listening, but she could not look up at him.

She swallowed hard. "He died fighting in the war shortly after that," she said, her voice breaking. "I . . . had . . . just discovered that I was carrying his child."

She looked up at Walking Thunder and the confusion in his eyes pained her. "Walking Thunder, I was not married, yet I was pregnant," she said, a sob lodging in her throat. "I was desperate. I was full of shame. I . . . I . . . felt trapped. I . . . felt . . . so alone."

She sighed remembering the lonely hours and days. "I went to my parents and confessed my condition to them," she said, tears streaming from her eyes.

"My father was filled with rage. He was ashamed of me."

Walking Thunder placed his hands on her shoulders. "And the child?" he asked thickly. "Where is the child now?"

"Someone else is raising her," she answered, wiping the tears from her face. "When my father began making plans to give my baby away to uncaring relatives and for me to marry someone much older, someone I . . . I . . . loathed, I . . . ran . . . away. I hid from my father, and gave birth to my child while among strangers. Having no way to raise my child, I did what I had to do. I . . . gave her away."

Davinda yanked herself free of his grip, which had strengthened the more she had confessed. She turned away from him and hung her head. "I chose whom I wished to leave my baby with and . . . and . . . left her on the doorstep so that she would be found quickly and taken in."

Walking Thunder was taken aback by everything she had said. He was stunned to learn what she had lived through, and to realize what she had given up. He knew her well enough to know that it had all been done for the right reasons, she was good through and through. Everything she confessed to having done had been out of caring for others. She had left nothing for herself except pain and loneliness.

When he had first seen her, he was aware of the agony in her eyes. Only recently had it changed to something calm and wonderful. He had helped her through her grieving and now he would help her put her past behind her. Walking Thunder could not find it in his heart to hate Davinda over anything she had told him.

"The reason there is no chain on my locket is because it is with my daughter. I . . . I . . . put the other half of the locket among her blankets before I left. I . . . had . . . hoped it might lead me to her one day, or her . . . to me."

Walking Thunder still said nothing. Despair and fear grabbed at Davinda's heart. Sobs wracking her body, she turned and ran away from him. He caught up with her and swept an arm around her waist. He swung her around to face him. Placing a gentle hand to her face, he wiped away her tears with the flesh of his thumb.

"Do you not know that my love for you is as lasting as the stars in the heaven?" he asked. "Do you not know that nothing you could say could turn my heart against you? My woman, speak no more of it. Put it behind you. Look to the future. Our future. Marry me and let me make up to you all of that which has given you pain and regret."

Davinda was flooded with a joyous bliss she had never felt before. She was relieved that what she had told Walking Thunder had not turned him against her. "How can I be so lucky to have someone like you love me so unconditionally . . . so endearingly?" she said, her voice quivering with emotion.

"Loving you comes as naturally as breathing," Walking Thunder said, smiling. "And do not forget that it is not only Walking Thunder who is lucky to have you in his life . . . there is also Little Fox. He needs you. He can fill up the emptiness in your heart left by having been forced to leave your own child behind."

"He has already filled me with joy," Davinda said, melting into his arms. "Take me home, Walking Thunder. Please . . . take me home."

10

Words had been spoken which sealed Walking Thunder
and Davinda's hearts. They were now man and wife.
As the special day had darkened into night, the dancing and singing continued.

The feast had been bountiful. The day before the
women had roasted meat and pounded it with
chokecherries and plums. Until the early moon had
settled toward the west, thin-horned as a young deer,
they had stooped over the fire, which sent off the tan-
talizing aromas of roasting ribs.

Other women had busied themselves mixing flour
for fried bread. They twisted the dough around sticks
to cook over the coals. All night long the smoke from
the vast fires had drifted in small, blue spirals into the
nearby canyons.

Today, her wedding day, Davinda felt an intense
happiness inside her heart. Proud and deliciously
content, she sat on the fur-laden platform next to the
outside fire beside Walking Thunder. She was
dressed in a snow white antelope skin dress, ornamented with elk tushes. Her deerskin leggings were
fringed and adorned with bells and brass buttons.
She felt beautiful.

She gazed adoringly over at Walking Thunder. Except for bands of fur around his upper arms and his brow, he wore only a breech clout. He sat tall and square-shouldered, his arms folded comfortably across his chest, his eyes on the dancers—his eyes filled with peace.

He looked at Davinda. "My *nito-ke-man*, wife," he said, as he took her hand in his. "The dancers are almost exhausted. They soon will depart to their lodges." He smiled at her. "We will then retire to ours. It will be the first full night of our marriage, *nito-ke-man*. Perhaps we will make a child?"

"Yes, we could give Little Fox a brother or sister," she said, her voice revealing her enthusiasm. She looked past the crowd to Flower Woman's lodge. Little Fox would stay there tonight.

"I shall miss Little Fox," she said.

"This is *our* night," Walking Thunder said, leaning over to brush her lips with a kiss. "Only ours."

Davinda reveled in the bliss of being loved so much. She touched his cheek. "My darling," she whispered.

The Blackfoot began to sing much more loudly and dance more vigorously as the tom-toms droned song upon song. The women were dressed in their best gowns, and the men wore breech clouts, with their bodies heavily painted.

At intervals the rest of the people, who had only until now observed, rose and danced with the others. They danced bending their knees and swinging and swaying their bodies. The women held their arms and hands in various graceful positions.

Then everyone, except the bride and groom, joined a long, snakelike procession and left the outdoor fire.

They wove in and out and around the lodges of the village, one by one dropping away to enter his or her own private lodge until there were none left.

Davinda was surprised how quickly the ceremony had ended.

Walking Thunder rose to his feet. He swept Davinda into his arms, then carried her to his lodge. Instead of placing her on their bed at the back of the tepee, he placed her on a thick pallet of furs beside the lodge fire.

Slowly, meditatively, he undressed her, then stood before her and slid off his breech clout. Gently he took Davinda by the wrists, laid her down, then blanketed her with his body. "I love you," he whispered.

His lips came to hers in a quavering, passionate kiss, leading her, mind and soul, to a sweet valley of joy. His hands cupped her breasts. His lips nibbled first one nipple, and then the other, drawing throaty gasps from Davinda.

When he slid his arms beneath her, she moved toward him and twined her arms around his neck. Nestled close to him, she pulled his head down and their lips met in a sweet, leisurely kiss.

When he entered her with one deep thrust, she shuddered with pleasure, then moved her hips rhythmically with his. Between their kisses, he whispered fierce words of love to her, some in his Blackfoot tongue, and some in her own.

Desire washed over Walking Thunder. He could feel it welling up inside him, filling him, spreading into his loins. He was close to losing his last vestige of rational mind as the pleasure mounted.

He thrust deeper as Davinda's hands stroked his hair. She moaned in her mounting ecstasy. They gripped each other as their spasms came in hot torrents. In a frenzy of kisses, their hands were all over each other's bodies, touching, caressing, gripping. And then it was over, ecstasy sought and found.

Davinda lay beside Walking Thunder, her face hot with the aftermath of pleasure. "It was over too quickly," she murmured. "And the night has just begun."

"Do not sound so disappointed," Walking Thunder said, laughing huskily. He slid her beneath him. He gazed down at her and lost his heart and soul in her passion-filled violet eyes. "Yes, the night has just begun, but so has our lovemaking. We shall make love, rest awhile, and make love again. Do you not see the importance now of having left Little Fox with Flower Woman?"

"Yes, I do." Davinda said, giggling.

Walking Thunder smiled down at her. Framing her face between his hands, he said, "My woman, I knew that Old Man would hear my heart's sadness over having not been able to find the perfect woman who fills my heart and home with sunshine. I told Old Man many times my feelings. He listened. He sent me you."

"I'm so glad that he favored me over everyone else," Davinda murmured. She closed her eyes and sighed when Walking Thunder kissed her.

Davinda had waited a lifetime for such a love, herself, for such a man, for such joy and peace.

She could not help but wonder, though, what her daughter might be doing at this very moment, and whether or not she might grow up and find someone as wonderful as Walking Thunder?

But she knew that she might never know the answer to these questions. She could only pray her daughter would someday find the happiness she had found.

PART 3

Daniel's Song

1

Sarah Collins hammered in the last nail, then stood back to admire her handiwork. She'd chosen a green sign with dark green script, a faint outline of gold on the letters, and little decorative curlicues on the corners. The frills had cost a little more but they looked elegant without being pretentious.

Piano Lessons: 50¢

"There," she said out loud, "I'm officially in business."

Well, after a fashion she was. The sign was up, she had a piano, and she'd brought her music from home with her. She'd be "in business" when she had her first music students.

Shivering in the brisk October air, she went back inside the house wishing she could play hooky, but crates demanding her attention were waiting to be

unpacked. She had been lucky to find the old brownstone that sat along the waterfront. The owners had
turned the building into rental property. Once the
house had been quite elegant. Sarah had four large
rooms on the main floor with a tiny entry, a sitting
room that she'd turned into a music room, a small
kitchen, and a parlor that served as a bedroom. A
scarred spinet piano she'd purchased at an auction at
Curly's bar dominated the sunny alcove. Lillian
Periwinkle, a matronly retired librarian, lived in the
rooms above her. Lillian had made it clear she
expected not to hear a note of music after five o'clock
in the afternoon.

Still procrastinating, Sarah went into the kitchen to
make herself a cup of tea. Waiting for the teakettle to
boil, she stood at the back door, studying the skyline.
Saint Louis, Missouri. How had she ever gotten the
courage to come so far, to a place she'd never been
before, where she didn't know a single soul? But then,
she'd been doing a number of things lately that were
out of character.

The idea to move from Mooretown to Saint Louis
started two years ago. She'd celebrated her twenty-
ninth birthday and her parents invited all their
friends, expecting her to announce her engagement to
James Thurlow. But the evening before she'd
informed James she couldn't marry him. What a
ruckus that had caused! She cared for James, just not
enough to marry him. James was hurt, and she felt
badly, but once it was done, she felt somehow
. . . free. Absurdly so.

She wasn't sure how to tell her parents what she'd
done. They were elated when James had started

courting her. In their opinion, a schoolteacher was the perfect match for their daughter. Sarah thought so, too, until the night she realized she didn't love James. She wanted to love the man she married with all her heart, and James just wasn't that man.

Katherine and Michael Collins were upset with her. Michael, the town blacksmith, was furious. Katherine cried, and Sarah was disappointed in herself. They had done so much for her, even though she wasn't their own. One night, during a howling storm, Michael had heard a knock on the door. When he went to investigate, he'd discovered a small bundle on the doorstep. Just hours old, Sarah was wrapped only in blankets, with half of a locket tucked in among her wrappings. Michael took the child in, and then enlisted Katherine's help in caring for her, since he hadn't know the first thing about babies. Eventually they married—and Sarah liked to think that she had played an important role in their union.

The Collins saw to it that their precious children received the best they could provide, including music lessons for Sarah from a man who'd studied abroad. They'd been delighted to discover that their Sarah had a natural aptitude for piano and voice, and they never begrudged the nickels they'd hoarded to pay for her lessons.

Sarah thought of the sacrifices they'd made on her behalf. The shocked looks on their faces when she broke the news that she was not going to marry James still haunted her. But she stuck to her decision.

Her parents finally recovered from the initial disappointment, though they didn't understand her "foolishness," especially since she was nearing thirty. She'd tried to explain how she felt, but at the time she wasn't sure herself. Could she call it restlessness? Not unhappiness, because she was never unhappy a day in her life. She was always surrounded by love. So how could she explain this recent need to be on her own, this unsettled feeling of not knowing who she really was?

For nearly thirty years she'd been Sarah Collins, but who had she been before that? She was someone's daughter, maybe even granddaughter or sister. Why had her mother given her away? Why had she left her on a stranger's doorstep?

Had her mother been afraid, alone, heartbroken to give up her child? The war had been raging at the time, she knew that. Had there been a romantic tryst between her mother and father that resulted in her conception? Was her father dead? It wasn't an unusual story, she supposed. She'd heard of such things happening, though Katherine tried to shield her from such tales. Was her natural mother alive today? Had she died in childbirth? So many questions, and Sarah had no answers. Maybe that's why she felt so restless.

She loved Katherine and Michael deeply. It wasn't that she wanted to leave them, or deny how much they meant to her. It was just that . . . well, something was missing in her life and she wanted to find it.

It sounded melodramatic when she said it, but it was as near as she could come to identifying the unsettled feelings she'd had the last two years.

It took some talking, but she'd finally persuaded her parents that she needed to be on her own, to see if she could teach music and earn enough to support herself. They'd finally agreed, thinking she would end up an old maid. But when she announced she was moving to Saint Louis, Missouri, the declaration brought on a renewed flood of tears from Katherine and disgruntled mumblings from Michael. Far into the evening she'd heard the sharp ring of hammer against iron as he worked through his disappointment.

In the end they finally gave her their best wishes, and she'd boarded the train for Saint Louis.

The first day, she was exhilarated by the new adventure, then reality set in. What if she failed? What if she couldn't make her own way, what if there were no students, what if her students hated her and wouldn't continue their lessons? What if what if what if . . . By the time she got off the train in Saint Louis, she was convinced she didn't have a prayer of carving out a life.

But then she'd found the brownstone along the waterfront.

Evenings, she strolled along the river and watched the boats travel up and down. Last week she'd found a sign painter and purchased the wonderful sign she'd just hung from a pole a handyman set in the ground for her. She gained two pupils the first week; two more joined her this week.

With any luck at all, by the end of this week she would have the fifth pupil she needed in order to make a living.

"Excellent work, Daniel. Excellent!"

Porter Hayes, founder of Hayes, Brussels and

O'Ryan law firm, tossed the file onto the mahogany desk and smiled at the tall, dark young man who stood in front of his desk. Daniel Eaglefeather was a unique gentleman. When he was recommended as a law clerk, Porter hadn't been at all sure he wanted to mentor an Indian who was not long off the reservation, but he'd been persuaded by glowing letters of endorsements. When he'd met Daniel Eaglefeather, he'd been impressed by his quiet intelligence, and by his level of education. He was continuing his studies at the university and needed a job.

Daniel presented himself on a Friday morning. Porter remembered the day very clearly. The tall, powerfully built Indian wore an ill-fitting new charcoal suit. Porter knew the suit had been purchased without proper alteration, but Daniel had stood proudly before him. His long blue-black hair was parted in the middle and drawn back, secured with a leather thong; indeed, he still wore his hair the same way today. Daniel Eaglefeather, of Blackfoot descent, never failed to cause a stir in a courtroom.

Though he usually mentored men with more education and experience, Porter decided to take a chance on the Daniel. He'd not been at all disappointed.

"Daniel, you've blossomed in the atmosphere of the legal community."

"Thank you, sir."

Each day brought the Indian more maturity and the confidence of experience. At just under thirty years old he was far and away the most promising lawyer he'd ever taken under his wing. If the truth be known, Porter enjoyed teaching Daniel Eaglefeather the ways of the law, and the ways of polite society. Porter would miss him when he left the firm.

"Your time with us will be up soon, Daniel. What do you plan to do?"

"I'm going home for a visit." Humor danced in Daniel's coal-black eyes, eyes that could pin a witness to his chair. "Then perhaps hang out my own shingle."

Porter chuckled. "Then I'll have to make you a better offer to keep you from becoming my rival."

"Actually, I haven't made up my mind about what I want to do," Daniel said, growing serious again.

Daniel had discussed his indecision with Porter about whether to work on the Blackfoot reservation, representing his people, or work in the legal community, perhaps attached to the Porter law firm. There was yet time to decide. He still had classes he wanted to finish at the university, though right now he wanted to go home to see his father and mother.

Returning to the office space that had been his for the past eighteen months, Daniel straightened the things on his desk, then began locking up for the night. He had seen a sign this morning that had given him an idea for a gift for his mother. One that only he could give her.

The sign advertised piano lessons. The price was right, so he was going to accept the challenge.

Smiling, he tucked a stack of briefs into a satchel, and left the building.

Sarah was just finishing her four o'clock lesson when a knock sounded at her door.

"Jane Ellen, continue your scales. I'll be right back."

The pretty blond girl with pigtails squinted at the sheet music. "Yes, ma'am."

Jane Ellen was a charming ten year old. She appeared to be the most promising of Sarah's new pupils, though this was only her third lesson.

When she opened the door, Sarah stepped back, startled to find a tall gentleman standing on her doorstep. Coppery skin stretched over high cheekbones, and intense black eyes stared back at her.

An Indian. Her pulse started to race.

"May I help you?"

"I want to talk to the piano teacher."

"I'm Sarah Collins. How may I help you?"

"I want to learn to play a song on the piano."

If he'd said he wanted to fly, she wouldn't have been more surprised.

"I—I don't understand."

"I want to learn to play a song on the piano," he repeated. "Can you teach me?"

A muscle jumped in his jaw, the only evidence of his discomfort when she hesitated.

"Well— Won't you come inside? I'm just finishing a lesson."

"Thank you."

She opened the door wider, and he stepped inside the foyer, bringing a scent of cold air. His six-foot frame towered above her, and she felt a shiver of anticipation. What was an Indian doing on her doorstep, and why would he want to learn to play the piano? She directed him to a chair in the corner of the music room and returned to the piano bench to sit beside Jane Ellen, her knees suddenly weak.

Her eyes occasionally darted to the bench where he sat quietly observing her.

In her experience, Indians were dangerous. They didn't dress in nice suits, and she'd never heard of one wanting a piano lesson. Just having him in the house made her nervous. If she didn't need a fifth student so badly, she'd tell him to leave. But she would be foolhardy to turn him away. Lord knew when the next student might come her way, and she had rent to pay.

Ten minutes later Sarah said good-bye to Jane Ellen, watching her leave with misgivings. The Indian was still waiting on the bench.

Returning to the parlor, she smiled. "May I offer you tea?"

"No, thank you. I would like to discuss how many lessons it would take for me to learn to play a certain song on the instrument."

Sarah opened her mouth to speak, then closed it.

"I'm sorry." He edged forward in his chair. "I should introduce myself. I am Daniel Eaglefeather. I am a clerk for Mr. Porter Hayes at his law firm."

When she didn't respond, he said, "I am finishing studies at the university."

Remembering her manners, she stuck out her hand. "I'm pleased to meet you, Mr. Eaglefeather. You want to learn to play the piano. That could take some time—"

"I only want to learn to play one song."

A frown creased her forehead. "Only one song?"

"Yes. I wish to learn to play 'The Fox.' Do you know the song?"

"I'm familiar with the song, but wouldn't you like to play something easier? I have this nice beginner's—"

"No," he insisted. "I want to learn to play 'The Fox.'"

When she looked puzzled, he explained. "It is a song my mother sang to me as a child. I want to play the song on the piano for her birthday when I return home this summer."

"I see." She didn't, but it didn't matter. It was a noble gesture, but perhaps he could find someone else . . .

"How long will it take me to learn this song?"

"Well, it's hard to estimate how long it will take. Each person's learning ability is different."

"I learn very quickly," he assured her.

The sincerity in his eyes was so strong she was tempted to throw caution to the wind and teach him the song.

"Generally students begin with the rudimentary scales, progress to simple tunes, then learn the left hand, then they're ready for more complicated pieces. Usually after a year to eighteen months, if they show ability—" She noted his large hands, long, tapered fingers. He would easily reach an octave.

"I do not have the time for that," he interrupted. "I only want to learn one song. Can you teach me?"

"By summer!" She was flabbergasted. She could barely have him playing scales smoothly in that short a time.

"Mr. Eaglefeather—"

He stopped her again. "I learn very quickly. Please. I will work hard to achieve my goal."

Though his request was outrageous, there was an

earnestness in Daniel Eaglefeather that tempted Sarah to accept the challenge against her better judgment.

"Can you come on Tuesday and Thursday?"

"Yes."

"You said you worked—"

"And take classes. I will arrange my schedule to accommodate the lessons. Playing the song for my mother is important to me."

Sarah eyes softened. "You must love your mother very much."

Daniel Eaglefeather nodded. "I do."

"Well then, can you come at four-thirty? I have to finish my classes before five." Because of the old sourpuss who lives above me, she thought.

"I can be here at four-fifteen, if that would be more convenient."

"Four-fifteen." She smiled, nodding. He seemed nonthreatening—nice, actually. "That will give us forty-five minutes each day."

"Can this be accomplished in such a short time?"

"I can't say. It depends upon your aptitude, and how complicated you want to make your presentation of the music. Let's try it for two weeks and see how things come along."

"Very well. Shall we begin tomorrow?"

"Tomorrow will be fine, Mr. Eaglefeather. I'll try to locate the music to your song."

Daniel rose. "I will return tomorrow."

Sarah followed the tall young man to the door and stood watching him stride down the street, fascinated. He walked with a long, self-assured stride, his broad shoulders straight and confident. A shock of coal-black hair, held back by a leather thong, hung down his back, reaching nearly to his waist. She shuddered, recalling his dark, intense eyes that looked right through her.

Whirling, she shut the door and locked it.

2

Daniel arrived at four-fourteen, one minute early, the next day. Sarah was suffering through Peter Butcher's sixth lesson. At nine years old, Peter was more interested in frogs and worms than Chopin, but his mother's heart was set on her only son playing the piano. And what Sophie Butcher wanted, she was accustomed to getting, even if it meant wearing a body down with her whiny voice to get it.

Peter's disinterest in piano lessons was surpassed only by his lack of talent. The words "gently" and "softly'" were foreign to the boy. He insisted on pounding the keys without any thought to tone or tune. At the end of their lesson on Tuesday, they'd just gotten into the scales, but Sarah had been attempting to teach the dynamics along with notes. She believed the ability to feel music was as important as technique. Peter had no interest in either.

"Peter, listen as I play. Hear that? Soft, then loud. Try to *feel* the music."

Peter pounded the keys with enthusiasm and no attempt to do what she instructed musically.

From the corner of her eye, Sarah could see Daniel. He sat ramrod straight in a chair in the corner, out of the way, but she could see that he was watching with amusement her attempts to corral Peter's enthusiasm.

As much as Sarah needed the students, Peter was not interested in playing, not even for his own amusement.

"That will be all for today, Peter," Sarah said, her head pounding.

"I am so pleased with his progress," Sophie Butcher chirped, then leaned in close. "Are you aware there's a strange man sitting in the other room?"

"I'm aware Mr. Eaglefeather is in the other room."

Sophie ignored Sarah's response and went one. "In just a short time I'm sure Peter will be playing like a seasoned professional."

Sarah doubted that.

"If he will practice," Sarah cautioned, "and pay attention to the dynamic markings I've made on his scale pages."

"Oh, he will. Peter, stop that! Miss Collins doesn't want you digging in her ferns."

At that moment, Peter managed to tip the table on which her newly purchased plant rested. Quick as a wink, Daniel reached out and rescued her Boston fern from certain destruction. Sarah smiled her thanks as she trailed Sophie and her Peter to the door, aware of Sophie's censuring glares at Daniel.

With a sigh of weariness, she turned back to the music room.

"Mr. Eaglefeather, we'll begin with acquainting you with the piano, then progress to some scales so your fingers will become accustomed to the keys, spacing, and so on."

"This is necessary for me to play the one song?"

Daniel Eaglefeather was an impressive man. She had never seen a man more handsome, more physically compelling than he. Today, he wore a chocolate-brown suit with a boiled white shirt and string tie. It was obvious, by his speech and manner, that he was well educated.

"If you want to do it well, it is."

"Then let us proceed."

She indicated the piano bench, and he came to sit beside her. Her normal method of teaching was to sit beside the student, often placing her hands on his until he was comfortable with the keyboard, but she hesitated to adopt this method with Daniel.

You're being absurd, she thought. *He's a student. You're a teacher. Teach.*

The piano she'd purchased was an item left over from an estate sale, as Curly had told her. An old model, it was square with heavy legs and sides, richly curved rosewood. It had been badly neglected in storage, but she'd oiled it and had it tuned, and she was rather proud of its sound.

"A piano is a keyboard instrument that is capable of making loud, demanding sounds like thunder, or soft, tinkling sounds like a brook."

After careful thought, she decided to teach in terms he could understand. As she explained, he simply stared at her.

"It has four essential elements: strings, you see there, the upraised lid; action, the hammer hitting the strings; soundboard, which amplifies the sounds; and framework, which holds the whole thing together. There are eighty-eight keys. The piano is a direct evolution from the harp or lyre.

"You'll note that the keyboard has both black and white keys, the black keys divided into groups of twos and threes. The low sounds are on your left, the high on your right. When you read music you see a sign at the beginning that looks like a large S. That's the clef sign that means 'higher sounds,' which is for the right hand. This sign here," she pointed to a chart she used for this purpose, "that looks like a feather—"

"A feather?"

"Yes." She smiled. "A feather is the clef sign that means 'lower sounds' or the left hand. We'll start with the right hand, then add the left-hand sounds later."

Daniel spread his hands lightly on the keys, and she was pleased to see that he could easily reach an octave.

"Music has a language. The music language uses the alphabet—A, B, C, D, E, F, and G. I won't go too deeply into that, since your goal is to play a single song, but should you want to continue your studies you'll need to know the language."

"It is true, but I think it won't be necessary."

"Well, as it happens, I may be able to find the music to the piece you want to learn. It's a Scottish tune that mothers sang to their little ones in the nursery. It did appear in print, though, about 1832, so perhaps my friend at the music store can locate a copy. Meanwhile, we'll start on some basic scales so you can become familiar with the keyboard."

"As your student before me?"

Sarah glanced up in surprise, then saw the glint of humor in his obsidian eyes. She couldn't help laughing.

"I don't know what I'm going to do with him. He comes twice a week only because his mother demands it."

"Perhaps I will be a better student."

"I'm sure of it," she admitted, suddenly aware how close they sat, her skin warming each time his gaze touched her. "Now, the scales."

Sarah's fingers rippled lightly up and down the piano keys, explaining as she played. Before she realized it, the clock in the hall struck five.

"That concludes our lesson today. Do you have a piano on which to practice?"

"There is one available at the university. I've already spoken with the music teacher."

"Why didn't you take a class there?"

"He did not have the time to take on more private students."

"Well, practice will help you learn more quickly—"

"I will practice an hour two days a week after classes, and before going to my work."

Daniel slid off the stool, and she followed him to the door.

"Perhaps when you come next week I will have located the music for your song. If not, I can teach you to play it by ear."

"You can do that?"

She smiled at his surprise. "Oh yes. I was very fortunate to have an excellent teacher who encouraged my natural ability. It may take a few days, but I could compose the melody if necessary."

"I will look forward to Thursday."

By the time Daniel arrived for his second lesson, Sarah had been able to find the music to "The Fox." It was indeed the Scottish piece her new friend at the music and book store remembered. It had been published by James Balantyne in 1832 in a small collection he edited. After reading the words, Sarah could see why little children had enjoyed having it sung to them. The story was about a father fox who killed a duck and goose and had a great feast for his ten children.

Daniel had diligently practiced his scales, proving he was indeed an apt student.

Teaching him was going to be a pleasure.

3

"How are you today, Sarah?"

Elinor Hastings rested her forearms on top of the board fence separating her yard from Sarah's. The friendly widow had poked her snow-white head over the fence the first day Sarah arrived to look at the living quarters. Elinor's lively smile, rounded cheeks, and inquisitive bright blue eyes were among the reasons Sarah chose the brownstone. Little did she know Elinor was nosy.

"Good morning, Mrs. Hastings. It is indeed a fine day."

Sarah was poking around in a neglected flower bed, wondering whether it would be worth the effort to clear it and plant roses this spring.

Elinor was in a chatty mood this morning. "I see you have a new student. Rather old to learn the piano, isn't he?"

"Are you talking about Daniel?"

"That tall young man who comes on Tuesdays and Thursdays? Do you have another adult student?"

"No, Daniel's the only one. He's doing surprisingly well to have never played before."

Swatting a fly, Elinor adjusted her hat against the windy day. "Well, my dear, I'm uncomfortable saying this, but since your mother isn't here to guide you, I must. You have to be careful. You never know what those people will do."

Sarah sat up straighter. The portly little busybody was peering at her curiously, her eyes bright with zealous indignation.

"'Those' people?"

Elinor nodded as the wind blew a lock of silver-white hair over her forehead. Swiping it back, she said, "He's Indian, isn't he?"

"Yes," Sarah admitted, although she found it hard to think of Daniel as anything other than a polite, well-educated man.

Elinor sniffed. "No self-respecting man would wear that mass of black hair slicked back and tied with a leather strap. Makes no difference that he wears white man's clothes, he's still a savage."

Sarah felt her hackles rise as she calmly put her tools aside, suddenly out of the gardening mood. Elinor had no right to talk about Daniel that way. Prejudice still ran rampant toward the red man, but Sarah wouldn't tolerate it. Daniel came to her for her services, and she wouldn't say anything bad about him, any more than she would say mean things about Peter.

And she could say an earful about Peter.

"Mr. Eaglefeather is a gentleman," she said. Dusting her hands free of dirt, she got up.

Elinor leaned closer, whispering through the slatted boards. "You watch yourself, dearie—you never know when one of them will turn on you." She shivered. "I've heard stories—"

"I'm sure we've all heard those stories," Sarah interrupted. If Mrs. Hastings kept it up, she'd have her scared to death. Daniel came twice a week and he had never done anything to lead her to believe that he meant her any harm. "If you'll excuse me, I think I hear Jane Ellen."

Sarah went inside and furiously cleaned the old iron stove, working off her anger. How unjust people were, how prejudiced against a man they'd never met. *Sarah Collins, you don't know him either,* her conscience reminded.

You don't know what kind of man he is. Anyone can dress in a fine suit and pretend to be a gentleman for forty-five minutes a day.

Sunday, Sarah dressed in her best blue cotton with the white lace collar, put on the black wool cape her mother had made for her two years earlier, and walked to the church two blocks down the street. One thing Katherine and Michael Collins insisted upon was being in church every Sunday, unless illness prevented it.

Though she'd been in Saint Louis a little under two months, Sarah's musical talents had already been called upon during the morning services. Word spread quickly that she was teaching piano and voice. Three students alone had come from the congregation. One was Peter Butcher.

"A fine message this morning, pastor," Sarah said as she exited the church.

"Miss Sarah, Miss Sarah!"

Peter Butcher skidded to a stop in front of her.

Patting Peter's carrottop head, Sarah smiled. "Hello, Peter. Have you been practicing your scales?"

Peter scuffed his shoes in the dirt. "No."

"I'll expect to see some improvement on Tuesday."

Sophie Butcher waddled up behind her son. "Oh good. I hoped to see you today, Miss Collins." Sweat beaded the woman's forehead as she fanned herself with her handkerchief.

"You wanted to talk to me, Mrs. Butcher?" Sarah couldn't imagine why the woman was so warm. It was bitterly cold outside.

"I just wondered if you were aware," she leaned closer, "that young man who comes in when Peter is finishing his lessons," Sophie glanced to either side and leaned closer yet, "is an . . . *Indian*," she finished in a whisper.

"I know," Sarah whispered back. "But more than that, he's a student."

Straightening, Sophie looked put out. "You don't care?"

"No. Why should I?"

"Have you ever wondered why he came to you?"

The woman's attitude irritated Sarah. "I assume because I teach piano."

"Humph. Because you're a lovely young woman," she stepped closer, close enough that Sarah could smell a hint of vanilla. "A white woman," she hissed. "Alone."

"They have no sense of decency," a woman put in who was standing in back of Sophie.

"They run naked on the prairie, you know. Don't be surprised if that young buck shows up someday wearing nothing but a loincloth."

Sarah's hand flew to her breast, and her pulse started to race. "I have to go. I have a roast in the oven." She walked away without looking back.

She hurried along, Sophie Butcher's words ringing in her ears. First Elinor, now Sophie. Was there any truth to the women's warnings? Was it possible that Daniel would revert to his "savage" self and come to a lesson buck naked as Sophie suggested? After all, what did she know about Daniel Eaglefeather, except that he spoke well, was well educated, and clerked at a prestigious law firm? She knew nothing about Indians. She'd heard tales, like everyone else. Tales of savagery, of cruelty she couldn't imagine from those who had come west on wagon trains years before.

The weather turned fine briefly. Sarah decided to poke around in the yard again. Lillian Periwinkle sat in her rocking chair on the front porch, wrapped in a large blanket.

"Good afternoon, Miss Lillian. Taking in some fresh air?"

"I hate winter," the old woman said, her lips pursed as if she'd just sucked a lemon. "Hope I don't live to see another."

Sarah pulled her shawl closer. "Have you been having some health problems?"

"No, not yet."

Sarah smiled, indulging the eccentric retired librarian.

"We could all be killed in our beds if you keep inviting that savage into the house," Lillian warned.

Taking a deep breath, Sarah tried to ward off her irritation. Lillian was obviously referring to Daniel.

"I know Peter Butcher is a little scamp," she began deliberately, "but I'd hardly call him a savage."

"You know who I'm talking about, young lady, and it isn't Sophie's boy!"

"You're talking about Daniel Eaglefeather?" Who wasn't lately!

"Eaglefeather?" Lillian scowled. "Is that the heathen's name. Well," Miss Periwinkle sniffed, "if I come home one day to find you scalped—"

"My, the wind seems to be picking up," Sarah observed. She wasn't going to stand here and listen to this. Between Elinor and Lillian, she would end up being scared of Daniel. "Would you like for me to help you back into the house? You don't want to get a chill."

"I don't need any help, but you'd better mark my words, Miss Collins. That Indian will cause you nothing but heartache."

"Yes, Miss Periwinkle."

"If you wake up some day to find yourself scalped—"

Helping the old woman out of her chair, Sarah ushered her into the house, echoing exactly what her mother would say if she were here. "I'll have no one to thank but myself."

"Humph. That's right."

Humph, Sarah thought. She still liked Daniel, no matter what.

Monday arrived. As she tutored three students, Daniel Eaglefeather was never far from her thoughts.

On Tuesday she suffered through Peter's lessons,

her ears tuned for the "savage's" arrival. By the time four-fifteen rolled around, her stomach was tied in knots.

When he knocked, she hurried to answer the door, knowing Sophie Butcher was watching her. As she led Daniel into the music room, Sarah saw Sophie sink further into her chair. Getting up, she gathered her purse and hurriedly ushered her son out the door.

If Daniel noticed Sophie's hurried departure, he didn't mention it. Taking his seat at the piano, he spread his fingers over the keys properly and began to play his scales.

After a moment he looked up.

Sarah was rooted to the spot, staring at him.

A frown shadowed his handsome features. "Is something wrong?"

"Oh." Snapping out of it, she hesitantly approached the bench. "I think I'll just stand today."

"Stand?" He looked puzzled. "I'll move over."

"Thank you. I'll just stand."

Sarah realized that the busybodies had gotten to her and she resented it. Nevertheless, she planned to keep a safe distance from Mr. Eaglefeather this afternoon.

As Daniel emerged from the old brownstone it was nearing dark. A cool breeze blew in off the Mississippi. Turning up his collar, he turned in the direction of home.

Sarah was different today. He'd felt the change the moment she opened the door and stared at him, as if she expected to find him naked and brandishing a tomahawk.

The thought brought a bitter smile to his lips. Sarah's neighbors had been talking. They were filling her full of stories of the uncivilized plainsman.

A pity, he thought. Concern shadowed his smile. Sarah was nervous all through the lesson. She was careful to keep at least a foot between them, so careful she nearly toppled off the end of the piano bench once. When their fingers accidentally touched, she jumped as if shot. She was so tense it made him anxious and the lesson went poorly.

It wasn't the first time this had happened, yet each time it did he was disappointed. A room suddenly growing quiet, men directing their wives or daughters to the other side of the street.

When would people learn that just because he was Indian, instead of Irish or German, that he was no less civilized than they.

At first people's reactions had made him angry, but then he'd realized that the response was the residual fear of early years when this part of the country was very young. Both sides, white and Indian, had suffered from ignorance, from betrayal of the U.S. government as they continually broke the contracts made with the many Indian tribes of the Plains.

But his people, the Blackfoot, were from the north. His people in particular had little to do with the conflict between the states. He'd been raised on the reservation by his uncle Walking Thunder and his aunt Davinda, a white woman he called mother. They'd been unaffected by the conflict in the country just below them. He'd lived as the typical Indian boy, learning to track and hunt, learning the secret rituals of his people, going on his spirit search to find his warrior name.

He'd been taught the ways of the white man by his Davinda, a woman he loved most dearly, until he was sent to live with Davinda's close friend in Hampton, Virginia, where he'd attended Hampton Indian School.

Now, at nearly thirty, he was enjoying his position as law clerk and looked forward to finishing his classes.

Had Sarah asked, he would have explained his situation, but when there was no occasion to discuss who he was and what he planned to do, he chose not to talk about himself. Other's unfounded fears were of no concern to him.

What did concern him was how Sarah might react to the busybodies. It was important for him to learn the song to play for Davinda, his mother.

As the first star appeared in the eastern sky, Daniel looked up. His days were filled with work, school, studying, but at times he longed for someone like Sarah to share his nights—his bed.

But Sarah was forbidden to him. He had seen the way a red man's love for a white woman had hurt Davinda, even though Walking Thunder's love for her was strong.

Daniel Eaglefeather would put no woman through the agony of loving a red man in a white man's land.

No, Sarah was forbidden to him, even though she made his blood rush like a mighty river.

4

"Peter! Please don't slam the front do—" Sarah cringed as the lace curtains on the parlor window gyrated wildly from the sudden impact.

Sophie had ushered Peter out the door, mumbling something about Peter being hungry, and when Peter was hungry, Peter was cranky.

"And when Peter's cranky, Sarah's cranky," Sarah muttered as she stacked sheets of music.

The knock startled her, and she spilled the music she'd just stacked. After hurrying to the door, she opened it and pulled Daniel inside.

"Is something wrong?" he asked.

"No, I just didn't want Miss Periwinkle to see how handsome you look in that brown tweed suit and dark brown overcoat. She might get jealous and . . . "

"Shoot me?"

Sarah laughed, realizing how unfair it was of her to feel awkward around Daniel when he's been nothing but decent and well-mannered toward her. "Probably. But at least you would die with your clothes on."

"What?"

"I've been told you will show up at my door dressed only in a loincloth, and that you will ravage me."

"I must say the thought has crossed my mind."

"Daniel!"

"Miss Collins, I do believe you're blushing," Daniel teased. He removed his overcoat and handed it to Sarah, then took his seat at the piano. "You may want to leave the door open, just in case."

"That won't be necessary. Please begin your scales."

Daniel recited the notes as he played. "C, D, E, F, G, A, B, C."

"Now play 'The Swing,' then I promise you can begin to learn 'The Fox.'"

Sarah counted, "One, two, three, four," as Daniel played the notes perfectly with a smug grin on his face.

"It's like dancing," Daniel said, "only I dance better than I play the piano."

"You know how to dance?" Sarah loved to dance. "Do you waltz?"

"No." He considered the question. "Rain dances, mostly."

"I've never done one of those," Sarah murmured.

"Or a good war dance is most enjoyable."

"Stop playing with me, Daniel Eaglefeather."

"You told me to play, and that is what I'm doing."

"If you want to learn 'The Fox,' you'd better get serious." Sarah sat next to him on the bench. "And if you work hard on your lesson, I will serve you tea and shortbread."

Daniel played with diligence.

"Peter, please don't pull Kitty around by the neck!" Sarah's voice sounded sharper than she'd intended, but the boy would drive a body up the wall.

A loud *meeeowwwww* went up as a vase hit the floor and shattered.

"Peter!"

Sophie was now dropping Peter off for his lesson, then going to visit a lady friend a few doors down. Even Sophie couldn't take the forty-five minutes of piano hell.

Without Sophie there to monitor Peter's behavior, he was out of hand. He refused to listen to Sarah's instructions, ran through the house knocking over plants and knickknacks, and tormented the cat. Kitty was racing around trying to escape and the racket was intolerable.

Overhead, Miss Periwinkle thunderously thumped the floor with her cane.

"Peter!" Sarah shouted. "Go sit on the foyer bench until your mother comes!"

"I don't have to!"

The boy stood in the middle of the room, arms crossed in defiance. Sarah crossed her arms just as defiantly and stared at him. "Go to the bench, don't get up, and don't say another word."

Sticking his fingers in his mouth, he made a cross-eyed, distorted face at her.

Sarah was nonplussed. "I once knew a little boy who did his eyes that way and the look froze on his face."

"You did not!"

Shrugging, Sarah began to straighten sheet music. "Did too. He was so ugly, his parents were forced to give him to a sideshow."

"Huh-uh . . . Is that true?" Peter demanded.

Sarah wasn't about to set his mind at ease. "Keep making those faces and you'll see."

An openly belligerent Peter stomped to the bench in the foyer and threw himself on it, his lower lip stuck out. Sarah mentally dared him to get up, but for once he obeyed.

The front door opened, and Sarah looked up as Sophie entered the parlor. "Mrs. Butcher."

"Mommy, Mommy, Miss Sarah is being mean to me!"

"Don't whine, dear." She patted her son on the head. "I have been wanting to talk to you, Miss Collins. I don't feel Peter is progressing as well as he should."

"Mrs. Butcher, I don't think Peter's heart is in his music."

"Well, at least he hasn't given it to an Indian."

Sarah forced a smile, her hands fisted at her sides, her eyes fixed on Sophie.

"Mamma!" Peter shouted. "Miss Sarah said you were going to put me in a sideshow! Are you gonna do that?"

"Of course not, dear. Wait for me outside." Once Peter was gone, she began again. "Of all the nerve! Insulting Peter like that is as unforgivable as your cavorting around with that Indian!"

"Mrs. Butcher—"

"Don't you Mrs. Butcher me! I've decided this will be Peter's last lesson with you."

"I'm sorry you feel that way, but perhaps you're right. Peter's talents might be better used elsewhere."

"Good day, Miss Collins!"

Sarah resisted the smile that pulled at her lips. "I suggest you buy him a drum."

"If you don't stop seeing that savage, you won't have a student left!" She huffed out the door, not bothering to shut it behind her.

December arrived on the heels of a howling wind and snow flurries. Elinor Hastings and Miss Periwinkle had kept their vigil of Daniel's comings and goings. Mrs. Butcher had been true to her word: Sarah had lost half her students.

Daniel's progress was nothing short of remarkable. It was either her ability as a teacher, or the natural grace of his long, adept fingers. But either way, he'd soon master "The Fox" and have no further need of her. The thought bothered her, and she decided tea was in order.

It was Saturday night and Daniel said he'd try to drop by after he finished the paperwork Mr. Hayes had piled on him, but she didn't expect him for another hour.

Suddenly she heard someone kick her door. It flew open with a burst of frigid air and a frightening-looking man covered in snow stood in the doorway.

"Who are you?" Sarah managed, her stomach in her throat.

"I'm Ace, and I've come fer my pi-anna."

"Well, Ace, I think you have the wrong address. That is my piano," Sarah said gesturing toward the spinet with as much courage as she could muster.

"Nope. It's mine."

"I bought that piano at an auction."

"Reckon you wasted yer money, 'cuz she's mine. Curly, over at the saloon, was keeping it fer me 'cause I'd had a run of bad luck at the card table that night, but I aim to take 'er back. It was right nice of ya to keep 'er fer me, but Ma's waitin'. She 'spects it back fer Christmas. So step aside, missy."

Ace staggered past her, and the smell of whiskey all but knocked her over. She doubted the man had ever seen a bath or clean clothes. She watched in horror as he started to push her piano across the floor. It sounded like fingernails on a chalkboard, scratching the hardwood surface she'd spent so much time polishing.

"Please, Ace. Let me play it one more time before you take it away." Sarah prayed Miss Periwinkle wouldn't let her down. She stood in front of the piano and pounded on the keys as hard as she could, relieved when the thump of the cane interrupted her beat.

"What in the blazes is that?" Ace stared at the ceiling, swaying back and forth.

"Hurry Ace, you have to leave. My fiancé lives upstairs and he's very jealous. If he finds you here he'll shoot you."

"Shoot . . . m-m-me?"

"Go! Now! Come back in the morning to get the piano, he'll be in church." Sarah pushed the filthy man toward the door, her heart pounding.

"Go! He's coming!" she yelled when Lillian thumped right on cue. Ace tried to turn back. "Hurry or your mother will never see her piano or you again!"

With the help of Sarah's final push out the door, Ace fell down the porch steps and rolled all the way to the curb. He pulled himself up using the fence, then wobbled to the wagon. Sarah ran toward him to make sure he didn't turn back again. She muffled a laugh with her hand when Ace, looking like a snowman, stuck one foot on the wheel spoke to climb up.

Ace grabbed the reins to pull himself in as the horses bolted and took off with a lurch, knocking Ace headfirst onto the floor of the wagon in front of the seat. The driverless wagon pulled from her view, and she chuckled at the sound of Ace's whiny voice shouting obscenities into the wind.

Sarah jumped when a hand touched her shoulder from behind.

"What's wrong, Sarah? You're shaking."

"It's cold."

"It's more than that."

"We'd better get inside, this could be a long story."

Once inside, Daniel loomed over her. "Sarah Collins, you'd better tell me right now what that man wanted. I know he upset you. Did he hurt you?"

"No, Daniel. Calm down. Do you know a man named Curly who owns a saloon downtown?" She watched him nod. "That man who just left says Curly was keeping his piano—and he thinks my piano is his."

"Why would he say that?"

"I was going to Rose's Dress Shop one morning when I saw a sign outside the saloon that said, Piano for sale—Cheap. I thought it was an auction. I needed a piano for my lessons because the one I had been using was borrowed. So I went inside and talked to Curly."

Daniel shook his head. "I've dealt with Curly in court."

"Well, he said this guy ran up quite a gambling debt one night, and the only way he could pay his debt was with his mother's furniture left over from her estate that he was moving to Illinois."

"Let me guess, Mother is still alive and wants her furniture back."

"Curly said he was keeping the brass bed, and he already had a buyer for the grandfather clock, and I bought the piano."

"Did you get a bill of sale?"

"No. I didn't know I needed one." Sarah sighed. "Can Ace take my piano?"

"No. I'll take care of Ace."

Daniel left abruptly without another word, and Sarah had the feeling he was about to get himself into trouble. There was nothing he could do at this hour on a Saturday night at Curly's except start a fight. She couldn't let him risk his life and profession over a piano.

Sarah grabbed her cape and headed for Curly's.

Daniel ducked, then flipped Ace over his back into a pile of crates in the dark alley, but two others grabbed him from behind and held his arms. Three more men approached from the front and took turns landing blows in his stomach, ribs, face, and back. He spit the metallic taste of blood from his mouth in time to receive another hard blow to the jaw.

A woman's high-pitched scream cut through the air.

She screamed again and again until the men assaulting Daniel fled into the darkness.

Daniel felt a soft hand on his forehead and tried to focus. "Sarah?"

"Of course it's me. What other woman would come to the aid of an Indian in a dark alley?"

"You shouldn't have come, I was—"

"You were outnumbered. Now let's get you home. Where's your coat?"

"Gone." Daniel coughed.

She helped Daniel to his feet and they walked toward his home. The trip up the back stairs was a bit difficult, with one step forward and two steps back, but they finally reached the landing.

"The keys are in the front pocket of my pants."

"You want me to reach in . . ." Sarah grimaced when Daniel held up his bloody, swollen hands. "This is definitely going to slow your piano playing, Daniel Eaglefeather."

"At least you'll still have a piano for me to play."

"I'm afraid to ask how, but I thank you." Sarah wrapped her arms around Daniel and kissed his cheek, even though he groaned.

"Must you give my neighbors something to gossip about?"

"Sorry."

Daniel wiped his mouth on the sleeve of his shirt, then pulled Sarah into his arms and kissed her. She tasted like honey, and smelled even better. How he wanted her. He slid his hand down her back and pressed her hips against his. Her body, rigid at first, melted like butter as he held her tight.

Sarah, sweet Sarah. He pulled back. She deserved a

man she could love, a man she could be proud to be seen with. Not stealing embraces in the dark, hiding from the neighbors, and finding herself the center of gossip. No. He'd sworn he would never put a woman through that.

Walking Thunder and Davinda had endured much to be together. He'd experienced firsthand the cruel acts of hatred against any man who touched a white woman, and he couldn't put Sarah through that.

Daniel felt Sarah's hand slip into his pocket for the key. His intentions were good, but he didn't feel strong enough to send her away. At least not tonight.

There was just enough light from the streetlamp out front to let Daniel find his way to the bed.

"There's a kerosene lamp on the table, but pull the shades before you light it."

Sarah did as he instructed, then poured water from the pitcher on the washstand into the basin, picked up a towel, and walked to the bed. She set the bowl next to Daniel and began to wipe his face.

She watched him cringe. "I'm sorry, but I need to clean these cuts."

Her blue eyes were intent, her hands soft, her touch light. She was the most beautiful woman he'd ever seen, and he wanted her. Yet it could never be.

"I'm sorry I got you involved in this. I wouldn't have told you, but I thought there was something legal you could do. I never dreamed you'd . . ."

"Sarah, men like Curly and Ace don't respect the law. I handled it in the only way I could."

"No piano is worth your life. Besides, I have no more students left . . ."

"That's my fault, Sarah. I never should have insisted

you teach me. I knew what could happen. But you'll be safe from now on. I'll not take any more lessons."

"So you're going to give in to all the bigots? I never took you for a man who would give up so easily, Daniel Eaglefeather."

Sarah's wiping became rougher, and he grabbed her hand. "It's not about giving up. Don't you see, sweet Sarah? It was me today, tomorrow it could be you. Keeping company with an Indian could only mean grief. I'd rather die than see anything happen to you."

"No one's going to die. We'll just stand up to them."

"Sarah. In case you haven't noticed, I'm the only Indian for miles." He raised her hand to his swollen lips and placed a kiss on the back. "One man can make a difference, and that's what I plan to do. But not here, not now."

"When, Daniel? Is there ever a right time and place?"

Daniel wiped a tear from her cheek. "When I return to my people on the reservation. I can fight for their rights, rights the government wants to take away."

Sarah stood and paced the small, one-room living space Daniel called home. "What about playing 'The Fox' for Davinda? I thought that meant a lot to you."

"It does, but—"

"But nothing. I've lost enough students, I can't afford to lose you as well."

"So it's my money you want after all." Daniel laughed, but when he did, the cut on his lip started bleeding again and he gasped for air.

"Look what you've done." Sarah rushed to his side and wiped away the blood. She sat on the bed and began to unbutton his shirt and noticed his eyes grow wide. "Don't you get any ideas. I'm just trying to see how badly they beat you."

Daniel knew he had a couple of broken ribs, and from the ashen expression on Sarah's face when she opened his shirt, she knew it too. She ran her hands lightly across the purple and blue skin at his sides, then up and down his chest. Her touch set him on fire, causing his need to grow firm and hard.

"I think you'd better go, Sarah."

"Nonsense. You need someone to take care of you and—"

"It's not safe for you to stay here any longer."

"Why? Those men won't come looking for you."

"I'm not worried about those men. I'm worried about myself, being alone with you." He reached up and traced the delicate line of her jaw. "Do you understand now?"

Warmth flooded her cheeks. "I'll leave, but only if you promise to see me tomorrow. This matter of lessons isn't settled yet."

"I'm in no condition to argue."

With regret, Sarah left Daniel alone with his injuries. She wished he hadn't risked his life for her piano, but she loved him for it.

Loved?

Had she fallen in love with the virile Indian? The only love she'd ever known was that of Katherine and Michael, not the love between a man and a woman.

What she felt for Daniel went beyond friendship. When he touched her, he awakened feelings she never knew she had. He made her feel warm and cared for. When her hands roamed his muscled chest, she'd felt sensations within her own body she couldn't explain, sensations she didn't want to end.

But he sent her away. He said he was afraid to be alone with her. Was it because she wasn't his kind? Or had he felt the same stirrings she had? Their relationship had become closer, beyond that of student and teacher. But then Daniel said he could no longer be her student. Could he really mean it?

What would she do if he stopped coming? It wasn't the money, it was Daniel. There had to be a way to continue his lessons. She couldn't bear not to see him, but the decision belonged to him.

Sarah paced the floor of the music room waiting for that familiar knock. She'd skipped church, not wanting to miss Daniel if he should come in the morning. The clock chimed four times, and she stared out the window wondering when the snow would stop falling.

The only good thing about the snow was that it kept Miss Periwinkle in. Lillian never ventured out in bad weather, but she was about to wear out her window shade. Even if Daniel came, who could recognize him in a blizzard?

She walked into the kitchen when the teakettle began to whistle and checked the shortbread in the oven. As she pulled out the tray, the long-awaited knock sounded. She dropped the sheet of cookies on top of the stove and rushed to open the door.

"Oh, Daniel!" She threw her arms around his neck and hugged him, snow melting into the fabric of her heavy cotton dress.

"What did I do to receive such a welcome?" he asked, removing his hat.

Daniel hung his overcoat and hat on the wall rack in the foyer. "I sure could use a cup of tea."

Sarah ran into the kitchen to rescue the screaming teakettle. "Have a seat," she said, setting the tea and shortbread on the table.

Daniel sat and held the cup with both hands, and let the steam rise up his face. "It's cold out there."

"Enough about the weather. How do you feel?"

"I'll live. Right now I'm too cold to tell."

"Then let's talk about your decision regarding your piano lessons."

"There's nothing to discuss," Daniel said, taking a sip.

"Nothing to discuss? I'm not going to let you quit now. You're just learning how to play 'The Fox' and—"

"Slow down, woman. Did I say I was quitting?"

"Last night you said you would no longer take lessons from me." Sarah ran her finger along the edge of the plate. "Does that mean you've found another teacher?"

Daniel tilted up her chin with his finger. "No, Sarah. You will still be my teacher, but not here." He watched her smile turn to puzzlement when he held up a key.

"Don't keep me in suspense, Daniel."

"You remember my mention of the music teacher at the university?" He watched her nod. "This is the key to a private practice room we can use any time after hours."

"How did you manage that?"

"First of all, Mr. Grayson likes Indians. He confided there was one in his family. Second, I drew up a will for him and he's returning the favor."

Daniel stood and walked around the table. He pulled Sarah to her feet and lowered his head. The moment his lips touched hers the sound of shattering glass broke them apart.

5

Daniel pulled Sarah to the floor. "Stay down." He crawled to the table and shut off the kerosene lamp. "Don't move until I return."

He rushed outside in time to see a lone rider lope away in the snow. The icy wind cut through his shirt as if he were naked. There wasn't much he could do now except reassure Sarah that she was safe with him.

Back inside he lit the lamp and helped Sarah to her feet. "He's gone." Daniel brushed a stray hair from her face, but didn't stop there. An easy tug on her upswept curls sent long blond strands cascading down her back. His fingers threaded themselves through her silky locks.

"Some braves prize a blond scalp above all other colors."

"Do you?"

"Only if it's attached to someone as beautiful as you."

This time when he lowered his lips, he took the kiss he'd longed for. Sarah smelled of vanilla and tasted like shortbread. He controlled the burning need within, but he didn't know how much longer he could. She kissed him back so passionately, her body so willing, he wanted to carry her to the bed and claim her as his own.

Daniel ended the kiss. "I'd better take care of the broken glass."

"I'll get the broom," Sarah said, heading for the kitchen.

When he surveyed the damage on the music room floor, he spotted a rock amidst the shattered glass and noticed a crumpled piece of paper underneath it. He picked it up, not surprised to read: "If you see that Indian one more time, he's dead." His fist closed around the note, and he shoved it in his pocket.

"Here's a broom," Sarah said, returning from the kitchen.

At least she hadn't seen the note, he thought, taking the broom from her outstretched hand. "I'll need to board up that window. Can't let the snow blow in like that."

"I'll see what I can find."

Sarah disappeared into the other room and Daniel swept the glass. He would have been worried if the note had threatened Sarah, but it was him they wanted and he could handle himself.

Walking Thunder and Davinda had warned him things like this would happen and tutored him in ways to deal with white men's threats. But they never expected their son to become involved with a white woman, especially since he knew their story so well. His only concern was Sarah.

❧

At seven o'clock Sarah and Daniel met by the music department, and Daniel let them into the private practice room with Mr. Grayson's key.

"This is wonderful," Sarah said, when Daniel turned on the light. "There isn't even a window for anyone to spy on us." She ran her hand across the top of the highly polished upright piano. "Only this fine instrument, a few chairs, and us."

"As it should be." Daniel took his seat at the piano.

Sarah listened intently as he played through "The Fox" with only minor hesitations. He was making such wonderful progress, it was hard to conceal her pride.

"I think it's time you teach me to sing the words."

"You want voice lessons?"

"I only want to sing 'The Fox.'" Daniel smiled. "It can't be as hard to sing as it is to play."

"We'll see." Sarah gave him a smile, knowing how he was going to react to her next statement. "All right, then, let's begin by singing scales."

His grimace matched her expectations.

"Like this." She played one note five times and sang, "La-la-la-la-la." Sarah sang each note several times up and down the eight-note scale. "Now you try."

Sarah anticipated hearing Daniel's rich baritone.

"LA-LA-la-laaaaaaaaa-LA," he sang.

The hair on her arms stood up. She'd heard better sounds from the brakes on a train!

"No, now listen closely, Daniel. La-la-la-la-la. Listen to the tone and try to match it."

"La, la, la, LA, la," he croaked on the same discordant note.

Sarah hit the note more sharply, hoping it would penetrate the tone he was making. "La-la-la-la-la."

"LaaHah, Laalah, Lahhhh!"

Tone-deaf. God help him, he was tone-deaf! If he attempted to sing "The Fox" or anything else, he'd embarrass himself and anyone with the misfortune to witness it. She watched him look at her proudly.

"How was that?"

"Honestly?"

His eyes searched hers. "I want you to always be honest with me, Sarah."

"We-el-l, your mother will love it, but you're tone-deaf, Daniel."

"I am? No one ever told me that before. I really wanted Mother to hear the words."

The disappointment mirrored in his eyes only made Sarah more determined. If she could teach him to play "The Fox," surely she could teach him to sing. "Don't worry. Next week is Christmas, we have plenty of time."

Unexpected tears burned at her lids. She couldn't say the month without getting teary-eyed. "I'm sorry, Daniel. I just realized how much I'm going to miss you."

Daniel slipped his arm around her shoulders. "And I will miss you, Sarah Collins. Perhaps you would like me to sing for you?" Sarah began to laugh. "Am I really that bad, or do you enjoy it so much?"

"Let's say I can do without your singing, but I can't do without you." She watched his gaze grow soft and warm, his lips moving toward hers. Her eyes closed as his mouth found hers, his arm pulling her to his chest. She felt the rapid beat of his heart, and knew he wanted her the same way she wanted him.

Her stomach turned upside down and every inch of her body tingled with desire. She felt dizzy and weak, but his strong arms held her firm. If only this feeling could last forever, but she knew he would slip away from her, return to his people.

Daniel's body was so warm and alive against her, his kiss so powerful and possessive. She hugged him tightly. It was better to have these few short memories than none at all. Sarah pulled back before repressed tears surfaced.

"I think it's time to continue your lesson."

Sarah played the notes while Daniel attempted to sing.

Sarah sat in the crowded church trying to concentrate on the Christmas Eve service. It was difficult with everyone around her whispering and pointing fingers. What was wrong with all of them? She hadn't done anything to be ashamed of. But that's exactly how they wanted her to feel.

She took her place at the piano to play the final song, "Silent Night," while the congregation sang, their unrelenting eyes fixed on her. It was as if she were a criminal.

Where was their Christmas spirit? Their compassion and understanding? This was her first Christmas without Katherine and Michael, which was enough to deal with. Now it seemed the entire community had turned against her. She tilted her head back, finished the song, then took her seat for the final prayer.

As she walked down the aisle, women turned their backs to her and the men shook their heads. She saw the pastor in the doorway bidding a Merry Christmas to several of the parishioners.

"Sarah," the pastor greeted her, "I've been meaning to tell you—Mrs. Kirk will be taking over as pianist the first of the year." He looked away. "I'm sure you understand."

"I understand perfectly, Reverend."

Sarah bit her tongue and walked away, clutching her bag so tightly her knuckles turned white. She wanted to give everyone a piece of her mind, but it would be useless. They'd judged her, and nothing would change that.

She wanted to scream at the top of her lungs. Instead, she picked up her pace and wondered what Katherine would say if she were here.

The walk home was cold and lonely. She opened the door of the brownstone and took a deep breath of relief, closing it behind her. She leaned against the hard wood and thought how her little Christmas tree filled the room with the fresh scent of pine, remembering Christmases past. Why hadn't she insisted Daniel come over? They were both alone, very alone, while the rest of the world spent time with their loved ones.

Sarah heard the sound of a match, then a flame came into view across the room, and her heart nearly jumped out of her chest. Relief spread through her when she saw the face she loved in the faint flicker of light.

"How did you get in?"

"I'm resourceful, remember?"

"I certainly do." She smelled sweet smoke floating in the air. "When did you start smoking a pipe?"

"When I became a man. I believe I was twelve." Daniel lit the kerosene lamp and smiled at Sarah in the doorway. "I'll not smoke if it bothers you."

"Please do. I like it. It reminds me of my father."

"How was church?"

"I'd rather not discuss that right now." Sarah removed her cape and tossed it on the bench. She walked toward Daniel. "I'm so glad you're here."

"I couldn't let you spend Christmas alone."

"Do Indians celebrate Christmas?"

"They do when their mother is white."

Sarah leaned against the piano. She hadn't realized Davinda was white. Daniel had always called her by name, or Mother, never mentioning her color. He'd said he thought of Walking Thunder and Davinda as his blood parents, and she'd never considered the possibility that Davinda was anything but Indian.

"Have I shocked you?" Daniel asked.

"By scaring me to death? Yes. I had no idea you were coming."

"No, Sarah. You know what I mean."

"I never gave your mother's heritage a thought, and you didn't mention it. All you said was that she didn't discuss her life before meeting your father. I just assumed she came from another tribe."

"I only see her as my mother. The color of her skin isn't important."

"I wish the rest of the world thought the way we do."

Daniel walked to Sarah and took her hand.

She faced him, his copper skin glowing in the subdued light, his dark gaze loving and tender, the silence between them filled with emotion.

He reached into his coat pocket and pulled out a small box tied with red satin ribbon. Sarah smiled when he placed it in her hand.

"Open it," he said softly.

Her hands shook as she untied the bow and lifted the lid. "Oh, Daniel, they're beautiful!" She removed the two sterling silver combs and watched them glisten.

"I want you to wear those, and your finest dress next Thursday when you go to see *Romeo and Juliet* at the opera house." He handed her a ticket.

"Daniel, this ticket is for a private balcony box. I can't accept this, it's too expensive. Besides I won't go without you."

"Oh, but you will."

"No, you take this ticket and sell it to someone else. Besides Thursday is your lesson night, and neither you nor I can afford to miss it."

"I'll pay for the lesson, but only if you attend the opera."

"It's not the money, it's—" Before she could say another word, Daniel's lips brushed hers, and his kiss made her forget everything but the taste and feel of him. The butterflies in her stomach were overactive tonight, and so were her emotions.

Tears pressed against her lids and escaped against her will. She didn't care. Daniel had saved her from dire loneliness and filled her with holiday love, a love she prayed he shared.

Daniel's mouth moved to her cheeks where he kissed away her tears. "Sweet Sarah. Don't cry. I want you to be happy, especially tonight."

"You've made me happy, Daniel, that's why I'm crying."

"The ways of women have always been a mystery to me."

Sarah wiggled from his embrace and walked to the tree to pick up the only gift there. She heard Daniel's footsteps stop behind her and felt his hand on her shoulder. "This isn't much, but I made it myself."

Daniel took the gaily wrapped package from her.

She watched him rip it open with a child's enthusiasm, and felt her heart race with pride as he removed the gloves she'd knitted.

"Thank you, Sarah."

"I wish it could be more."

"Being with you is all I need, but you've given me so much more. A gift from your heart." He pulled her into his embrace and kissed her deeply.

Sarah sighed in contentment. It was a perfect Christmas, because she held in her arms all she ever wanted.

Thursday night Sarah sat alone in her private box as the lights dimmed and the first act began. She never would have come if Daniel hadn't been so insistent. And of all the plays to see, *Romeo and Juliet*, doomed lovers, never to share a life together, a story that ran all too parallel to her life. If society were different, she could enjoy an evening on the town with the man she loved, like the other women here. But that could never be.

A warm tickle on her bare shoulder made her jump. When she turned to her right, nothing was there, but when she turned back, Daniel was in the chair next to her, a smug expression on his face.

"You scared me!" she whispered angrily into his ear.

"You scare me, too—especially in that dress. You look beautiful, sweet Sarah."

"What about you?" she replied, trying to keep her voice low. "You're the most handsome man here in that black suit, and . . ." She felt his finger touch her lips.

"This night is for you. We'll talk later."

Daniel took her hand in his; the feel of him was so exciting. She wanted to kiss him for arranging this special night, for caring when no one else did, for being there when she needed him. If this was love, it was wonderful.

6

Daniel closed the book and leaned back, resting his booted feet on the edge of the desk. He'd be leaving for Montana in a few months, and the prospect filled him with both joy and sadness.

Joy that he would be seeing his family again, and that he would play for his mother, but sadness that he would no longer be able to see Sarah. His sweet Sarah. How could he leave her?

Over the months, love had crept in. He hadn't meant for it to happen. She filled his heart and made him feel complete. Sarah had lost virtually all her students because of him, and had become an outcast from her church and community. Through it all, they had grown closer, but he felt guilt. Other than his adoptive parents, he knew of no match between a white woman and an Indian that ever stood a chance of being happy.

He stood and looked out the window. The city was quiet this early on a Sunday morning, and he was glad. He needed time to think, time to decide.

Daniel recalled his first encounter with Sarah

Collins. She had been so afraid. Afraid to have him in her home, and afraid to ask him to leave. Taking piano lessons may have been the worst decision he'd ever made. Because of it, he had ripped two lives apart.

Sarah had fallen in love with him despite his efforts over the past weeks to avoid her, except for lessons. He'd stayed away from her for many weeks after the opera, hoping the attraction would cool. It hadn't. They both knew he didn't need more lessons. He could play "The Fox" perfectly, with feeling, and he'd never be able to sing. Yet he needed to see her, to hear her voice, see her smile. He was in love with her and he couldn't, wouldn't deny it.

But Sarah wasn't a fool, she sensed his feelings, but never said a word. She'd sit next to him at the piano, her light rose-scented perfume tempting him, her lips pulling him, and the thought of leaving her tore him apart.

No, she hadn't fallen in love with him by accident. That was his fault as well. He'd pursued her as any man would a beautiful woman. That night at the opera had been magic, at least until he reached home. He'd taken every precaution not to be seen, he even left before the last act and waited in the buggy in the darkness behind the opera house.

Three men jumped him at his door. It was quite a fight, but he'd won. Sarah hadn't questioned him taking two weeks off from lessons to let his hands heal. He'd told her it was because of his studies and work. She understood, she always did. The thought of deceiving her didn't make him feel any better, but he had to spare her the ugliness that went along with their relationship.

He'd insisted on a lesson today and she'd agreed.

Sarah hadn't questioned the fact that it was Sunday. But he wasn't sure how to ask her to go with him to Montana. It might be foolish, but he wanted her by his side, to be his woman, forever. It might be too soon to tell her of his love, ask her to marry him, so he'd just ask her to go with him. Yes, he'd ask her today, before he lost his nerve.

The campus was deserted when Sarah arrived. There were times she wondered if anyone studied here.

She began to pace and worry about Daniel. Something was terribly wrong between them, had been for several weeks now. Oh, he still came for lessons, but he made obvious mistakes which gave him excuses to continue. But enough was enough.

He had pulled away from her. She no longer felt the same close bond they had come to enjoy. Instead they barely talked, and he no longer stole kisses. And even worse, he avoided her touch, and that was more than she could bear.

It was past time she dismissed him as a student. It didn't matter that the neighbors never saw Daniel, she was still called "Indian-lover" everywhere she went. Whether she heard the name, or only saw the resentment in their eyes, it was all the same.

She'd been willing to give up everything for him. Now she had lost everything because of him. The pain of being with him and not talking or touching had to end. He'd made it clear he didn't care for her, so she would tell him today. It was over.

"Play the notes again, Daniel."

"I'm trying, Sarah."

"Listen to the tune—hear the chords. Now sing it again."

Daniel sang, even though his heart wasn't in his music. For the first time it hurt to hear the words roll off his lips.

> The Fox went out on a chilly night,
> Prayed for the moon to give him light,
> For he'd many a mile to go that night,
> Before he reached the town-o, town-o, town-o,
> He'd many a mile to go that night,
> Before he reached the town—before he got to—
> before . . .

"I'm sorry Sarah, my mind wandered."

"Sing the second verse," she said tersely.

Daniel tried his best to sing the words.

> He ran till he found a big, big pen,
> Where the ducks and the geese were put therein,
> Tonight two of you will grease my chin,
> Before I leave this town-o.

He suddenly stopped playing, and the music faded away as he looked at her. "Would you sing it for me?"

"You're doing . . . fine. Your mother will be pleased." Sarah stood and put a safe distance between them. "Daniel, I think this will be your last lesson. You no longer need me."

Daniel sat silently for a moment. Finally, he looked up. "What are you saying, Sarah?"

"You're an educated man, you figure it out." Sarah picked up her cloak from the chair and swung it around her shoulders, but it hung on something. She turned to find the material in Daniel's hand. "Let go! I'm leaving."

"Not until you tell me what's wrong."

"If you don't know, Daniel Eaglefeather, then there's no point explaining."

She only called him by his full name when she was happy or mad, and with fire dancing in her eyes and her lips pursed that way, he couldn't call her happy. Even when she was angry she was beautiful, and he wanted her even more.

"Where are you going?"

"I haven't decided, but I'll be leaving Saint Louis. There's nothing left here for me."

Daniel watched her wipe at tears and couldn't resist. He pulled her into his arms and held her tight even though she struggled against him.

"Let me . . . go!" she snapped.

"Not before you agree to go to Montana with me." He felt the struggle of her body cease and the one in her mind begin. Had he gone too far in his ruse to push her away? He prayed not, but he couldn't blame her for hating him.

"Sarah, please listen to me. I've treated you badly, and for that I'm sorry. I was only trying to protect you."

"Protect me from what?"

"Falling in love with me."

"You should have thought about that before you stole kisses, gave me gifts, and took me to the opera! No, you're like all other men, and the color of your skin doesn't matter!"

"Sarah, please—"

"Release me this instant!"

"Not until you agree to go to Montana with me."

"You really are a savage if you think I would go off with a man who cares nothing for me!"

With a hand on each shoulder, he pulled her to his chest and kissed her hungrily, passionately, with every ounce of his being. But Sarah wasn't responding. He pulled back and gazed into her eyes.

"Look at me, Sarah. Look deep into my eyes and see my soul. I love you, Sarah Collins. I want you to be my woman, to trust me, to love me."

Sarah stepped back, turned, and walked out the door.

Daniel grabbed her hand to stop her. "I will wait here tomorrow at seven for your answer. Sarah, sweet Sarah, I love you." He released her hand and she ran as if she were running for her life.

He slammed his fist against the door. He'd never forgive himself for hurting her, but he had to face the truth. He'd lost her forever.

Sarah paced the music room anxiously. Daniel was the most infuriating man she'd ever met. He made her fall in love with him, then pushed her away. Now he claim to want her. For what? He said to be his woman. What did that mean? Did she even care?

Of course she cared, she cared too much. But could she believe his proclamation of love? A month ago she would have, but now? He was a bit late. Protect her? Indeed. If he'd asked her to marry him, the decision might have been simple. The church may have pushed her out, but she still had her morals.

No. She couldn't go off with an Indian to live in Montana, a wilderness she knew nothing about. His people wouldn't accept her any better than hers had accepted him. It was useless. He could wait until the cows came home. She wasn't going.

She picked up her music satchel to pack the rest of her music. When she opened it, a ticket fell on the floor. She picked it up, her hands shaking. "Paid passage for one. Date of departure June 3rd. Time: 9 A.M."

Daniel Eaglefeather could wait a lifetime, she wasn't going to be on that boat.

Daniel leaned against he rail of the upper deck, his eyes trained on the boarding ramp. Where was she? Would she forgive him? Four months was a long time to be apart.

The joy of returning home and playing "The Fox" for his mother was little consolation for a broken heart. He turned from the rail as two men in white uniforms lifted the boarding plank. It was over. Sarah wasn't coming.

The key to the stateroom turned and Sarah's heart raced. How would Daniel feel seeing her after she'd not spoken to him since the night he asked her to come? She sat on the bed and adjusted her hat.

She gasped when the door flew open and Daniel's imposing form stood in the doorway, silhouetted by the morning light behind him. His face was obscured until he stepped inside and closed the door.

"Have you nothing to say, Daniel?"

His eyes said whatever words were missing. Moving quickly to her, he pushed her back on the bed, his mouth devouring hers, his fingers deftly working loose the buttons down her back. He lifted his head, tossed her hat across the floor, and pulled out the two silver combs that held up her hair.

Easing her dress down quickly, he removed her undergarments slowly, exposing skin inch by inch. Every new exposure was thoroughly kissed and touched. When his mouth found her breast she moaned.

He raised to look at her. "Sarah, sweet Sarah. You're so beautiful. You're not angry with me?"

"I should be very mad at you for the agony you put me through."

"I'd deserve it for being so stubborn."

"Oh Daniel, I love you!"

There was no more need for words. She watched him stand and remove his clothes, her gaze fixed on every inch of sinewy muscle, his bronze skin begging for her touch. When her perusal found the part of him that was man, she knew what he meant by need.

He lay down beside her and caressed her bare skin with his fingertips, slowly, sensuously, the look of love heavy in his dark, penetrating eyes. His lips moved slowly down the creamy column of her throat, then kissed the soft mound of flesh, tasting one nipple then the other.

With tortured slowness, he lowered himself into her, his hands molding her slender hips against his. She accepted him with all the love her soul possessed and wrapped her arms around his back, feeling his strong muscles tense.

Daniel had a magnificent body. All the butterflies she'd felt in her stomach settled in her womanhood. Her breath caught in her throat when he penetrated her, but it was the most delightful pain she'd ever felt. Pain that faded to ecstasy and beyond. Sensations sparked through her, igniting a fire that would burn a lifetime.

Later, she lay contented in his arms, her hand resting on his damp chest, drifting in and out of awareness.

This is what love is all about.

She had nearly drifted off to sleep when Daniel sat up. The sound of a match striking caused her eyes to open. Daniel was staring at her nakedness, his gaze raking her from head to foot. Self-consciously she reached for the blanket.

"Don't," he said, pulling the cover from her grasp. "I want to look at you. You're beautiful. So perfect."

"I'm beautiful when I'm with you," she whispered, letting her fingers drift over his thigh.

His gaze softened tenderly. "What made you change your mind?"

"I love you."

He kissed her cheek and ran his fingers through her hair, then down her neck, threading themselves around a thin chain around her neck, tracing the outline of an oval locket. "What is this?"

"A treasured possession."

"What happened to the other half?"

"I don't know, this is all there was."

His eyes mirrored his bewilderment.

"The locket was among my blankets when I was left

on Michael's doorstep. It's the only thing I have of my birth mother."

"That's odd," Daniel murmured, turning the locket over in his hand. The faint light glistened off the tarnished gold as he held it higher.

"What's odd?"

"I feel that I've seen this before."

"You've probably seen me wear it."

"Probably, but . . ."

Sarah's fingers drifted up his thigh, and she laughed as he forgot the locket, concentrating all his attention on her.

7

Sarah stood on the deck looking across the Missouri River as the ship plowed through the murky waters. She sighed, wondering what her life would be like living among Indians on a reservation. But then, Daniel hadn't said much about their future.

Daniel walked up behind her and placed his hands on her shoulders. "What are you thinking about?"

"The future."

"I hope it's the future as Mrs. Daniel Eaglefeather."

Abruptly Sarah turned to face him. "Are you asking me to marry you?"

"I can't have you living in sin." Daniel stroked her blond curls that blew in the breeze. "You have sacrificed much to be with me."

"I've sacrificed nothing. When you love someone as I love you, it's not a sacrifice."

"Be that as it may. I want you to be my wife, Sarah Collins."

"Oh, Daniel. Yes! Yes, yes, yes!" She threw her arms around his neck and kissed him, barely able to breathe in her excitement.

Daniel pushed her back gently and smiled. "You honor me. But I must warn you it will not get easier. Just because we're married won't make the white man accept us."

"We'll deal with that. We have so far."

"I'm afraid you will grow tired of being treated so unfairly because of your love for me."

Sarah stroked his cheek. "I have nothing without you, Daniel."

He pulled her close. "I love you, sweet Sarah."

Their kiss was long and passionate, their minds on love and their future together.

That evening, the ship's captain closed the book and announced, "I now pronounce you man and wife. You may kiss the bride."

Daniel bent his head and kissed his bride, barely able to contain his smile.

"May I be the first to wish you two luck?" the captain interjected.

"Thank you, sir," Daniel responded. "I know you were reluctant to marry us, but . . . "

"It isn't hard to see that you two belong together, son. Just take care of this beautiful lady," he said, kissing the back of Sarah's hand. "She's mighty special, and I can see by looking at the two of you that whether I married you or not, you'd be together."

"Thank you, Captain," Sarah replied.

"Now get! The two of you need to be alone, and I have a ship to run." The captain laughed.

❧

"Sarah, my love. We must dress for dinner."

"But I want to stay here, with my husband."

"Your husband needs food," Daniel said, rolling out of bed. "We have many weeks left on this boat before we reach Montana." He walked to her side and slipped his arm around her. "Plenty of time to make love, day and night if you wish, but right now it's time for dinner."

"It's just that . . . well I . . . like it."

Daniel grinned. "No excuses, wife. Get yourself dressed. I'll meet you in the dining room." He kissed her on the cheek and gave her a loving tap on the rear, then left the stateroom.

Sarah sighed. It was time to face the world as Mrs. Eaglefeather, and she was proud of her new name. She just didn't want the magic to fade, the magic of their love. She bowed her head and thanked the Lord for Daniel. He'd saved her from loneliness and given her a love so deep she felt it in her soul.

As she dressed for the evening in her emerald green gown, she knew she'd found true happiness. She swept up her hair and secured it with the silver combs, then headed for the dining room.

Daniel stood when she approached and pulled out her chair. "This is my wife, Sarah," he announced proudly.

The other two couples mumbled their introductions as the waiter served the first course. One was a middle-aged pastor and his wife on the way to a mission field, the other newlyweds who were so enamored with one another they didn't notice who was with them for dinner.

Sarah knew how they felt. If she'd had her way, she

and Daniel would still be in their cabin making love. But they did need to eat.

The pastor was interested in Daniel's opinion of the area they were going to, and asked many questions and apologized for doing so.

The food was adequate, and the conversation interesting, though the newlyweds had little to say and left early, just as Sarah wanted to do. But Daniel seemed to be enjoying himself, and, as he said, they had plenty of time.

Daniel squeezed her hand under the table and occasionally sent her looks that made her blush. After their time together, she knew exactly what those looks meant, and the excitement they stirred was delectable.

"Well, it's growing late," Pastor Evans said, laying his napkin aside. "We had a long trip over land, and my wife grows weary."

"If you want to visit, Charles . . ."

"No, no, I think we're all in need of a good night's rest." The couple bade them good night and left in search of their cabin.

"Quite interesting companions," Daniel said. "Especially the young couple. Did you catch their names?"

"I believe he said 'honey,' and she called him 'dearest.'"

Daniel's laugh caught the attention of their nearest dining companions. He pushed his empty coffee cup aside. "Are you ready for a night of dancing?"

"I thought we'd go back to the cabin and . . ."

"I'm happy you're so eager for me. But tonight we celebrate our marriage on the dance floor. Then I shall

take you to the cabin and make sweet passionate love
to you."

"Daniel!"

"Yes?"

Sarah laughed and took his hand. "I love you."

A full silvery moon glistened off the water as the
steamship slipped along in the humid early June
night.

"It seems like we're floating on air," Sarah
remarked, leaning on the rail, looking ahead at the
wide expanse of river before them.

The only sounds were of water brushing the bow
and the occasional twitter of a bird disturbed by their
passing. The low murmur of voices and music were
barely audible from the deck below.

"I love traveling by boat. It's so restful."

Daniel slipped his arm around her waist and pulled
her closer to him. "Have I told you how glad I am that
you're here?"

"At least a thousand times."

"I was so afraid you wouldn't come." He looked
deeply into her blue eyes, "Tell me again why you
changed your mind."

"Because I realized I loved you and couldn't live
without you."

"I will never tire of hearing those words."

"Daniel, how is your mother going to feel about
you showing up with a wife? A white wife at that."

"She'll welcome you with open arms. You two now
have something in common, you both love, and married, an Indian."

"Lately, I've begun to wonder more and more who my real parents were. I'd like to thank my birth mother for giving me to such wonderful people to raise me, but I also want to know why she gave me away."

"You may never know."

"I realize that," Sarah said, running her hand along the polished wood railing. "That's why helping you give your mother the gift of music means so much to me. It's like I'm doing it for my own mother. I know that sounds odd, but it's how I feel. I don't want to take anything away from what you're doing, it's just . . ."

"You're not," he said, leaning closer. "You're helping me." He brushed a kiss across her parted lips, tasting her sweetness, then tasting it again.

Sarah clung to him, her fingers clutching his lapels, her mouth clinging to his, her stomach doing those familiar somersaults in anticipation of things to come.

The boat trip was long, but Sarah relished every moment. She loved having Daniel to herself.

The whistle sounded as the boat docked. There was a large crowd on shore, waving and laughing as the passengers walked down the plank. Daniel walked behind Sarah, laden with luggage.

Within the hour she and Daniel were riding along a dusty trail in the wagon he'd secured, their luggage bouncing in the back. "How far is it?"

"We'll be there for supper," Daniel said, snapping the reins on the horses' hindquarters.

They drove for hours through treeless plains covered with buffalo and blue grama grasses, nothing like the river valley with its aspen and cottonwood trees. Sarah clasped her hands together nervously. What if Daniel's mother didn't like her? What if his people didn't accept her?

"Don't worry," Daniel said, laying his large hand over hers.

"Easy for you to say."

"She'll love you," he said, stealing a kiss. "Just like I do."

"You look more like an Indian than I've ever seen you look," Sarah commented. His tight leather breeches hugged his muscled legs like a second skin, and the linen shirt, open at the neck, revealed more chest than she was used to seeing when he was dressed. His sleeves, rolled to the elbow, highlighted the strength of his forearms. He wore a leather hat with a wide brim and a snakeskin band, his feet encased in leather moccasins, the top decorated with blue and red quills in an intricate design.

"You don't like the way I look?"

"If you looked any better, I'd have to make you stop this wagon!"

Daniel pulled the team to a stop, jumped from the wagon, ran to the other side and lifted her down.

"What are you doing?"

"I'm going to make love to my wife." He eased her down into the thick prairie grass.

"Here? Now?" she panted, her heart racing. "What if someone sees us?"

"They'll have me to answer to."

Daniel undressed her with a fury, then shed his clothes. He kissed her with such passion that she melted beneath his touch. His body felt hot under his caresses, but not as hot as she felt. The feel of his bare skin against hers sent shivers down her spine, and when he entered her, she forgot everything except the love he gave.

"How do I look, Daniel?" Sarah asked, securing the combs in her hair for the tenth time.

He laughed.

"I look that bad?"

"No, that good. Maybe I should stop the wagon again and—"

"Don't you dare!"

"You're lucky I'm so anxious to see my parents, or I would."

Sarah smiled. She knew he was serious, he'd proven that once today, the memory of his body on hers still so fresh she blushed. "Behave yourself, Daniel."

"Where you're concerned, never."

She laughed and stared at the horizon as dark blocks changed into buildings, seeming to appear like magic out of the wilderness.

"It that it?"

"Uh huh."

Her chest tightened until she could hardly breathe. Daniel leaned over and kissed her.

"You worry too much, my love."

She tried to smile and failed.

A dog barked as they drew near, setting up a chain reaction to a dozen or so more trailing out to greet them, along with a group of children of various sizes. Shining black hair framed round brown faces.

Curious black eyes studied them as Daniel drove the wagon down a rutted street.

A church with a steeple sat on the left along with a trading post and a mercantile, with what looked like a school on the right. Cabins, some with porches and fences, some without, stretched out behind the store buildings, with a dozen or so tepees dotting the horizon.

"It's much larger than I imagined," she confessed.

"An Indian village is laid out in a circle, all the openings facing east to greet the sun each day. They have continued that tradition here.

"I probably shouldn't tell you this, but an Indian woman owns the house." He smiled. "She can throw her husband out when he displeases her. Fortunately, Walking Thunder has pleased my mother and has never had to find a place for his pallet."

Women of varying sizes and ages came to their doors to see what the commotion was about, some recognizing Daniel and calling out to him, all curious about the woman he'd brought with him. The children and dogs trailed behind the wagon, a lot of laughter, talk, fussing, and barking creating quite a parade through town.

Sarah's blond hair was twisted up in a bun to keep it off her neck, and she'd donned a bonnet that matched her cornflower blue dress. She felt dusty and ill prepared to meet Daniel's parents, but unless she missed her guess, the couple waiting in the door of the cabin were her new in-laws.

The woman was slim and blond, her hair in one long braid that fell over her left shoulder, and the Indian next to her looked very much like Daniel, save for age and a touch of gray.

"Daniel!" the woman called brightly, stepping off the porch and running toward them.

Daniel leaped off the wagon and grabbed his mother around the waist, swinging her off the ground and around in circles.

"Daniel," she shrieked lightly, "put me down!"

He set her on the ground, his arm around her shoulders.

"And who is this you've brought with you?" Davinda asked, her husband walking up behind her.

He helped Sarah from the wagon. "Mother, Father, I'd like you to meet Sarah Eaglefeather, my wife."

8

Davinda's hand flew to her mouth, and Sarah thought she'd faint. The woman was at least forty, but she seemed much younger, even though Sarah couldn't tell if she was laughing or crying.

Chief Walking Thunder grasped his son's arm. "There is always room in our family for more. I'm happy for you, son."

Davinda's hand fell to her side and she turned to Sarah. "Welcome to the family, Sarah." She threw her arms around the young woman and squeezed her tightly.

"Daniel, you devil," she teased, "you said you might bring a friend, you never mentioned a wife."

"It's a long story, Mother. Let's just say that things changed on the way here."

"Come dear," Davinda said, taking Sarah's hand. "I'm sure you'd like to freshen up. It must have been a hard trip," she said, pulling a piece of prairie grass from under Sarah's bonnet.

"It was," Sarah said, feeling heat rise in her cheeks. "I thought I'd walk for a bit, but I fell in the grass. I must look a sight."

"You look fine. Daniel, why don't you take Sarah to the guest house. I readied it just in case. Now you'd probably like it for privacy."

"That would be nice. Thank you." He kissed his mother on the cheek.

"Don't be late for dinner, we'll be eating in an hour."

Daniel settled Sarah into the guest house then carried in the luggage. Having a wife felt good, but he wondered why women needed so much baggage. He burst through the door, his arms full, and laughed when Sarah jumped.

"I didn't mean to scare you."

"I'm sorry, I'm a bit nervous."

"The worst is over. You have already met my parents, and they love you. So what's the problem?" he asked, staring at the half locket around her neck.

"No problem. I'll just change and brush my hair so I won't be late for dinner."

Daniel dropped the luggage on the floor and pulled Sarah into his embrace. "There's one more thing you need to do before dinner," he said softly, toying with the familiar-looking locket.

"What's that?"

His lips found hers and he groaned as Sarah understood what he wanted before dinner. She had learned to please him in every way, and he found it difficult to let such a willing partner out of his arms. He loved her with his very life, and he would spend the rest of his life making her happy.

❦

Davinda was a wonderful cook—roast beef, potatoes, carrots, and apple pie hot from the oven.

"Daniel's favorite dinner," Davinda said with a fond look at her son.

"It was delicious," Sarah said, laying aside her fork.

Davinda spent the evening reminiscing about Daniel as a boy, much to his embarrassment, but he was proud of the way she felt about him. Sarah glanced at him a few times with an amused giggle. Though Walking Thunder was quiet, he laughed along with the rest of them.

Daniel watched as Davinda and Sarah talked. He was amazed how quickly they'd taken to each other. How very alike they were; both blond, both had the same blue-violet eyes. Strange how he'd chosen a woman to marry who was so much like Davinda in looks and temperament.

He wondered why Sarah always wore her locket under her clothes rather than letting it hang on the outside. She'd said it was left among her blankets by her real mother, so why hide it? The locket. There was something about the memento that bothered him, but he couldn't think what it could be—until he remembered Davinda's box on the mantle.

While the others talked, he walked to the fireplace and lifted the lid on the cedar box. How many times as a boy had he seen Davinda open this box and look through it, searching for the gold earrings he'd given her for Christmas the year he was ten, the braided bracelet he'd made from leather he'd cured himself. But at the bottom was what he'd searched for.

Locating a worn leather thong, he pulled it out and let it dangle from the tip of his finger. The locket his mother had worn when she first came to the tribe. The locket she refused to take off for a very long time, but then had put it in the box and never taken it out again.

He remembered her saying it was a time of putting away, of closing the book on the life she'd once known, a life before Walking Thunder.

The locket was the same as Sarah's . . . half a locket, when fit with the other half, would make a whole. "Well, I'll be damned," he said, clenching the locket in his hand.

"What is it dear?" Davinda asked, walking toward her son, Sarah close behind.

Daniel knew that what he was about to do would bond them all together for life in a way no one expected, and heal two hearts. "Sarah," he said softly, "let me see the locket around your neck."

Hesitantly she pulled the chain from beneath her dress and let it fall.

Davinda's eyes widened and she suddenly paled, looking faint, until Walking Thunder slipped his arm around her.

Daniel let his mother's locket dangle from his finger and Sarah stared blankly. Unconsciously she reached for the leather thong and held it to her own.

"Daniel?" Sarah said in a questioning voice.

"Yes, sweet Sarah, they fit."

Tears rolled down Davinda's cheeks. It was rare that his mother let him see her cry.

"This half must belong to my mother." Sarah swayed on her feet and Daniel's protective arm slid around her shoulders.

Chief Walking Thunder stepped forward. "Daniel?"

Davinda stared at Sarah. "I put that locket among my daughter's blankets when I left her . . . "

"On a doorstep," Sarah finished, hardly able to comprehend what this all meant.

"Oh, dear Lord," Davinda whispered. "Could it be?"

"Mother?" Sarah asked, her eyes full of wonder.

"I had to give up my child," Davinda began softly, her voice smothered by a sob. "It broke my heart. That's why . . . the locket . . . the two pieces. And like that locket, my heart was broken." Davinda reached for Sarah and threw her arms around her. "Oh, my precious child, I've found you!"

Sarah and Davinda clung to each other as if they would never let go.

Between bouts of tears, Davinda told her daughter the story of how she'd conceived, and how her young lover was killed in the Civil War. In a broken voice, she told how her parents were determined to keep her secluded in their house for the duration of her pregnancy, and how they wanted to give her baby to distant cousins who needed more hands to work their farm. "I ran away the night I went into labor," Davinda said. "I made it as far as the outskirts of Mooretown where a farmer and his wife helped deliver you. By then my father had caught up with me, but I knew what he would do if he found you, so I ran away again. I roamed the streets until I nearly collapsed, not wanting to leave you, but knowing it was best. I finally made my way to the Collins house, where I left you on the doorstep, praying the people there would give you a good and loving home. Oh, Sarah, my heart was breaking as I kissed you good-bye. I broke my locket in half so that you would always have a small part of me with you."

"Oh Mother." Sarah went into her arms, and mother and daughter knew they would never be separated again.

When the excitement quieted down, Davinda reached for Daniel's hand and brought it to her cheek.

"What a wonderful gift you have given me, my son. My life is now complete."

"Not quite. I have one more surprise for you."

"Daniel! I'm not sure I can take any more!"

Daniel grabbed Sarah's hand. "It's time for Mother's surprise."

Sarah grinned through her tears. "Don't you think she's had enough surprises for one night?"

"Not yet."

Daniel ushered everyone from the cabin over to the schoolhouse and took his place at the piano. "Sarah will sing first," he announced with a smile.

Sarah stood next to the old spinet and gave Daniel a nod. He began playing and she beamed almost as much as Davinda, *their* mother. She sang the words, thinking how she'd told Daniel it would be like doing it for her real mother, not knowing she would be doing just that.

> He ran till he got back to his den,
> Where little ones waited, eight, nine, ten.
> 'Daddy' they said, 'better go back again,
> For it must be a very fine town-o, town-o, town-o.
> 'Daddy,' they said, 'better go back again,
> For it must be a very fine town-o.

When they finished, Davinda sat, tears streaming down her cheeks in glistening rivulets.

Sarah smiled at Daniel as the proud wife she was. He'd played better than she'd ever heard him play.

"Well, Mother?" he asked.

Davinda was speechless. When she finally found her voice, she asked softly, "When did you learn to play?"

"Sarah taught me," he said, smiling at his wife. "That's how we met."

"You have a lovely voice, Sarah, thank you. This meant so much to me. Daniel's name is Little Fox, had he told you?"

Sarah smiled. "No, he hadn't."

"Sarah also taught me to sing," Daniel said, breaking into the second verse of "The Fox" with gusto, slowing only as laughter drowned him out. He stopped and frowned at Sarah.

"My dearest son," Davinda began, "you play the piano beautifully, and I couldn't be more touched by your precious gift, but you sing like a ruptured walrus."

Daniel burst into a belly laugh that set off Walking Thunder, Sarah, and Davinda. Finally he managed, "Sarah warned me not to sing!"

"You married a very wise woman, my son."

Sarah threw her arms around Daniel's neck, "Maybe you need more lessons."

He pulled her close and whispered in her ear, "Maybe I do."

EPILOGUE

Daniel knelt beside the crib, looking down at his twin daughters. "They're beautiful, like their mother."

Sarah fairly glowed with pride. Two years had passed since she'd married Daniel. Two years in which she'd fallen more in love with her husband every day.

Daniel was working near the reservation to help his people. The government welcomed him as a liaison.

They'd built a small house on the side of town closest to his work, and Sarah had begun teaching piano as well as playing in the small church each Sunday. Never had she felt so complete, so content.

The door opened, and Davinda and Katherine slipped inside the room, followed by Chief Walking Thunder and Michael.

Sarah reached for her two mothers' hands. "My darling mothers, I'm so glad you're here."

Davinda hugged her daughter, then went to the crib. Falling to her knees beside it, she reached inside to gently touch the tiny hands.

"They are so perfect," she murmured. "Absolutely perfect."

"They are God's miracles," Katherine crooned, laughing when one of the babies latched onto her finger and held on tightly.

Michael lifted one of the babies in his burly arms and kissed it on the forehead. "Look here, Mother. We've got two more to love."

Rising, Davinda took a package from her pocket. "I have a gift," she said, opening the packet.

Taking out two lockets, she broke one in two, threaded a thin chain on each half, and placed them around the necks of the two babies. The second locket she slipped over Sarah's head.

Daniel and Sarah looked at one another questioningly. "Mother?"

Davinda smiled. "These lockets are a symbol of our love for one another, once separate and now together. And for the love these two little girls will share while growing up. One day they will be grown and married, and maybe apart, yet still a part of one another. And you will always be a part of them, the three of you together in spirit."

"Thank you, Mother. It is a most special gift."

Davinda turned to Katherine, slipping a third locket around her neck. "Thank you for raising our child and giving her so much love."

Katherine smiled. "No, it's I who should thank you."

In the background, Daniel began to croon a familiar tune—

> Then the fox and the wife without any strife,
> Together they lived for the rest of their life,
> All in the town-o

Davinda smiled. The circle was complete.

Walking Thunder rested a broad hand on Daniel's shoulder, his eyes filled with pride. "Son, you cannot sing. Please stop trying."

They all broke into laughter, hugging each other.

The circle was, indeed, complete.

LORI COPELAND is the bestselling author of over forty novels. She has also penned a novella for HarperMonogram's *Seasons of Love* anthology. She is the recipient of numerous awards, including the *Romantic Times* Career Achievement Award for Love and Laughter. Lori Copeland currently lives in Springfield, Missouri.